Sofia

Sofia

Joseph Sciuto

IGUANA

Publisher: Meghan Behse
Editor: Lee Parpart
Front cover design: Meghan Behse

Front cover image courtesy of Shutterstock.

ISBN 978-1-77180-352-6 (paperback)
ISBN 978-1-77180-353-3 (epub)
ISBN 978-1-77180-354-0 (Kindle)

This is an original print edition of *Sofia*.

To all the pediatric oncology and critical care nurses, to the cancer researchers, and to the courageous children who fight this terrible disease.

And to 7jane, my Goodreads friend, whose insights and wisdom into Asperger's syndrome was inspirational and enlightening.

Chapter 1

I woke up one morning with a stinking pain in my neck, and when I touched the area, I felt a bunch of lumps. This seemed odd, but I figured I'd probably slept funny. So I changed into my running gear, and went for my early morning seven-mile run through the lovely, tree-lined streets of Studio City, hoping to work out the kinks. When I returned home, the pain had backed off a little, and I didn't think about it until five hours later. I was sitting at my desk, in my book-lined study, writing the opening scene to a new screenplay, when I suddenly felt like I'd been hit in the neck with a poison dart. When I felt the area again, the lumps felt bigger and the pain was more intense. Naturally, I did the first thing any sensible person would do: I went to my refrigerator and grabbed an ice-cold Budweiser. That first liquid anesthetic was followed by several more until I forgot all about the pain. Beer, beautiful beer, had been a surefire remedy ever since I was a teenager, and it performed its usual magic.

I stopped writing for the day. It was a golden rule of mine never to write with a buzz, despite any urge I might feel to finish a scene or work out an idea. If the idea was that good it would wait until the next day when I sat down at my desk sober. I made myself a peanut butter and jelly sandwich, downed a few more beers, and went out to sit by the pool. It was a beautiful, sunny southern California day, and after a few minutes of lounging, I fell asleep. I woke up hours later, as the sun was descending through the trees on my property. The twilight hour was and is my favorite part of day, and to celebrate I walked into the kitchen and grabbed some more liquid reinforcement. Armed with three more ice-cold Budweisers, I sat back down in the chair by the pool and marveled at the relaxed beauty all around me. When the pain suddenly returned, I added a few shots of Jack Daniels Old No. 7 to the mix, and after a while everything went back to normal.

The lights around my pool popped on, signaling the end of a lovely evening. I walked back into the house, hit the remote control that turned on a looping playlist of Beatles hits, and walked into the kitchen singing along to "Penny Lane." I made myself two more peanut butter and jelly sandwiches, had a few more beers, lay down on my living room couch and fell asleep to something from *A Hard Day's Night*. I woke up at around two in the morning with the pain back in full force and the lyrics to "Help!" in my ears. I sleepily registered the irony as I clicked off the music, took two aspirin, and climbed into my bed, where I fell right back out as if I'd never woken up.

At six in morning I got up, put on my running gear, and went for my daily seven-mile run. I returned home, ate my usual breakfast of cereal with chocolate milk, took a shower, and sat down at my desk to start working on the screenplay. I could afford to be pretty relaxed about this one. It was a sequel to my last screenplay, and like the last one, it would be directed by my longtime friend and collaborator, Nick Jones. Like six out of seven of our other collaborations, that movie had been a box office smash, and I couldn't think of any reason why this one would be any less popular. It's amazing how much success one can achieve in the movie business just by sticking with whatever formula made you a fortune in the first place. All you need to do is change the locations, re-name the characters, throw in a few adorable cats and a litter of puppies, and add a buxom woman in a bikini. Then you'll have a nice backdrop for your swashbuckling male lead to escape certain death, win over the babe, and prove his sweetness with the cats and the puppies. Or something like that.

Just as I was getting my groove on, reworking one-liners that always got a laugh or a tear, the pain came back with such intensity that I grabbed my neck and spat out a stream of obscenities that I won't repeat here. I looked at the clock on my computer, and after thoughtful consideration, I decided that it was too early to go to my usual liquid remedies. So I did the next best thing: I called my doctor's office. His lovely receptionist picked up on the first ring. At first she didn't recognize my voice, and she tried to tell me that the next available opening wasn't for another week. After I revealed who I was, she miraculously found an opening, but only if I could get there within two hours. Amazing how doors open when you've had a string of hits. It didn't hurt that the receptionist was an aspiring actress who fit all the qualifications required of the lead actress in the script I was writing. Also helpful was the fact that I'd promised to get her an audition with the director when casting started. I thanked her profusely and hopped in my car, stopping on my way to the office to pick her up a box of expensive chocolates.

When I entered the doctor's office I was greeted with a wink and smile from the receptionist, Caroline. I handed her the box of chocolates, and she smiled broadly, saying, "Oh how very thoughtful. You shouldn't have," in a tone that clearly indicated that she was glad I did. There was no doubt about it: She was hot. But I had a rule never to date or sleep with any girl that could be mistaken for my daughter. This limited my possibilities, but one had to draw the line somewhere, and I was very good at drawing lines — so good that at the age of forty-three I hadn't been on a date or slept with a woman for nearly twenty years. No one believes that, but I would swear on a stack of Bibles that it's true.

After checking in, I was escorted by a different nurse to the examination room and told to change into one of those god-awful gowns that give the whole world a look at your hairy butt. I did as she said, sat up on the examining table, and allowed her to take my blood pressure and my temperature, and ask a bunch of questions about the medications I was on, and whether I had ever had any thoughts of suicide.

"Of course, I have," I said. "I'm a writer. The thought of killing myself is pretty much a constant refrain. But I have the perfect remedy: beer and more beer."

She tried to smile but it just wasn't in her nature, unlike the receptionist, who kept passing by the open door, smiling and winking at me. "Besides, what do thoughts of suicide have to do with the nagging pain in my neck?"

"It's a new law. As medical professionals we are required to ask such questions."

"Is that so," I replied, as she looked up from the iPad she was using to take down my information. She just looked at me and said, "The doctor will be in shortly," then closed the door and left me in the room.

After about five minutes, Dr. Joshua Souter entered the room. He had the same distracted and vaguely displeased look he always wore, and I could have sworn that the brown mole next to his nose had doubled in size since my last visit. He looked surprised to see me. "Is it already a year since your last physical?"

"No! I'm here for something else," I said, but he was already staring down at his iPad and may or may not have heard me. Dr. Souter had been my primary care physician since I arrived in Los Angeles over twenty years ago, and the years hadn't been kind to him. He seemed to be aging at about twice the normal rate. Over the last couple of years, he also seemed to be slipping a bit, mentally. If I didn't know better, I might think it was the onset of early Alzheimer's. I thought about switching doctors, but I was loyal to a fault, so I stayed on as his patient.

He put his stethoscope up against my chest and back and told me to take deep breaths. I did as he said, but I made it clear that I thought he was looking in the wrong place. "The pain is not in my chest or around my heart," I said. "It's in my neck." I pointed to the spot, but he ignored my comment and leveled me with a suspicious gaze.

"I know why you're here, and all I can say is, back off. Until I perform a total and complete examination on my receptionist and have satisfied my libido, you can just stay away. You don't see me hanging around your staff and picking off the good-looking ones."

This was weird, even for Dr. Souter. I took a moment to absorb the accusation before trying to set the record straight.

"I don't have a staff and I'm certainly not here trying to pick up your receptionist."

"Then explain the chocolates, which, by the way, were delicious. I had a few before coming in here."

"Happy you enjoyed them, but believe me, I have no interest in your receptionist."

"And the promise of a part in your next movie?"

"The promise of an *audition*," I said. "I needed to get in here and see you. I'm seriously worried about this pain in my neck. I would have told her anything. Besides, I thought you were happily married."

"I was, until that bitch of a wife switched to a new gynecologist and started sleeping with her."

"Your wife is having an affair with her female gynecologist?"

"Isn't that what I just said? Jesus, Joe, keep up."

"Sorry," I said, then immediately wanted to take it back.

Dr. Souter kept talking at me, his eyes focused on some midpoint between us.

"At first I tried to handle the situation calmly. I told her that it was only natural for a woman or a guy to want to experiment after twenty-five years of marriage. And so I suggested that I join in on the action, if only as an observer. That way it wouldn't seem so seedy and underhanded."

"That sounds reasonable," I reassured him, no longer feeling very sure of what was reasonable and what wasn't.

"Well, the bitch went insane and accused me of being a pervert. Me! Can you believe that? Like I was having an affair with another guy. Screaming that I was the worst lover she ever had. That after twenty-five years she still hadn't achieved one orgasm with me. Well, let me tell you, Joe, as a medical professional, I will swear under oath that that bitch achieved multiple orgasms while having sex with me. I've always been a caring and sharing lover, except of course on those nights when I had one too many martinis and was just too exhausted to even start to fulfill her insatiable desires."

He picked up a photo of his wife and handed it to me. She was a fairly attractive, middle-aged lady with shoulder-length hair and a good figure. When I raised my eyebrows in approval, he said, "She didn't always look like that. When I first met her, she looked like a cross between a frog and horse. Amazing, what a skillful plastic surgeon can accomplish. After spending all that money, what do I get?

A slap in the face, while some young gynecologist just out of medical school gets to enjoy my hard-earned investment and I'm left to chase after my receptionist."

"Hey, not for nothing, but the receptionist isn't such a bad consolation prize." I was beginning to feel like I needed a shower, but I couldn't stop consoling him, and Dr. Souter was lapping it up.

"You're right there, and I'm fairly certain she hasn't had any work done."

"I just wouldn't introduce her to your wife. She might not want you as part of the group, but she might think differently about the receptionist, and then you'll really be left out in the dark." In for a penny, in for a pound, my mother used to say.

"Good point," he said, putting the picture of his wife back on the counter. "So, the pain is in your neck?" I pointed to the spot and he touched and felt around the area. "You have swollen glands. Have you had a fever or a cold lately?"

"No. Are swollen glands usually accompanied by a kind of stabbing sensation?"

"Sometimes, but not usually." He once again felt around the area and I jumped with pain as he touched what felt like a loose lump.

"I doubt it's anything, but there's no point taking a chance. I'm sending you to an ear, throat, and neck specialist. He's just down the hall from here, and he's a friend. He's the best in the business, and I happen to know he has an opening right now." Dr. Souter sent the specialist a message on his iPad and two seconds later the device pinged. "He can take you in ten minutes. Dr. Benjamin Casey. The son-of-a-bitch has won more money off me on the links than anyone else I play golf with. I'm quite certain that the second house he is buying in Malibu was paid for by me."

Dr. Souter moved closer to me as I started pulling on my clothes. He lowered his voice to just above a whisper. "Tell me what you think of this, Joe. When the receptionist finally succumbs to my charms, the examination will be taking place right here on this table." He spread his hand across the roll of paper I was just sitting on as though he were explaining a five-course dinner extravaganza to a guest. "I was thinking of putting a hidden camera right between these journals and taping the whole thing and then showing it to the bitch."

"I don't know," I said. "That sounds a bit unethical if you don't let the receptionist know that you're taping her during such an intimate act."

"You're right. I'll get the receptionist's consent and then after I make a few copies I'll give her one and she can use it as her audition tape. Actually, I'll make a note to send a copy to you. You can learn a lot from a doctor's know-how."

I tied my shoes, shook the doctor's hand, and got out of there. "Good luck," he yelled after me.

Dr. Casey's receptionist buzzed me in, and the doctor greeted me at the door to his examination room. He looked more like a movie star than any movie star I had been around over the last twenty-five years, and I have been around quite a few. He was tall and handsome, with dark, straight hair combed back like Clark Gable. He was perfectly tanned, apparently the result of many hours spent on the golf course beating Dr. Souter out of the rest of his money that he didn't spend on his wife's plastic surgery. Dr. Casey had a relaxed and confident manner and I would bet my life savings that he wasn't worried about any of his former wives or girlfriends having lesbian affairs behind his back.

Instead of a doctor's white coat, he wore an expensive suit. Once we were in the exam room, he took off his jacket, stretched his hands and fingers as though he was ready to shuffle a deck of cards, and touched the area around my neck where I'd told him I was having pain. At first it felt like a massage, but when he pressed down hard on one of the lumps I nearly screamed with pain. "Dr. Souter might not be much of a golfer but he's a fairly intelligent physician for someone who did not graduate from Johns Hopkins. He was smart to send you right over."

"What do you think it might be?" I asked.

"It could be something or it might be nothing," he said in a matter-of fact manner that did nothing to relieve the anxiety I was feeling. "Thankfully, you have come to the best." When he said it, I believed him, and it didn't even sound like bragging. He pushed a button on a phone console and said, "Jennifer, could you please button up your blouse and come to my office? I'd like you to walk a patient down to radiology for an MRI. I'm sending them all the instructions they need right now." He picked up his iPad, recorded the instructions on audio, and sent the message.

The mention of buttons on a blouse had me curious, and when Jennifer walked in, I suddenly understood why she'd been assigned to patient relations. The blouse was some sort of form-fitting, candy-stripe affair that seemed to have been tailored to hug every curve. Her soft blond hair fell loosely around her face to just beyond her shoulders. Her hands glittered with a new French manicure, each nail ending in a subtle sliver of white. I couldn't believe that this goddess, whose figure could re-energize a corpse, would be escorting me to radiology. She introduced herself with a sweet smile and guided me down a hall.

"Come here a lot?" I punted, and with that old chestnut, I got to hear her incredible laugh for the first time — a completely natural, genuine laugh that went on a little longer than you expected it to and that made you feel like a million bucks.

"Not usually, but today has been busy. Already, I have had to take five patients down, and each one is scheduled to undergo surgery tomorrow."

"Surgery?"

"Oh, don't worry. It's a simple procedure. Dr. Casey performs them all himself — a simple biopsy to see whether the growth is malignant or benign. If I suspect correctly, and you're number six, I would not eat a big dinner tonight and certainly nothing after twelve o'clock. You'll be put under for a short time and not everyone responds to anesthesia very well."

The fact that she seemed to be getting a little ahead of herself did nothing to dull her radiance. I watched her lips move and nodded mutely, trying not to gape at her too openly or appear too concerned about the possibility of going under the knife.

We entered the radiology department and the chief technician had me change into my second butt-baring gown of the day. Why they can't design one that wraps all the way around the body I will never understand. As I changed, Jennifer chatted with a staff member. When I came out, the staffer directed me to lie down on the MRI table and strapped me in. I was feeling anxious, and thinking that it would be great to have Jennifer be a little closer, when she suddenly walked over and took my hand in hers. Then she used the other hand to unfasten the top two buttons of her blouse. My anxiety level was still dropping as they rolled me inside the MRI tube. A voice warned me not to move, and instructed me to "close my eyes, and think of pleasant things." That wasn't hard to do after getting a bird's eye view of Jennifer's gifts to the world.

The fifteen minutes inside the tube flew by quickly. They rolled me out, untied me, and said to change back into my clothes. I did so, then walked back out into the reception area to find Jennifer waiting for me. I was surprised to see her there and told her she didn't need to stay, but she was adamant.

"I couldn't leave you there," she said. "You looked like a lost puppy. Besides, I need to walk you over to the lab so they can take some blood."

"Will you hold my hand?" I asked jokingly as she turned toward me and smiled.

"I'd love to," she replied, and being the *pig* I was and am, I couldn't help noticing that she had refastened the top two buttons on her blouse. We entered the lab and a technician took two vials of my blood while Jennifer sat across from me, crossed her legs, and once again unfastened the top two buttons of her blouse.

We walked out of the lab and I asked, "I thought you were going to hold my hand?"

"I took an educated guess and thought you might like the view better looking across at me. Was I wrong?"

"Not at all. Where to now?"

"Well, I'm going back to my office to eat lunch. Would you like to come along? If the doctor hasn't left for the day to play golf, he'll most likely look at your MRI and blood work in the next four hours."

"How about I treat you to lunch? You've been exceptionally sweet."

"That sounds great, but I need to ask, do I also get a box of chocolates?"

When I laughed, Jennifer said, "Dr. Souter's receptionist has a big mouth. She's really sweet and hopefully one day she will get her big break."

We stopped at her office door, where Jennifer excused herself for a few minutes and went inside, closing the door behind her. I sat down in a chair in the empty reception area, and thought about what a strange day it had been. Events were moving quickly, and Jennifer was proving to be a nice distraction, but the words "malignant" and "benign" were getting bandied about, and it was a lot to handle in a short time.

For a moment after Jennifer walked out of the office I didn't recognize her. She had changed out of her nurse's uniform and into jeans, a sweater, and a pair of loafers.

She caught me staring and put on a pout.

"What, you don't like?"

I realized that for the first time since meeting her, I was focused on her face. And what a face it was — smooth and oval-shaped, framed by loose blond curls that fell past her shoulders. Her big, blue eyes were wide open and full of curiosity and confidence.

"You're stunning," I said, then immediately questioned whether I was even a writer. Was that really all I could come up with?

She laughed, and said, "Are you telling me you like me better in this outfit than in my nurse's outfit?"

"Well, I don't know, but I think there should be a law against that other one."

"It is a regulation nurse's uniform."

"Perfectly tailored to maximize your assets."

"My assets! Hmm, well," she said, "at the moment it pays the bills."

"Are you also an actress?"

"No! God, no! I'm a registered, specialized nurse with a whopping student loan that I've barely began to pay off, and I turn thirty in a month." She put her arm in mine as casually as if we were best friends. "So, where do you usually take a girl when you want to impress her?"

We went to Morton's Steak House, a high-end restaurant with excellent food. The lunch crowd was just emptying out and we were seated right away. We both ordered ice teas, even though I was dying for a cold beer. The change in Jennifer's appearance was so startling that I totally forgot about the very real possibility that I might have a serious medical problem.

"So, are you a native Californian?" I asked, and Jennifer started to laugh.

"Seriously Joe, an accomplished writer like yourself asking me, with my accent, if I was born here."

"How do you know I'm an accomplished writer?"

"Your little girlfriend, who you bought the chocolates for and promised a part in your next movie, read off your list of credits to me."

"I didn't promise her a part in my next movie, just an audition."

"Oh, is that what they call it now? Is she your dinner date?"

"No, I was hoping we might be able to extend lunch into dinner, unless you already have a date for tonight?"

"Or a husband who might not be very pleased that you are hitting on his wife."

"If you're married or have a boyfriend, I sincerely apologize."

"Not to worry, I have neither. Would that have actually stopped you?"

"Yes. I would still have wanted to be your friend, but that's a line I won't cross."

She looked at me skeptically and once again started to laugh. When I didn't say anything more about it, a new expression crept onto her face, and I couldn't tell if she was sizing me up or getting to like me. I just looked back at her, not feeling anxious or nervous — just calmly studying her face as she studied mine. I couldn't get over how genuine she seemed. She was as natural as a child chasing a butterfly in a field of lilies.

"So, are you in between marriages or going through a nasty divorce?" she asked.

"I've never been married, but I do have one daughter. Her name is Sofia."

"You didn't want to put a ring on it?"

"Put a ring on it? Oh — no, it wasn't like that," I said. "Long-ish story."

"Sorry," she said. "It's none of my business."

"No, no," I said. "I don't mind telling you. Sofia's mother was … difficult. Unpredictable. We were together for such a short time, and by the time we found out she was pregnant, we both knew it was over. Three days after giving birth, she handed me my daughter and said, 'Good luck,' and I never heard from her again."

"Oh," Jennifer said. "It wasn't pre-arranged, was it?"

"No! And please, if you ever meet Sofia, never tell her what I just told you. As far as she knows, her mom passed away when she was two. She's eighteen, and that is a secret I plan on taking to the grave."

"Into the vault," she said, using her fingers to turn an imaginary lock.

"I appreciate that."

"You raised her yourself?"

"That's right," I said. "No nannies. I changed all her diapers, sterilized her baby bottles and fed her ten times a day, and stayed up all night with her when she had her crying fits. It was no big deal."

"No big deal?" she said, looking surprised. "I don't think I've ever heard any parent say that before. Ever."

"Well, I never really struggled financially as a writer, and my job allowed me to be home all the time. Almost from the moment I moved out here from the Bronx, I was able to sell my scripts."

"You must be very good at what you do."

"To tell you the truth, I think I was very lucky. I have known many writers who were far better than me who have never sold anything."

"Still, taking care of an infant had to interfere with your social life?"

"Sure," I said. "But raising Sofia has always been my greatest joy."

As soon as I said the words, my eyes welled up, and the image of my beautiful daughter erased everything else from my mind. It was my Sofia that was the child chasing the butterfly, and it was my out-stretched hands that could not catch her and bring her back into my life. Jennifer reached across the table to grasp my hand, and as she did so, a couple of tears escaped down my cheeks. I turned away.

"Oh my God, look at you," she said.

"Sorry," I said.

"You're sorry?" Jennifer sounded incredulous. "I think it's wonderful that you love her so much. And what an accomplishment to have raised her on your own."

I dried my eyes and looked across at Jennifer. I was amazed to see that her eyes were welling up too. I started to apologize again, this time for upsetting her. "I never do this. I never get emotional. At least not in public. And never in the company of such a beautiful and charming lady."

"Of course not ... tough guys from the Bronx don't let other people see them cry."

I was grateful to her for changing the subject. "So you do know a little about New Yorkers?"

"A little, from the movies."

"Yes, of course, from the movies," I said. "So what part of the south are you from? Tennessee, Kentucky, Georgia...?"

"Kentucky, just outside of Lexington. Have you ever been?"

"No, but I have seen plenty of pictures. It looks beautiful."

"That usually depends on who is taking the pictures and what they're trying to sell."

"That could be said of just about any place. You take pictures a half-mile from the Santa Monica Pier, day or night, and it looks heavenly. You walk up to the pier and down a few streets and it is quite filthy and disgusting and populated with the forgotten people, the homeless, the mentally disturbed, and disabled veterans. I guess you saw pictures of the pier from half a mile away?"

"I haven't seen any pictures of the pier, nor have I been there. Maybe one day you can take me there and we can walk through the dirty parts. I'm not easily frightened."

"Okay, then, it's a date. Whenever you wish."

"I'll check my calendar and let you know."

The waiter checked on us several times, but we were so absorbed in conversation that we hardly noticed the service. I found myself wanting to know more and more about Jennifer — her job, her life, anything.

"So tell me more about your work. What specialized field of nursing are you in?"

"Pediatric oncology."

"Children with cancer," I said, immediately impressed and humbled by her decision to join what must be the most grueling area in all of medicine. "I cannot even begin to imagine how difficult that must be."

"Not all the children are critical. In fact, I don't like to think of any of them as terminal. I never give up hope on them. And there is nothing more rewarding than seeing the little runts walk out of the hospital with the disease in remission or totally eradicated."

"Wouldn't it have been a lot less stressful just to become a maternity nurse?"

She put her two lovely hands under her chin, smiled, and moved close to me and whispered, "That's the type of job I could see you going into if you ever get tired of writing. After all, you have all that experience with Sofia. Besides, you would look adorable in a nurse's uniform."

"But not nearly as adorable as you."

"Oh please, every time I put that Halloween costume on, I feel like retching."

"Really? It had a completely different effect on me."

"I noticed," she said.

"How, again, did you end up working for Doc Hollywood?"

"I came out here about six months ago and interviewed for a job at UCLA Medical. I got the job, found an apartment, put down first and last month deposits that nearly wiped me out, and I flew back home to pack all my belongings. A few days before I was to come back out here and start at UCLA, my mother had a stroke. It was a life-or-death situation for weeks, and UCLA was very considerate, but after a month they had to fill the job. Thankfully, my mother is doing much better now, but when I eventually flew back out here I was desperate for any job, and Dr. Casey was the first one to come along."

"Did you have to audition?"

She laughed and replied, "Yes."

"And were you mortified?"

"Oh, for sure, but I really was desperate. Besides, I'm from the south, where you can still call a girl *sweetie* and *honey* and not have a lawsuit thrown at you. Thankfully, he's never asked for any favors. Personally, I think he's in love with himself."

"Yes, as someone familiar with such a person, I think you've hit it right on the head about Dr. Casey."

"Don't get me wrong, you don't build a profession like his without being a really good doctor. I mean, you've seen it for yourself. He has his own lab and staff, a radiology department at his disposal, and an operating room where he performs routine surgeries. Patients like to get results right away, and if you have the money, or are privileged to have great insurance, he can provide it all for you in a day."

Jennifer reached into her purse and took out her cell phone. As soon as she turned it on, it beeped several times. After she put on a pair of reading glasses that only enhanced her beauty, she read the email and looked at me.

"It's your lab results."

"Great! I'm no different than your other patients, so give it to me straight."

"Well," she said, "your white blood count is up, not significantly, but enough to suggest that something is not right. And your MRI reveals a mass behind your glands. The doctor suggests a biopsy. He can fit you in at two o'clock tomorrow."

"And your expert opinion?"

"In the short time I have been there, I don't think a day has gone by without him doing at least one biopsy. He already has those five scheduled for tomorrow. They usually turn out to be benign growths that he is able to remove totally, and in a couple of days, after the results come in, you get the peace of mind you're hoping for."

"No same-day results for the biopsy?"

"No, that is much more specialized. Let me put you down for tomorrow. I can be your ride home, unless you prefer a limo?"

"No! I definitely prefer you."

"Great! And once we get you back home, if you're a good boy, I can even cook you a real southern-style dinner, if you'd like that."

"If I'd like that? Um, let me think," I teased, which caused her to pull a face.

"You're a young woman of many talents," I continued. "Not only do you play the part of the sexy nurse who transforms into the lovely, studious, *pediatric* nurse sitting across from me, but you're also a chef."

"Never said I was a chef."

"Do you know how to turn on a stove and cook over a flame?"

"Yes!"

"Well, in the city of Los Angles a professional woman who also knows how to turn on a stove and cook over a flame is considered a chef."

"Guess you haven't had many home-cooked meals over the years."

"Not since my mother got sick and stopped coming out to visit."

"And your mother never taught Sofia how to cook?"

"The only way my lovely daughter could find the stove would be if she accidently noticed her reflection in its polished exhaust vent."

"Interesting," Jennifer said. "Well, that settles that. Tomorrow you get a homemade dinner." She looked down at her email and scheduled my biopsy for two o'clock. She looked back up, smiled and said, "I'm finished for the day. Doc Hollywood is off to play golf and it's time for a relaxing glass of wine. It's not easy acting the part of a sexy nurse. And how about you, Mr. Hemingway? Surely you wouldn't let a lady drink alone?" I picked the wine list off the table and handed it to her.

"Hemingway! Ha! Hell of a comparison," I said. "Get a bottle. Whatever you like."

She tried to order a house merlot, but I guided her toward a wonderful bottle of Far Niente chardonnay, and she was happy to try it for the first time. To go with it, we started with crab cocktails, and for our main course we both ordered porterhouse steaks with sides of sautéed mushrooms and garlic mashed potatoes. Jennifer ate only a small portion of her steak and had the rest put in a to-go box. She said the steak would add flavor to the feast she was going to cook for us tomorrow. We stopped at one bottle of wine because we both had to drive. I paid the bill and Jennifer followed me back to my house where I parked my car. We drove back to her place and from there we took a taxi to her favorite Mexican Restaurant on Ventura Boulevard, Casa Vega.

It was not even four o'clock when we entered the restaurant, yet it was already crowded. Jennifer was excited because it was happy hour, and all margaritas were half-price. I don't think I had thought about happy hour since I was still living with my parents over twenty years ago in the Bronx. Coming into a lot of money, as I did in my twenties, has a way of distorting your reality. Never having to worry about money is different; among other things, it has a way of sheltering you from many of life's little pleasures. It suddenly occurred to me that Sofia, who had never lacked for anything, would never experience the thrill of landing a cheap margarita at a happy hour. It wouldn't mean a thing to her.

The restaurant was dark, despite the early hour, and we sat at a side table for two with a lit candle in a small red bowl. Almost immediately, a waiter brought us chips and salsa, and while he was there, Jennifer ordered a strawberry margarita. I tried to order a Budweiser, but Jennifer cancelled that plan and told the waiter to bring us another margarita. "You need to forgive him; he doesn't get out much," she told the waiter and then turned to me and said, "You walk into a Mexican restaurant that serves the best margaritas in the world, find out they're half-price, and like a true Yankee from New York you order a beer."

"What can I tell you? I like beer."

"And I like Dom Perignon, but you don't see me ordering it."

"If that's what you like, order it. I imagine it would go wonderfully with your margarita."

She laughed, and I suddenly felt chills running up my arms. What was it about that laugh? Every time I heard it, I felt like the luckiest guy in the world. It made me want to try to be funnier, just to pull the sound out of her body. It wasn't her physical beauty. In a city like Los

Angeles you pass pretty girls every twenty feet. Jennifer had something else going for her. She glowed from inside.

The waiter returned with two margaritas, each one sporting a skewer of fresh mango pieces and a single blackberry. Jennifer tasted hers right away and rewarded the waiter with a look of ecstasy. "Still the best in the city," she said. "Thank you." Then she looked across at me, took another sip, and playfully passed the tip of her tongue around her lips. I looked down at the strange drink in the broad-rim glass with the long stem and hesitated. "What are you waiting for?" she asked. "I promise it won't kill you — unless of course you're allergic to strawberries?"

"No!" I replied as I picked up the glass, moved the skewer to one side, and took a sip. "Not bad, actually. Not bad at all." I wasn't a big fan of fruity drinks, but in the presence of this amazing young woman I would have drunk rat poison and given it four stars. I took a bigger sip this time — a manly swig of margarita — only to be hit by a sudden brain freeze. My hand flew to my forehead and I grimaced.

"Oh, honey," she said, laughing, as she reached across to take my other hand. "Slow is better."

As I recovered, I reached into the glass and pulled out the fruit skewer and deposited it on my side plate.

Jennifer smiled and patted my hand. "Don't you worry, my little warrior writer. I won't tell anyone that I saw you drinking a girlie drink. But I happen to know that even Hemingway loved his margaritas while sunbathing in Key West."

This perked me up. "So you like Hemingway?"

"Of course I like Hemingway. Surely, you didn't take me for a Fitzgerald girl?"

"I wouldn't presume, but I'm happy to hear it," I said, telling the whole truth now, and starting to feel my forehead coming back to life. "*The Sun Also Rises* is my favorite book of all time."

"What a coincidence. Lady Brett Ashley is one of my favorite female characters of all time. Even though I'm nothing like her, I can assure you that deep inside the unconscious of all females, there is a part of us that wishes we were like Lady Ashley."

"Really, a southern belle like yourself? I never would have thought."

"Oh, absolutely," she replied, raising a hand to her heart. "Even a southern belle like me would secretly love to be able to chuck off her clothes and jump into bed with a handsome, young bullfighter, if only once in this life."

Now it was my turn to laugh, and this seemed to make her happy and loose. She leaned forward, smiling, and rested her head on the table and looked up at me. Her eyes and lips were so inviting that I suddenly had no idea what to do. If I was writing this scene, this would be the moment when the male character reaches across to kiss this amazing creature, but it had been so long since I kissed a woman that I felt completely helpless. Paralyzed. It had just been me and Sofia at home for so long that I never even thought about dating. I'd thrown myself into work and parenting until romance became a distant memory. Even casual sex had seemed like too much work. The only love and passion in my life was what took place in my imagination. I could write these scenes, but I could no longer remember how to be *in* them.

Jennifer lifted her head off the table and cupped her chin in her hands, looking at me intently.

"Now it's your turn to tell me a deep, dark secret," she said. "I'm a big girl, so you can be a little dirty, but please, keep it under NC17."

"What if I don't have any deep, dark secrets?"

"Oh, please. Every writer has secrets, or they have nothing to write about."

I fumbled for my drink and took another big swig. This time I was okay; it had warmed up a little. "What if I tell you something about my daughter?"

"The aforementioned Sofia?" Jennifer replied.

"The one and only."

"Well, I guess that will do … even though I was hoping for something a little more romantic, like a tale of a beautiful señorita who, many years ago, was dumb enough to leave you on a beach down Mexico way, but whose image remains cemented in your mind."

"Sorry to disappoint, but nothing so exotic has ever happened to me. And if I did carry the image of a beautiful señorita from years ago, it would have been erased the moment I saw you walk out of your office in those jeans and that sweater."

"Really? Because I could have sworn you seemed mighty interested in me while I was in that sexy nurse costume."

"True, but that was for all the wrong reasons. I prefer the real you."

She smiled as she reached for her drink and took a long sip. Then she put her drink down, folded her hands in front of her, and looked straight at me.

"So tell me about Miss Sofia."

"Well …" I said, suddenly not sure where to begin. How do you talk about the air around you? How do you talk about the weather?

"This is going to sound superficial, but hear me out. The first thing everyone notices about Sofia is her beauty. She is strikingly gorgeous, and has been from the moment she entered this world. She has this full, dark, straight hair that glitters like black diamonds. Her face is oval and her skin is olive with golden undertones. Her eyes are both exotic and glamorously expressive, and her eyelashes — well, I've heard girls say they would 'die for them,' so there you go."

"It sounds like you are describing Sophia Loren."

"That's who I named her after — although I spelled it with an 'f' instead of a 'ph' — and I imagine she could pass for Ms. Loren's daughter, because, for the life of me, I can't understand how her mother and I produced such a creature. Her mother was pretty, but she had none of the qualities that are so blatantly apparent in Sofia. Her mother had blond hair, and her features were soft and pale, and her eyes were blue. And as for me, there is no resemblance or even a hint that I might be her father. The best guess I can come up with is that Sofia was the recipient of some latent DNA on my mother's side."

I took out my wallet and showed Jennifer a chronological pictorial of Sofia from when she was a baby, through childhood, right up to the present.

"My God, you weren't kidding. She is everything you described and more."

"Unfortunately, she's not so beautiful on the inside, or at least not these days. Not for about five years now."

"What happened?"

"She changed, and not for the better."

"How so?"

"It's hard to describe. I can only seem to approach it from the outside, through what I saw her do to my parents."

"What did she do to your parents?"

"She broke their hearts, and roughed up mine pretty badly in the process. They loved her more than anything in the world, and she turned on them. She was about thirteen when a total change came over her. At first, we thought it was just hormonal changes that all teenagers go through, but her behavior got worse, until my parents stopped coming to visit when she turned sixteen. The things she said to them ... I can't even repeat them. They were just abhorrent. How I stopped from beating her silly I'll never know."

"Because it's not easy to hit someone you love."

"No, but she would have deserved it. I loved my parents, and she treated them like dirt. A few years later, both my parents died, and Sofia refused to go to either of their funerals. In their final will and testament she was the only grandchild to be left with nothing. When I told her this she said, 'Like I missed out on some type of fortune.'

"So I told her, 'Eighty thousand dollars is what you missed out on,' and she said, 'Wow! I could have really used that money. Well, can't do anything about it now.' And that was it."

Jennifer was listening closely but not saying a word, so I continued.

"What I did not tell my daughter was that her grandparents left me eighty thousand additional dollars that, they stipulated, I could give to Sofia if she changed and showed the humanity and love she possessed as a child. She's now eighteen and she's still the same empty, ungrateful creature she was at thirteen. She's simply in love with herself and cannot pass a mirror without admiring her own reflection. Even worse, she seems to truly believe that her needs and opinions are the only ones that matter in this world. Everyone else can just stuff it."

We ordered two more margaritas and Jennifer's relaxed posture suddenly stiffened as she sat back in her chair. At that moment I thought, *How fitting that the one woman I could imagine falling in love with is going to be scared off by my psychotic daughter.*

But Jennifer's eyes remained fixed on me, and there was enough gentleness in them to make me think I could continue.

"It's not like Sofia was denied anything from the moment she was born. I took her to school and picked her up and I never missed a parent-teacher meeting or a school play she was in. She was allowed to have friends over whenever she pleased, though there weren't many friends in her life. We celebrated her birthdays and we always had guests over for the holidays."

Jennifer finally spoke up. "What was Sofia like as a little girl? I mean, how would you describe her personality?"

"She was a happy child, always giggling and giving out hugs. At night we would cuddle up and watch her favorite TV programs while eating popcorn. I used to think that if God never gave me anything else, he had already giving me the greatest gift … my Sofia."

"What do you think went wrong?"

"Well, it was like the lights went off inside her. Before that time, she was a straight 'A' student. In the end, she barely graduated high school. The child who I thought might one day become a doctor or a scientist, someone who could make a difference, didn't exist anymore. When she decided not to go to college I was actually relieved that she wouldn't have to face the rejection that would have come her way. Instead, she decided she wanted to become an actress, and according to her, 'surely one didn't need any stupid college degree for that.' We agreed that I would give her three thousand dollars a month to pay for acting lessons, rent, and living expenses. She moved out about a month ago and into an apartment with a bunch of friends … friends I still have not met and I seriously doubt exist except in her mind."

"Wow," was all Jennifer said. She seemed to be staring at a spot between us, thinking.

"Wow?"

She shook herself back into the present. "Sorry. It's a lot."

"I know," I said, then studied her face, which had already clouded over again. "What are you thinking?"

"Well, to be honest, I'm thinking that you're probably enabling her by giving her all that money. But I'm sure you must know that already."

"Believe me, Jennifer, I do know. But it was the only way I could be sure I would see her at least once a week. I don't just mail her a check. She has to come over to the house and pick it up. I give her seven hundred and fifty dollars a week. I have no idea what goes on in her mind. If she's short on money, I wouldn't put it past her to start peddling the only gifts she has, which are her beauty and her body."

"Has she seen a therapist?"

"I have made so many appointments with therapists and doctors over the years that I've lost count. She either refuses to go or says she will and doesn't show up."

"I can't wait to meet Miss Sofia," Jennifer remarked, to my astonishment.

"Why?" I asked as I took another swig of margarita.

"I have my reasons, trust me. Why don't you call her and tell her you need a ride to the doctor tomorrow? If she doesn't answer, leave a message, and then text her over and over again until she replies."

I followed her advice, calling Sofia and leaving a message. But when it came to texting, I handed Jennifer the phone and she did the honors. Every fifteen minutes, she sent a new text, each time telling Sofia that it was "very important" that she reply as soon as possible.

I was not an aficionado when it came to Mexican food. The few times I ate it were not very pleasant. But then, I didn't have Jennifer to do my ordering for me. She was like an FBI profiler, reading me for clues before she ordered an all-beef burrito and beef tacos with soft shells for me. After a few bites, I was a fan … either that or the margaritas were hitting me harder than I realized.

Jennifer insisted we leave at seven o'clock, as soon as happy hour ended. She was not going to suddenly spend double for the same drinks that we'd been having for the last three hours. Trying to talk her out of it was futile. Besides, she pointed out, it was better we stop drinking now because tomorrow I was having surgery.

I did not want the night to end. She was intoxicating and at the same time completely down to earth — a combination that left me feeling calm and excited at the same time. I had the waiter call us two cabs, playing it safe rather than sorry.

As we stood under the restaurant awning waiting for our cabs, we exchanged phone numbers. I had her promise to call me as soon as she got home. When the first cab arrived, I opened the back door and Jennifer slipped inside. I handed the driver a fifty-dollar bill and told him to keep the change. Jennifer naturally complained and said she could afford her own cab fare, but I waved off her objections and the driver smiled his thanks. I stuck my head in the back window to say goodnight, and as I looked at her face in the moonlight, all I could think about was how much I wanted to kiss her. Instead I froze and muttered something about what a wonderful day it had been, and how I looked forward to many more. The cab drove off and I saw her look back at me and smile.

Back at the house, I opened the refrigerator and took out a Budweiser as I waited for Jennifer's call. It was strange to think that this amazing day could end on a sour note if she did not call. I was starting to fret about that possibility when my phone rang and I heard her voice on the other end. It was like my guardian angel reaching out and touching me on the shoulder, alleviating my fears, inspiring dormant feelings of romance. We talked for over an hour and it was almost like she was still seated across from me at the restaurant. I could still smell her subtle floral perfume and see the dimples in her cheeks every time she laughed.

At one point during the conversation she warned me "not to drink too many more beers."

I stopped in mid-sip, put the bottle down, and asked, "How do you know I'm drinking a beer?"

She laughed, and I could sense her eyes sparkling with the knowledge of a discerning teacher. "Because I was naughty and kept you from having your favorite beverage all night."

"Those margaritas went down easily enough."

"Great, because they have a happy hour Monday through Friday and as long as I am working for Doc Hollywood I will be available."

"Wow! I could easily see margaritas becoming my favorite drink."

She laughed and replied, "Somehow I just don't see a boy from the Bronx replacing beers with margaritas."

"I could easily see a Frenchman giving up wine for margaritas if it meant sitting across from you every day for the rest of his life."

"Oh, that's the writer speaking now," she said with a giggle. "Or do you honestly believe I'm that perfect?"

"You're that perfect and then some."

"Please, keep talking. My head hasn't swelled this much … ever!!"

"Maybe I should just stop talking," I teased, as she continued to giggle.

"Oh no, please don't stop. I just love to hear how wonderful and perfect I am. It's not every day that a Hollywood big shot lavishes a hillbilly like myself with such an abundance of praise."

"I'm not a Hollywood big shot."

"Oh sure you are. Just ask Dr. Souter's secretary. If I didn't know better, I would have sworn she was your agent. And let's not forget the box of chocolates, while all poor little me got was half-price margaritas and a few tacos and chips."

"And a steak, crab appetizers, and a wonderful bottle of wine for lunch."

"Oh yeah, I almost forgot about that, it was so long ago. Isn't one of the mottos I hear going around this town, 'What have you done for me lately?'"

"Yeah, but I don't live by that motto."

"Does that mean I shouldn't expect a box of chocolates?"

"I'll buy you a hundred boxes of chocolate if that's what you really want, but you should know that the place I buy those delicious chocolates from never runs any half-price sales like they do at the Mexican restaurant. There's no happy hour in the truffle business."

"How unfortunate. If that's the case, you only have to buy me fifty boxes."

"So considerate."

"Thank you, I have always considered myself a very thoughtful person, but we *are* talking about chocolates. A girl's best friend, after jewelry, shoes, and clothes."

"You don't strike me as a girl who's obsessed with baubles."

"I'm not, but then when you're as perfect as me, why distract from the flawlessness with shiny accessories? That's not to say that if you gave me a diamond necklace I wouldn't gladly accept."

"But I would be the last person who would want to distract from your flawlessness."

"Not to worry — after wearing it once I would sell it and pay off my student loans. After all, it's exactly one month until I turn that awful age of thirty."

"Is that a hint?"

"It might be. Surely you don't expect me to come right out with such an outrageous suggestion."

"Your subtlety is duly noted."

"Thank you, kind sir, but all I really want for my birthday is a collection of half-priced margaritas and a cupcake with a single candle."

"And when you blow out the candle, what will be your wish, if you don't mind me asking?"

She hesitated for a moment and then replied, "That you and your beautiful daughter Sofia reconnect."

I knew at that moment that I could not let this one get away. I was suddenly choked up and struggling to keep up the banter.

"That might take a miracle," I said.

"No, not a miracle, but very likely a different approach."

"Please, enlighten me."

"I will, once I meet her."

"That might scare you off forever."

"I don't scare easily, and I never give up hope. It's like I told you, I wouldn't have chosen the profession I did without possessing both of those traits."

"Well, maybe once you stop working for Doc Hollywood and get a job in your chosen field in one of the many hospitals around town you can take Sofia on a tour. Meeting some of those children might re-awaken some of the lost humanity that I pray still exists somewhere in that shell of a human being."

I thought I felt her stiffen a little on the other end of the line. She was quiet for a few seconds, then said, "The children are not there to elicit sympathy. They're not display items in a museum."

"I know that, and I didn't mean it like that."

"How did you mean it?"

"Well, I know it's not the same as cancer, but I've been around disability a lot, and I think it helped me be a better person. I know how important it is to treat people with disabilities like everyone else. Growing up, my favorite uncle, Tony, had polio. He developed it as a child, and for the rest of his life, he walked with a very noticeable limp. Then there's my Aunt Jeannette, who was born developmentally delayed and spent her life in a wheelchair. She was never left out of any family events and just having her there made everything so much more special and fun, because she was such a naturally happy person. Neither of them was there to elicit sympathy. In fact, they would have been offended by the idea. They were never on display, but having them in my life was a reminder that it's a gift to be born healthy and in full control of your body. All I was trying to say is that I would love to see Sofia gain a better understanding of people who have it a lot harder than she does. She has never encountered anyone with a severe illness or disability. Or if she has, she has never shown any signs of acknowledging it."

"You don't know that," Jennifer shot back quickly. Her tone caught me by surprise. It was the first time, in the short but memorable time we'd known each other, that she sounded severe.

"Yes, I do. I'm her father," I replied, suddenly defensive.

"She could very well be a victim. You told me she refused to see a therapist and so you can't rule out anything."

I didn't like the sudden turn this conversation was taking. I knew my daughter, and I wasn't about to jeopardize my relationship with Jennifer over her. I had sacrificed a lot for Sofia, and would continue to do so until the day I died, but I was also beginning to feel that I deserved some happiness. Jennifer must have sensed my anxiety. She interrupted my train of thought with an apology. "You know, I haven't even met Sofia, so please forgive me for jumping to conclusions. I'm just a fanatic when it comes to keeping hope alive. I can't stand to give up on people."

"And that's just one of your many fine qualities."

"Oh yeah, I nearly forgot that I'm perfect! Thank you for reminding me." As she giggled on the other end of the line, my anxiety ebbed away.

I knew that we should both be getting to bed, but I didn't want the conversation to end, so I lobbed another question at her. "Did you always want to be a nurse?"

"I don't think so. I can't remember. But I do know that I wanted to go into a profession where I could make a positive difference in peoples' lives." Then she started talking about her dad, and about how he worked in a coal mine from the time he was eighteen until the day he dropped dead of a heart attack at forty-seven.

"I don't think I ever saw him leave for work without a touch of dread on his face or come home after a twelve-hour shift anything less than totally exhausted. And he was such a handsome and gentle man. He never developed the bad habits of the other miners. He barely drank, and he never smoked. He always said he inhaled enough coal dust underground that he didn't need to add nicotine to the mix. He provided for his family quite handsomely and, in the end, he provided for us with his life."

"I'm so sorry."

I could hear her sniffling on the other end of the line, and after a few awkward moments she said, "He never did get to see me graduate from college. He would have been so proud."

"Do you have any brothers and sisters?"

"No, only perfect little me and my mommy," she said, forcing her voice to sound brighter. "How about you? Did you always want to be a writer?"

"It was my dream to play for the New York Knicks." She started to laugh hysterically.

"Surely you're kidding?"

"No, that was my dream. What's so strange about that? I grew up on basketball courts."

"Basketball, fine, but the Knicks … they're so terrible! And as far back as I could remember they have always been terrible."

"That's not true. They had some great teams in the past."

"Like when, fifty years ago?"

She was almost right. My Knicks have not won a championship since the 1973-74 season. Actually, they have not won a championship in my lifetime, but I wasn't ready to admit that.

"My Kentucky Wildcats, a college team, could beat the Knicks."

"Okay, okay, you know that isn't true. No college team is going to beat a professional NBA team."

"I'm sorry, I didn't realize the Knicks were still considered a professional basketball team."

"Very funny!"

"I don't know why you just don't root for the Lakers. It's not like you haven't been living out here for over twenty years. They at least know how to win championships."

"I'm not the type who suddenly stops rooting for my team because they're going through a rough stretch."

"Oh, is that what you New Yorkers call it? Where I come from they call it a drought with no rain in the forecast."

"Wow! This is a side of you I never expected to see."

"And why is that? It's not like it's a rule that only New Yorkers are allowed to grow up playing basketball. For the record, basketball is second only to God and family in Kentucky."

"And let me guess, beautiful Jennifer grew up playing basketball."

"That's right. Anytime you want a real ass-kicking from a girl, I'm happy to oblige."

"Is that a challenge? A one-on-one, you and me?"

"That's right, and let me warn you, I don't play like a sissy. So if you're going to call a foul every time someone lays a pinkie on you, please don't waste my time. I can't stand crybabies on a basketball court."

"Well, since you are so sure of yourself maybe we should put a little wager on the game?"

"I don't need to put a wager on the game. Kicking your butt will be its own reward."

"For the record, what will you be wearing? Your sexy nurse outfit or your Kentucky blue uniform?"

"If it's the sexy nurse outfit you want me to show up wearing, I don't have problem with that, as long as you don't care about being embarrassed in front of onlookers as I kick your butt in heels. And if you so much as touch my boobs I will elbow you so hard to the head that you'll be seeing stars."

"But you just said that you like playing physical."

"Yeah, but in that outfit the upper deck is off-limits, unless of course you want an elbow to the head. It's up to you."

"Well, you're going to have to give me a little time to decide on the outfit. Do you play any other sports?"

"Yes, I'm a wonderful tennis player and I'm quite certain I can hit a baseball further than you and quite possibly throw one harder."

"You don't seem to have a problem with self-confidence."

"No, I don't. But it's not bragging as long as you can back up your words with action. I can't help it — being confident is simply part of being so perfect."

"And after I whip your butt, what is that going to do to your confidence?"

"Why would I even consider such an outrageous outcome? You're going to have to do a lot better than that to shake my confidence."

I opened the refrigerator and took out a beer. I twisted the top off and took a long swig.

I heard a sigh on the other end of the phone. "And that's the last beer tonight, right?"

"Besides being the female version of Michael Jordan, are you also a mind reader?"

"No, but I have excellent hearing."

"Of course you do. Just another attribute to go along with your already perfect self."

"If you say so. And no more beer, right?"

"Yes, mommy."

"Hmm. Not your mommy. But if that's a promise, I'll take it."

"That's a promise"

"Great. And don't forget, no late-night snacks. That includes peanut butter and jelly sandwiches."

I was starting to believe she really *was* able to read my mind, since I was quite certain I never mentioned my love for peanut butter and jelly sandwiches.

Before I could reply she remarked, "You had a small but discernable peanut butter and jelly stain on your shirt."

"You don't miss much, do you?"

"Nope. It's all part of being a good nurse."

"It's part of being a good writer, too. Maybe you should try your hand at writing."

"Maybe, but I would hate to infringe on your livelihood. But then who knows, I might decide to sit down one day and write my memoir. I can call it *Sexy and Perfect*. What do you think?"

"It sounds like you have already given it some serious thought."

"Not really. At least, not until today, when you pointed out to me how amazing I am."

We both had a laugh at that one, and after we finally said goodbye, I pulled the phone to my chest and slid down along the front of the refrigerator, grinning into space. I was dying for another beer, but I made a promise and, to be honest, I was getting a little paranoid about her ability to read my mind. I wasn't the type who believed in love at first sight, but I was fairly certain that I was in love with the perfect nurse from Kentucky, even though she made fun of my favorite team … a slight imperfection that I could probably learn to overlook.

I undressed and jumped into bed, then felt the back of my neck. The bumps were still there, but amazingly, since meeting the real Jennifer, not the actress playing the sexy nurse, I hadn't felt any pain. I checked my phone to see if Sofia had returned any of my messages or texts, and true to form, she hadn't.

Chapter 2

I woke up at my usual time and went for my run through the lovely neighborhood of Studio City. I felt like I was running on air as I thought about Jennifer and replayed our conversations in my head. Suddenly, all of the romantic and fun-filled possibilities that I had long ago given up on seemed to be within my reach again. After my run, I walked back into the house and just as I opened the door my phone rang. It was her.

"Hope I didn't wake you. I just wanted to remind you not to eat or drink anything before the procedure."

"Not to worry … sorry, I almost called you mommy again. I've been up since 5:30. Just came back from my seven-mile run."

"Really? You run?" She sounded genuinely surprised.

"Yes, I run. Is it that shocking?"

"No, I think it's great! I just thought you might want to use your exercise time a little more wisely, like maybe by picking up a basketball and fine-tuning those skills you brought with you from New York."

"I see you haven't lost your sense of humor," I remarked.

"You make it too easy."

"So happy I can keep you entertained."

"I appreciate that. I'll be at your house at 12:00."

"Why?"

"I'm your ride."

"I can just take a taxi. I don't want you to waste your lunch hour rushing over here and then rushing back."

"It's not a problem, and don't try to talk me out of it, unless of course you don't find me as perfect after a good night sleep and an eye-opening run."

"Just the opposite. I couldn't get you out of my mind. Those seven miles felt like two."

"Wow! My head is starting to swell again and it's much too early for that. I'll see you at noon."

"Thank you."

Jennifer arrived at exactly twelve o'clock in her vintage 1974 Dodge Dart. I walked out to meet her, grabbing my car keys. She was dressed in a simple summer dress and she was lovelier than I remembered. I remarked, "Not only perfect, but punctual."

"All part of the job. Come, get in."

"I have an idea. How about we take my car?"

"Why, what's wrong with my car?"

"Nothing, I had a car just like it when I moved out here but it's supposed to go up to 95 degrees and my car has air conditioning."

"You're amazing. Are you sure you grew up in the Bronx? You behave more like you were raised on the upper east side of Manhattan."

"No, I'm quite sure it was the Bronx."

She got out of her car and held her hand out for my keys.

"Are you sure you'll be okay driving an SUV as big as mine?"

She looked at me incredulously and replied, "I've driven tractors double the size of your precious SUV. And if you keep it up, you'll be driving in the trunk of my car."

We got into my SUV and Jennifer adjusted the driver's seat as though she had done it a million times before. "Now isn't this more comfortable?" I asked. "Feel that air conditioning. I even have SiriusXM, but none of the stations are tuned to country music. Sorry."

"Do I look like the type of girl who listens to country music?"

"I don't know, you *are* from Kentucky."

"Kentucky is considered the southeast."

"I knew that."

"No, you didn't. Before meeting me, you probably thought all people from Kentucky lived in log cabins and used outhouses."

"Are you trying to tell me you didn't grow up in a log cabin?" She looked at me and hit me on the arm.

"Another remark like that and I won't be so gentle. Do you have the Beatles channel on your SiriusXM?"

"Yes."

"Great — they're my favorite group."

I looked at her, dumbfounded. "My God, you really are perfect."

"What's that?" she asked over the engine noise.

"Oh, nothing."

I turned on the Beatles channel and the melancholy strains of "Girl" filled the space between us. We listened in silence until the deejay segued into another tune from the Rubber Soul album, "Drive My Car." The timing had us both laughing for several blocks.

"Do you think Sirius is watching us?" Jennifer asked.

"Clearly they've got the car bugged," I said.

"Next it'll be 'I'm Looking Through You.'"

"Ooh, good one," I said, genuinely impressed with her grasp of the Beatles catalogue. "As long as they don't play 'Nowhere Man,' we should be okay."

Then we had one of those moments you see in the movies where she stole a glance at me while I was looking out the window and I stole a glance at her while she was focusing on the road. I caught her looking at me out of the corner of my eye, but I pretended not to notice. It was funny because I had just included a similar scene in a script about a month earlier. I wondered if it was hokey at the time, but it didn't feel hokey now.

Chapter 3

When we reached the medical center, Jennifer parked in the garage beneath her office. She took the magnetic ticket, and before we even checked in, she had the girl at the desk stamp the ticket so we wouldn't get charged when we left.

I couldn't resist teasing her about her thrift. "Wow! That deal is better than a half-priced margarita."

Jennifer just looked at me and shook her head as we took the elevator up to Dr. Casey's suite. I asked, "So, are you going to go into your office now and re-emerge as the sexy nurse?"

"No! I'm finished for the day," she said, with a playful curtsy. "This is as sexy as I get today."

"Not that I'm complaining at all, but … those buttons … were *so* helpful."

She shot me a look that fell somewhere between stern schoolmarm and sweet girlfriend. I began to feel concerned.

"Aren't you going to be in the operating room?"

"No! He has his regular staff that he has been using for years. No need for ornamentation when the patient is going to be passed out and the crew needs to concentrate."

"You've got to be kidding."

"No, I'm not kidding. What would you want me in there for, to hold your hand?"

"Yes."

"Tough boy from the Bronx afraid of a little procedure?"

"No, tough boy from the Bronx smart enough to want beautiful girl to hold his hand."

"Sorry, but while they're cutting into you, I'll be out shopping for tonight's dinner. But I will wait for them to take you in before I go, and then I'll see you in recovery after it's all over."

Jennifer walked over to the receptionist and picked up some final paperwork I had to fill out before the procedure. I could not stop looking at her. In her white summer dress and flat leather sandals, she looked like some kind of princess who'd gotten lost on her way to the castle. As she stood there chatting amiably with her colleague, I suddenly marveled at how anyone could remain as pure as she seemed in this city of grifters and fakers. Half the people I'd met in LA could throttle the moral rectitude out of a saint, and yet here was Jennifer, as fresh and unaffected as a wildflower growing up through a crack in the sidewalk.

When my paperwork was ready, I was escorted to a room where I changed into a white hospital gown. Jennifer waited outside the room. As I let her in I walked backwards, conscious that my butt was hanging out. I sat down on the portable table that they would use to transport me to the operating room. She started to laugh.

"What's so funny?" I asked.

"You, that's what's so funny … I'm a nurse and I have seen plenty of naked butts. I'm sure your butt isn't much different than those of most men your age, unless of course you are trying to hide something from me."

"No, it's just that these gowns are so…"

"…revealing," she finished, with a giggle.

"That's the word I was looking for." I reached into my bag, took out my wallet, and handed it to her.

"Afraid someone might rob you while you're under?"

"No, but I'm not going to have you cook and on top of that pay for the food. If I don't have enough cash in there, just use the American Express." She opened my wallet and took out my American Express Centurion card. She playfully twirled it around her fingers.

"You know a guy can seriously regret handing a girl a card like this, especially one he just met."

"I'll take my chances."

She put the card back in the wallet and put the wallet into her purse.

"And please, whatever you do, don't forget to have the girl at the desk punch the garage ticket when you come back to pick me up. The last thing I want to do is pay for parking."

"You know, you're a real ass."

"Please, tell me something I don't know."

She stood up, looked at the watch on her wrist, and said, "They'll be in shortly." She reached over and kissed me on cheek. "When you wake up in the recovery room I'll be right there."

"But will you be holding my hand?"

"The whole time."

"Promise?"

"Yes, I promise." She opened the door and looked back and smiled. The next thing I remember was waking up in recovery and looking up into the face of an angel, and yes, she was holding my hand.

Chapter 4

I was still a little sluggish from the anesthesia as Jennifer helped me into the passenger seat of my car. I had a bandage across the upper part of my neck where they made the incision, but I had no pain. Jennifer told me that everything went well, but that they wouldn't have the results from the biopsy for at least two or three days. She said she had no doubt that they would find nothing.

She took the parking ticket out of her purse and handed it to the attendant sitting in the booth in front of the exit. There was no charge and I remarked, "I see you didn't forget to get it stamped."

"I don't forget things like that. Maybe when I qualify for an American Express Centurion Card, such things won't matter so much to me." She drove out of the garage and turned left onto the Boulevard.

"Did you get everything you need for the dinner tonight?"

"Yes, and I even went a little crazy and bought two bottles of the Far Niente chardonnay we had at lunch yesterday. Never have I spend so much money on wine before, but it was so delicious, and since it's kind of a special occasion I didn't think you would mind so much." She looked across at me and smiled. "I warned you that giving a girl a card like that could be dangerous."

I just stared at her, mesmerized.

"Are you okay? I could pull over if you're feeling nauseated?"

"Why would I be nauseated?" I asked, like a real idiot.

"Because you just had surgery. It's quite common."

"No, I'm feeling wonderful. What could possibly be wrong? I'm sitting across from the most beautiful girl in the world."

"Wow! That anesthesia really did a number on you." She laughed, and the magical spell she had already cast over me mushroomed into an all-encompassing cloud that I would have been content to live on forever.

Back at my house, Jennifer helped me onto the couch in the living room. That was the last thing I remembered until I woke up hours later with the smell of a homemade southern dinner being prepared in the kitchen. I walked toward the kitchen and stopped suddenly at the door. Right there on my terra cotta floor, a Kentucky beauty was cooking, singing and dancing to Andrea Bocelli's rendition of "I Can't Help Falling in Love With You" as the song streamed through the radio I kept on the counter.

The song ended and I started to clap. Jennifer spun around and smiled shyly like a little girl caught with her hands in the cookie jar. "Okay, I'm guilty of making a fool of myself, but it isn't nice to spy on people."

"The only thing you're guilty of is looking more perfect than any human being has a right to be."

"Wow! I see the anesthesia still hasn't worn off."

"No, it has."

"Are you having much pain?"

"Nothing a few beers and a homemade dinner won't cure." I opened the refrigerator and took out a Budweiser.

"Don't you dare!" Jennifer barked as she grabbed the beer out of my hand and put it back in the refrigerator. "You haven't eaten a single thing all day and the first thing going into your stomach is not going to be any type of alcohol, especially not after surgery." She stuffed a piece of delicious cornbread into my mouth. I swallowed it like a good little child, and she followed that with another piece.

"Delicious! Did you make it all by your lovely self?"

"No, I had it delivered all the way from Kentucky. Wiseass!"

"Exactly how many pieces of bread am I going to have to eat before I'm allowed an adult beverage?"

"When I decide that the only child in the room starts acting like an adult," and with that she shoved another piece of bread into my mouth.

"You know, if you keep filling me up with cornbread, I'm not going to have any room for the wonderful feast you have prepared." I pointed to a pan on the stovetop where she'd laid out four breaded, uncooked, pork chops on the bone.

"Pork chops, one of my favorite dishes … and on the bone and seasoned. A special recipe?"

"Yes, my mommy's very special recipe."

"Is your mommy as tough and beautiful as you?"

"Much tougher and tons more beautiful."

"What's her name?"

"Lou, and that's all I have ever heard anyone call her, including my daddy and my grandma."

Jennifer turned as an undeniable sadness came over her.

"But you have always called her mommy?" I asked.

"Yes, mommy." She took out a frying pan and put it on top of one of the gas jets. She turned the gas on and put cooking oil and butter in the pan. She lightly fried each of the pork chops and then put them into a separate pan that she placed into the stove.

"Is there anything I can do?"

"Yes, you can pour me some more of this delicious wine and pour yourself a glass."

I opened the refrigerator and took out the bottle of Far Niente chardonnay, then refilled her glass and poured one for myself.

"Well, at least I know what to get you for your birthday. A case of this delicious wine."

"Hey, what happened to the diamond necklace?"

"I'll get you that, too."

"I would hope so," she remarked, then started to laugh at her own audacity.

I heard the front door open and shortly after, the voice of my beautiful daughter, yelling, "Daddy, Daddy."

"In here, Sofia."

Sofia walked toward the kitchen and suddenly stopped as she noticed Jennifer. "Who's she?" she asked.

"Sofia, this is my friend Jennifer. Jennifer, meet my daughter Sofia." I turned to Sofia and explained, "Jennifer is also my nurse."

"So is that what they call girls in her profession these days?"

Jennifer put the slatted spoon she was using down on the countertop, took a few steps toward my daughter, and spoke to her calmly but firmly. "I'm going to let that insulting remark slide … only because I would like to get off to a good start with you. Your father told me how beautiful you were, and he was not mistaken."

Jennifer took a few more steps toward her and Sofia quickly moved around her and close to me. "Daddy, can I please have my money? I'm already running late for rehearsals."

"I can't take care of that for you right now, honey. Jennifer has been with me all day, driving me back and forth from the hospital, and then slaving over a hot stove so I could have a homemade meal."

Sofia had her phone in her hand and Jennifer snatched it right out from her hand. "What the hell," Sofia yelled.

"Your father left you eleven text messages and a number of voice mails last night, and apparently you didn't think it was important enough to get back to him."

"I was having trouble with my phone all last night."

Jennifer opened the phone and looked down at all the unanswered texts and messages ... all dated at about the time they were sent.

"You should get out of the habit of lying, Sofia, because the longer you continue, the harder it will be to tell the truth." Jennifer handed her back the phone and asked, "Why don't you join us for dinner?"

Sofia looked at me and I remarked, "You can either join us for dinner or wait until we are finished, but that might be a long time from now."

"I'll just come back later." She started for the door and Jennifer asked, "Don't you even want to know how your father's surgery turned out?"

"I'll find out later," she said, and walked out the door.

I looked helplessly across at Jennifer, who opened the oven and took out the pork chops. There was nothing in the world I loved more than my daughter; not even my infatuation with Jennifer came close to my love for Sofia. Yet, at this moment in time, I was wishing that I had put that girl in a monastery in the remote hills of Italy as soon as this insane behavior began. Not only would she have learned a foreign language, but they would have whipped her sorry little ass into shape. As an alumnus of Catholic schools I could vouch for their medieval methods of discipline.

"I apologize for my daughter's behavior," I remarked feebly.

"No need to apologize. You warned me and I intentionally egged her on. In just the short time she was here, I noticed that she seemed to totally space out at times."

"Like she is lost, disconnected."

"Exactly."

"So what do you think?" I asked.

"Oh, she needs help, but I have no doubt she is going to be okay, more like the girl you remember before this all started."

I left it at that, pretending to take comfort in Jennifer's reassurance, even though her optimism seemed unfounded. I set the table. It was the first time I had done that in years. I opened the second bottle of chardonnay as Jennifer brought over the plate of pork chops, mashed potatoes, and biscuits.

As I refilled our wine glasses, Jennifer put the radio back on, and like magic, Andrea Bocelli's rendition of "I Can't Help Falling in Love with You" came back on. She had put it on autoplay. Never in my life had a song represented everything I was feeling at that moment so perfectly.

I looked into Jennifer's eyes, raised my glass, and said, "To Lou and to the very special child she raised."

I cut into a pork chop, took a first bite, and instantly closed my eyes. It was absolutely delicious, as was the rest of the meal, and the dessert, blackberry cobbler, was a perfect mix of tart and sweet. The memory of my daughter's behavior receded with every bite and with every giggle and laugh we shared. We talked about old movies, music, literature, and what it was like growing up in Kentucky and the Bronx.

After dinner, we moved to the couch in the living room. I ordered two more bottles of Far Niente from a liquor store near the house that delivered. Jennifer had brought along a small overnight bag. She was going to sleep in the room my parents used to sleep in when they visited. She joked that this wasn't the beginning of a plan she had hatched to "move in permanently."

I replied without thinking, saying that the only thing that could make this night more perfect was the idea that she might move in permanently, and that no, I wasn't still high on the anesthesia.

She laughed and said, "Maybe not, but I'm pretty sure it's the wine talking now."

I reminded her that she had started on the wine before I had, and she replied that she was "raised on bourbon" and that where she came from, "the drunkards only drank wine and beer as a last resort."

"So what you're telling me is that you're not only a champion basketball player but a champion drunk."

She made a silly face and replied, "A champion drunk — no. More like a girl who can handle her liquor better than any guy she knows from the Bronx."

"And exactly how many guys do you know from the Bronx?"

"Let me think ... just one."

"If you're trying to get me to agree to a drinking contest, with bourbon as the weapon of choice, you can forget it. I concede right here and now."

"Well, that's very wise of you. It's good you know your limitations. It's a shame I'm going to humiliate you on a basketball court, but if you want to concede the inevitable and save face, we don't have to go through with that contest either."

"Not a chance of that."

"Well, then my only advice to you is what I told you earlier. Instead of going running tomorrow you might want to spend that time practicing on the nearest court. Actually, you might want to consider giving up all other activities and simply practicing day and night until we finally do play."

"Wow! Talk about overconfidence."

"It's not overconfidence, it's reality."

"And here I was thinking that I would go easy on you, but I am seriously going to have to kick your perfect little butt." She laughed as the phone rang. I looked down at the caller ID and it was Sofia.

"Wow! Hold off on the money and she suddenly remembers her father's phone number." I answered the phone. "Hello, Sofia."

"Hello, Daddy. Is that bitch still there?"

"Yes, the bitch is still here and if you call her that one more time there will be serious consequences." I looked at Jennifer as I placed the phone on speaker, without Sofia knowing.

"Let me just warn you, in another seven or eight years when she turns thirty she won't be looking so great."

"She will be turning thirty next month, and in another ten years I expect she will look as beautiful as she does right now."

"Hi Sofia, it's the bitch, and just let me say that that was one of the nicest things another girl has ever said about me. The idea that such a beautiful young lady as you thinks I look so much younger than I am is such a wonderful compliment. Thank you so much."

"Oh my God," was the last thing Sofia said before hanging up.

Jennifer laughed and then suddenly stopped and said, "I guess that wasn't very nice of me, but I couldn't help it."

"What do you mean? She called you a bitch and earlier in the night she insinuated that you were a hooker. I think you were within your rights to say just about anything to her, but I do appreciate that you wore your kid gloves."

"She's a troubled young lady, but I'm quite confident that with the right treatment she will turn back into the fun-loving daughter you remember."

I looked at Jennifer with an expression of open disbelief. This must have egged her on, because she raised her prediction to a promise.

"Have faith, Joe, I will get the daughter you knew back to you."

"I do have faith. Every night I pray to Saint Joseph to help my daughter. Maybe he put you in my path to help with Sofia; even though I like to think he put you in my path to also help me."

"I think the two things are connected."

"That might be too much for anyone to handle."

"I've been raised, and trained, to handle situations a lot more difficult than a troubled teenager and her concerned father. Were you named after Saint Joseph?"

"Yes, my mother had a special affection for him. As a child, she asked him for what she considered a miracle, and when she got what she asked for, she promised him that if she ever had a boy, she would name him after him."

"That's so sweet," Jennifer said.

I lowered my head and nodded sadly. "My parents were really wonderful. I was blessed, and it will always haunt me the way my daughter treated them. Always."

I looked up at Jennifer and couldn't help thinking about how I'd wanted this night to *not* be about Sofia, and how it turned out to have her fingerprints stamped over the entire gathering. I knew that Jennifer was smart and that she would know without me saying anything that if push came to shove and I had to choose between her and my daughter, it would always be Sofia. When her mother handed her to me and said, "She's all yours," it turned out to be a blessing until she turned thirteen, and since then it had been a curse. Despite every effort to understand the problem and to find her help, it was useless. The child was like an irritable zombie, and I could not help feeling responsible.

"A penny for your thoughts," Jennifer remarked.

"Is that all?" I asked.

"Oh, I'm sorry. I forgot you're rich and probably don't even remember what a penny looks like. How about a dollar bill? You still remember what they look like?"

"You know, besides being beautiful and intelligent you also have a wonderful sense of humor."

"Thank you, and don't forget my culinary skills."

"To think of it, you would make the perfect wife."

"Is that a proposition?"

"Yes," I replied without hesitation. "I would marry you right here and now if you said yes."

She laughed as she reached for the wine bottle. I gently grabbed her hand and said, "I'm not joking, and it's not the wine talking."

"But why? You hardly know me. For all you know, I could just be after your money."

"No, you're definitely not that. I ruled out that possibility at lunch yesterday. Nobody talks about sick children like you did yesterday if their one goal in life is to bag a rich husband."

"The reason I moved out here was because nurses in my field, in Los Angeles, make three times what they make in Kentucky."

"And that extra money you have earmarked for what, if you don't mind me asking?"

"For my mommy. The nursing home she's in is terrible and even though she doesn't remember me, she deserves the best. She sacrificed everything for me. It's the least I can do."

"I can easily help you with that, no strings attached."

"I know you can, but the answer is still no," she said, then looked at me intently. "Don't think for a minute that I don't appreciate the offer."

"Why is it that you can open your heart so generously to people you hardly know, yet refuse to accept other people's generosity?"

"Maybe it's because my whole life all I have ever heard is how us hillbillies are good for nothing, except for taking handouts. If I ever took money from you to help my mommy, it would be disrespecting everything she has stood for her whole life."

"I understand, but the offer has no expiration date in case you change your mind."

"Thank you. I think it's nighty-night for this girl, and I wouldn't be a very good nurse if I didn't suggest that you also should go to bed. After all, you're the one who had surgery."

"But I was the lucky guy who got to look at you before and after surgery, and on top of that have you cook for me."

She turned and laughed before disappearing into the bedroom that my parents used to sleep in when they came to visit. I waited a few minutes and walked into my bedroom. I got into bed and tossed for hours like a teenager, agonizing about everything that had gone wrong during the night, going over and over all of the excuses that the magnificent creature sleeping just a few rooms down from mine could easily use as a reason to cut this relationship off before it had a chance to really begin. Naturally, Sofia topped the list. What sensible woman would even consider becoming a kind of step-mother figure to a young woman who thought nothing of hurling insults and calling her a prostitute on their first meeting? For the first time, I sensed a new threat to my happiness in Sofia's cruel streak. Her behavior had plagued me for five years, but now I wondered if it might rob me of my one shot at happiness with an amazing woman. Jennifer seemed wildly optimistic about her chances of getting through to Sofia, but what would happen when my daughter stayed just as abusive as she had been the night they met? What then?

For the first time in hours, my neck started to throb. The whole time I'd been laughing and talking with Jennifer and enjoying her gorgeous home-cooked meal, I hadn't even noticed it. Now everything seemed uncertain again, and a dull ache kept me awake until the wee hours.

Chapter 5

Despite sleeping badly, I woke up at my usual time, and for the first time in years I heard music coming from down the hall. I pulled on my running gear and walked into the dining area where I saw Jennifer one room over in the kitchen, cooking, singing, and dancing to the music on the radio. She had on the same light blue bathrobe that my mother wore when she visited. Before I had time to clap, she spotted me watching her and said, "Hey there! I told you it's not nice to spy on people."

"Maybe not, but when the person I am spying on is as beautiful and charming as you, I can't help myself."

"The music didn't wake you, did it?"

"No! This is the time I get up every morning and go for my run."

"So you actually do go running every morning?" she asked with a taunting smile.

"Yes. Why would I lie to you?"

"Umm, let me think … male ego?"

"Do I come off as someone who has a large ego?"

"Not usually, except for the fact that you don't think this particular female could possibly beat you in a game of one-on-one."

"I'm not the one going around bragging about how great I am."

"I guess I have been laying it on hard, but that's just because I don't want to humiliate you and I'm hoping you will come to your senses and just drop out."

I leaned on the kitchen counter and leveled her with my gaze. "There is absolutely no chance of me dropping out. What are you cooking?"

"French toast. Want some?"

"How did you know that French toast is one of my favorite breakfast dishes?"

She reached into the pocket of her robe and pulled out a piece of paper, then handed it to me. Scribbled on the scrap of paper were the words "don't forget to pick up bread for Joe's French toast." It was my mother's handwriting.

"Oh my God, will you look at that." I stared at the note and felt my eyes start to well up.

"I'm sorry. I didn't mean to upset you!"

"No, no! I'm happy you found this. I'm going to keep it." I stared at the scrap of paper some more. "It's just so strange. It's like she led you right to it."

"Well, I wasn't going to say anything, but I think you might be onto something there."

"What do you mean?"

"Well, it was kind of uncanny. I saw the robe there on the hook, and it looked so comfy and warm that I just had to put it on. When I reached into the pocket I found the note. I immediately took off the robe and was putting it back on the peg when I had this overwhelming feeling that I was supposed to put it back on and make you French toast."

"Wow! A sign from above. Thank you for telling me that. I have no doubt that my mother would have loved you, and I can't help but think that she would have felt honored that you were wearing her robe."

"I hope so, because to raise such an amazing son she had to be quite a special lady."

"Aww," I said. "Did you sleep well?"

"Wonderfully. I didn't wake once the whole night."

"I apologize for some of the stupid things I said last night."

"Ahhh," she said. "I guess you slept well, too. I told you a good night's sleep would have you thinking logically again."

"I wasn't talking about the marriage proposal. That still stands. I would marry you today if you agreed."

She shook her head as she turned the pieces of egg-drenched bread over in the pan, then looked up, smiled, and moved her face about two inches from mine. "You can't even work up the courage to kiss me, yet you're ready to marry me."

I blushed like a teenager and replied, "I am so out of practice that I'm not even sure I remember how to do it correctly. I didn't want to fail miserably and lose you."

"If any other guy tried to use that excuse I would be laughing hysterically, but for some reason I believe you." She suddenly pressed her soft and lovely lips against mine and for a few moments I felt like I was floating toward heaven. She was the first to speak, while I just stood there, unable to open my eyes. "Now that wasn't so bad, was it?"

"Gah, no. Not so terrible. Think we can do it again?" She suppressed a laugh and once again pressed her lips against mine. Never again would the phrase *a kiss is just a kiss* have any meaning for me.

"Not to jump to conclusions or anything, but does this mean that you accept my proposal?" I asked.

She pulled back and looked me in the eyes. "One kiss and suddenly we're getting married?"

"Two kisses."

"Oh well, if it's two kisses, then I think we're already married in some states," she said. That got a laugh, and I put my hands on her waist. From the look in my eyes, she must have been able to tell that I wanted a real answer.

"Okay. To answer your question, what it *means* is that we're on the right track, but you need to give me a little time. I still have the question of my mommy. Until I can sort out her care, I can't promise anything."

"How about you move her out here and she can live here with us. I'm Italian and we love having a lot of people around, even if they don't speak much or simply babble on. It's not like any of us listen to each other."

She reached over and kissed me again and said, "I cannot tell you how much that means to me. But it would be sacrilegious to take a lady who spent her whole life in the south and move her to an alien place like Los Angeles."

"I understand. I built the guest house out back hoping my parents would move in, but I knew they would never leave the Bronx where they were both born."

She transferred the French toast to a plate and placed it on the kitchen table, along with a glass of orange juice and a little pot of syrup. She pulled out a chair for me and I sat down like a child at the kitchen table back home in the Bronx. I looked up at her, waiting for her to join me.

"Aren't you going to have some?"

"No, I ate some fruit before you got up. I never eat much in the morning." She sat down in a chair next to me as I cut into the French toast and took my first bite.

"Delicious, simply delicious."

"But not as good as mommy's?"

"Nothing is ever as good as mommy's, but you're very close."

"I'll take that as a thumbs up."

"A big thumbs up," I replied as I ate one delicious piece after another. Jennifer stayed next to me with her elbow resting on the table and her hand cupped under her chin. I finally stared at her in wonder and said what I'd been thinking since last night. "I need to ask you, how is it possible that you don't have a regiment of men after you?"

"Maybe I do, but after they get to know me, I scare them off," she said with a laugh. "Remember, I warned you."

"I'll take my chances."

"A gambling man, are you?"

"Only on things I'm sure of."

"I've heard that from other admirers, only to have them regret ever saying that."

"Have you ever been married?"

"No, no one has been stupid enough to walk me down the aisle. And on that note, none have had the pleasure of making love to me."

"So you're a virgin?"

"I didn't say that. It's just that no man who has promised to marry me has ever got me into bed first."

"Is that a warning?"

"Maybe, but then again I will be turning thirty in a month and with that comes a lot of soul searching."

"But I'm ready to marry you today before you ever turn thirty."

"Be happy that I'm giving you time to think over that rash decision."

"I don't need time. I've been in love with you since the second you walked out of your office and into my life, having ditched that ridiculous nurse's outfit."

"And that was a whole three days ago." She laughed as she cut off a small piece of my French toast and put it into her mouth. "Quite good."

"I told you it was delicious."

She ate another piece and asked, "What do you usually have for breakfast?"

"Cereal with chocolate milk. Peanut butter and jelly sandwiches for lunch and dinner."

"My God, you really do need a wife."

"Yes, immediately, before I turn into a peanut butter and jelly sandwich." She touched the bandage on my neck.

"How does it feel?"

"Fine. It doesn't hurt at all. Actually, it hasn't bothered me since we went out to lunch that first day. I felt it a little last night after we went to our separate rooms, but as long as I'm with you I don't even notice it."

"Great! Maybe I should send you a bill."

"Or just marry me today and I'll never have to worry about my neck again and you'll never have to worry about money again. You'll be able to drink margaritas any time you like. Happy hour will be a thing of the past."

"It's going to take more than money and full-price margaritas to make me happy."

"I know that, Jennifer. You have made that abundantly clear, and it's one of the many reasons I am madly in love with you," I said. "And just for the record, it's not like I come from money."

"No?"

"Not at all. Both my parents worked, and I grew up sleeping in the same room with my two siblings in our family's two-bedroom apartment. It was not until I came out here and got amazingly lucky with my writing that I was able to buy my parents their own home and make it so they would never have to worry about money again."

"They must have been so proud."

"Yes. And they were so happy until my daughter decided to go bananas. I swear, there are times I just feel like grabbing her and shaking her. She caused my parents so much pain." I looked across at Jennifer and it didn't take much to realize that while she might sympathize with my predicament, she didn't think much of my solution.

"I hope you know that I would never use violence, ever," I said. "It's just that you had to be there to understand the situation and its effect on my parents and me. Now, for the rest of my life I'll have to live with the guilt that I didn't throw Sofia into a monastery and teach her sorry butt a lesson she would never forget."

"And do you think your parents would have been happy with that decision?"

"Of course not. Despite everything, my parents believed that Sofia belonged at home, even if it meant that they couldn't visit anymore."

"They saw the bigger picture."

"Yes, I guess they did." I picked up my empty plate, glass and the silverware and walked into the kitchen. Jennifer followed and looked on as I cleaned the dirty dishes and dried them with a washcloth.

"When is the last time you used the dishwasher?" she asked.

"Probably not since Sofia moved out."

"I guess there's not much need for a dishwasher when you're living on peanut butter and jelly sandwiches, cereal, and beer." I looked at her as she tried to suppress a laugh.

"Are you making fun of my diet?"

"No, I guess if it worked for you in college, why wouldn't it continue to work twenty years later."

"So besides being the most beautiful, caring, and intelligent nurse, are you also a nutritionist?"

"Who, me? I guess you missed all the butter I put into your dinner last night and all the sugar that ended up in your breakfast this morning?"

"So you're trying to kill me?"

"Just trying to get a head start. What good would it do me if I killed you before we got married?"

"Oh, I see now. This goody-good girl thing has been one big act."

"Well, this is the town after all where young girls come in the hope of becoming starlets. So what do you think so far? Do I have what it takes to have my star on the Hollywood Walk of Fame?"

I softly ran my hands through her hair and looked into her eyes. "You don't need any star on any walk of fame; your star shines brighter than all the stars that have ever passed through this town." As we kissed, I felt a tear run down her cheek and touch my lips.

Chapter 6

I never looked forward to running but once it was over I was always happy I did it. After kissing Jennifer a bunch more times and holding her tightly, my run felt effortless. I could have run a marathon if it wasn't for the fact that I wanted to get home before Jennifer left for work.

I opened the door to the house just as Jennifer was coming down the hall from the bedroom, looking as beautiful as ever. She smiled pure sunshine at me and asked, "Did my Greek marathoner have a wonderful run?"

"As perfect as any run I have ever had, and all it took were a few kisses and the expectation of seeing you before you went off to work."

She walked over to me, started to fling her arms around me, and thought better of bringing her clean work blouse into contact with my sweaty T-shirt. Instead she leaned in from a few inches away and planted a passionate kiss on my lips. "I hope that helps you have a great day."

"Guaranteed."

She picked up her purse and headed toward the door. I reached for my car keys on the coffee table and flipped them to her. "Please, take my car. It is going to be hot today in the valley."

"How hot?"

"Mid-nineties," I said. "Besides, I am going to be working inside all day and I don't expect to go anywhere."

She tossed her car keys to me and said, "Just in case you need to make a run somewhere. You remember how to drive a classic?"

"It's something you never forget."

"Thank you." She opened the door and walked outside. I watched as she got into my car and drove off.

I took a quick shower and sat down at my desk. As much as I loved having Jennifer around, I also loved my work, and my peaceful work space. I inhaled deeply, taking in the intoxicating scent of the books all around me, and noted with pleasure that every volume was still arranged in alphabetical order, by author. It was Sofia who had insisted that my books be arranged in alphabetical order. She had taken on the task herself, and did a splendid job of cleaning each book and putting it in its proper place. I marveled at the memory, and wondered, not for the first time, what happened to the bright, helpful, loving and happy child who used to share my home.

I started writing, and like the running that day, it came easily. Amazing, what a beautiful and loving woman can do to a man's psyche. I wrote ten pages in half the time it usually took me to write five. The sound of a car pulling into the driveway finally broke my concentration. I looked out the window and it was Sofia. I watched as she walked toward the front door and felt myself cringing at the thought of having to deal with my irrational and abrasive daughter.

She opened the door and called, "Daddy, Daddy," like a little girl, and suddenly my worry seemed unfounded. I called back and she walked into the study and without hesitating she hugged and kissed me. "How are you feeling? I've been so worried."

I was so taken aback by her sudden change in behavior that at first I wasn't sure if it was my daughter or an imposter, or whether I was hallucinating or dreaming, or if she had become a great actress over night.

"Daddy, how are you feeling?" she repeated earnestly. The muscles in her face were actually moving and her eyes were alert and anxious.

"I'm fine, sweetheart. They just removed a little cyst. It's nothing at all."

"Oh, thank God. I was so worried." She abruptly started walking around the room and asked, "And that woman, is she still here?"

"No, Jennifer is at work, but she will be back later."

"Why? You don't need her. I can take care of you."

"Sweetheart, I don't need anyone to take care of me, but I appreciate the offer. You have your own life to live."

"No!" She snapped at me with such force that I nearly jumped out of my chair. That moment of normalcy was lovely, but who was I to expect it to last for more than a minute or two? "I don't like her!"

"And is there some reason why you don't like her?"

She hesitated; apparently she had not thought that far ahead. She clenched her hands, turned away from me, and smashed her fists against the bookcase in front of her, sending my books flying all over the place.

The violence of this outburst caused her to lose her balance, and I stood up just in time to catch her as she fell backwards. She was as light as a feather and yet she was able to muster so much anger that she cracked one of the bookshelves. I laid her down on the floor, amid the scattered books, and she immediately pulled her knees to her chest and started to rock back and forth. Her eyes did not so much as blink and the muscles in her face were as constricted as a tightrope.

I knelt down beside her and softly called her name as I wrapped my arms around her. "It's okay, Sofia. It's okay. I love you so much." I kept my arms around her as her body continued to quiver, and all I could think of was how miserably I had failed my daughter.

She eventually stopped rocking and the tenseness engulfing her body slowly dissipated, yet I kept my arms wrapped around my precious little girl.

Chapter 7

I carried Sofia into her bedroom and placed her on the bed. I took off her shoes and placed a blanket over her as she reached for her favorite stuffed animal, a white polar bear, dressed up like a scholar, which she named Lawrence. She hugged Lawrence tightly as she closed her eyes.

"Do you want me to call a doctor?" I whispered as I softly stroked her hair.

"No, Daddy. I'm just tired," she said in a weak voice. Hearing her call me Daddy again brought me right back to when she was just a little girl and this scene of tucking her into bed at night always made me feel like the most blessed man in the world.

I stayed with her for a few minutes until she drifted off to sleep, then walked back into my study. Amid the scattered books and broken book shelf I noticed Sofia's purse. I had always respected my daughter's privacy, and for the first time, I wondered if that might have been part of the problem. Maybe, if I had been like other parents and been willing to invade her privacy as needed when she was younger, I could have nipped this in the bud before she went off the deep end.

In truth, I had always been afraid of what I might find. I was still afraid, but it suddenly dawned on me that this kind of thinking made me complicit in my daughter's problems. I had allowed fear to stop me from understanding Sofia well enough to help her, and that would stop right now.

I locked the door, picked up her purse, walked over to my desk and opened it. The first thing I saw was a small compact mirror with a herringbone design in abalone. That was a normal enough object to find in a young woman's purse, but then I found another mirror, then another, and another, until I had laid out before me six mirrors of different shapes and sizes. This in itself seemed to confirm what I always knew — that my lovely daughter was *too much* in love with herself, or at least had a problem with checking her appearance far more often than was normal or healthy. Was it vanity? Self-loathing disguised as self-love? Some sort of personality disorder? I had no idea, but I knew that something was wrong. I took out a hairbrush, lip moisturizer, and her car keys and keys to her apartment. In the money compartment she had a single dollar and some change. This, despite the fact that I had always coached her to carry at least twenty dollars in her purse, as a foil to any would-be mugger. God forbid any thief would hurt her while looking for more money on her possession. Better that they find a twenty and run off.

I found a picture holder, and opened it. The first picture was of Sofia and me when she was ten years old. I was holding her and making funny faces and she was laughing hysterically. I remember my mother took the picture. I turned the picture over and the second picture was a duplicate of the first. I kept going through the holder and found that the third, fourth, fifth, sixth, seventh, and all the rest, were duplicates of the first picture. Who carries around ten identical pictures of herself and her father from eight years ago? Surely, she wasn't using that picture as a headshot.

I put everything back in the purse and placed the bag on my desk. That's when I noticed her cell phone on the floor. I picked it up and turned it on. The photo on the display was the same photo of the two of us that was in her purse. There was no password needed to open the phone, so I was able to go straight to her calling history. The only messages she had received over the last month were from me, and the only phone calls she had made were to me. I couldn't see any stored phone numbers for what looked like friends, an acting coach, or anybody in her acting workshops. But I did see that she had entered her new address in her contact list. I put the phone beside her purse and looked it up on the computer. She had refused to let me help her move, and had kept her new address a secret, but now I could see that she had only moved a few blocks away from our house.

I opened the door and looked in at my eighteen-year-old daughter sleeping, hugging Lawrence, a good-looking, scholarly polar bear who just happened to be a stuffed animal.

I walked into the kitchen, opened the refrigerator, and grabbed my surefire remedy for all maladies, downing one ice-cold Budweiser, then another and another and another. I thought about having a shot or two of Old No. 7, but decided against it, even though I knew the current situation called for it.

I could not rule out the possibility that my daughter was using drugs. Actually, I would accept that news gladly. At least there was help and treatment readily available, and if it meant having to lock the little miscreant in her room until she was thirty, that was fine with me.

I walked into the living room and sat in a reclining chair facing the hallway that led to the bedrooms. The one thing I was sure of was that Sofia was not leaving this house. At least, not until I was satisfied that she was okay, and I didn't expect that to happen anytime soon.

The sun was shining brightly through the sliding glass door that opened onto the pool. Through the glare I could see the reflection of the water in the pool and in it, the image of my lovely little girl splashing around happily as I tried to teach her how to swim. Memories were pressing on me today. I began to feel tired and weepy. I was surrounded by pictures of Sofia, with my parents, during much happier times before the sunshine left her countenance and erased the glow and joy from my parents' very existence. I could not help but blame Sofia, even though I never accused her.

I always felt that it was my responsibility to shield Sofia from anything that could hurt her — like the fact that her mother had handed her to me at three days old, said "good luck," and disappeared from her life forever. I even had a phony death certificate made up that I showed to Sofia when she was old enough to understand. I told her that mommy had been cremated and that her last wish had been to have her ashes spread over the Pacific Ocean. That way, I never had to deal with the question of visiting her mother's grave. Sofia had no recollection of her mommy and I told her that she had just turned two and I didn't expect her to remember.

Looking back, it was hard to understand how I ever became involved with Sofia's mother in the first place. We met on the set of my first movie, where she'd been a part-time makeup artist, and we lived together for six months in this house. But for most of that time, I knew it was a terrible mistake. As soon as she moved in, she gave up all pretense of working and basically turned into a recluse. She read constantly, but only books about handsome princes falling in love with lovely maidens, and she became addicted to video games. She would stay in her room for days at a time, only coming out long enough to get the take-out food she had delivered to the house several times a day, using up the last of her money. She would play games on her computer for hours, never returning phone calls or communicating in any way with the outside world.

The breaking point came when we discovered that she was pregnant. It was an unlucky break from one of the few times we'd been intimate during her first month in the house, and she immediately said she wanted to have an abortion. I could not believe what I was hearing, and I begged her to reconsider, since my Catholic upbringing had taught me that abortion was murder, plain and simple. But Sofia's mother didn't see it that way, and she hounded me for months, demanding that I give her the money she needed to end the pregnancy. I wound up shadowing her every minute of the day just to stop her from finding the money and having it done in secret. After she passed the date for a legal abortion, I gave her ten thousand dollars with the promise of another twenty thousand if she stayed away from all drugs, alcohol, and cigarettes. She stayed clean, as far as I know, but she became almost demonic, hissing and swearing at me every time we were in the same room together. I had to drag her to her doctor appointments, and I tried to force her to eat healthy food, but she resisted every step of the way. When all she would eat was pizza, I took to crushing prenatal vitamins and dusting the pies with them whenever I could intercept one at the front door. Those nine months were a kind of living hell, no doubt for both of us, but in the end, it gave me Sofia, and her arrival made all of the struggles of the year before fade into oblivion.

Now, however, Sofia was beginning to remind me of her mother, and I had been paralyzed by that fact for five years. Since I often think in terms of sports metaphors, I explained it to myself this way: There were times when it felt like my daughter had thrown me a wicked curve ball that not even Derek Jeter or the late Tony Gwynn could hit, but I knew that neither of them would have stopped trying. They would have taken all the extra batting practice they needed to figure out that ball and hit it out of the park. Now it was time for me to step up to the plate and get the job done. I had to get over my fear of the truth, understand the problem, and help with a cure. It was no longer a case of Sofia being rude or having a bad attitude. It was so far beyond those garden-variety complaints that I had to consider the possibility that she was ill. The proof was right here in front of me, in the photo, the phone records, the apartment and the meltdown she'd had before my very eyes.

My religious beliefs had prevented me from even thinking about supporting Sofia's mother's wish to have an abortion. I did everything in my power to protect my unborn child while she was still in that inhospitable womb. Now I had another job to do. I would stop at nothing to help my precious, grown Sofia, even if it meant forcing her to change.

I walked into the kitchen, grabbed another beer, and took a roll of black duct tape out of a cabinet. I walked into the study and did a passable job of taping the broken bookshelf together, then propped it up at the seam with a bookend made of stone. This would have to hold until I could replace the shelf. I had just started picking up the books and randomly placing them back onto the shelf when Sofia came up from behind me, holding Lawrence.

"No Daddy, you just can't put the books up there like that. Don't you remember, they go in alphabetical order according to the author? Please, let me do it." She handed Lawrence to me and told me to sit down. I watched as she patiently and meticulously put the books back in their correct order. She then turned to me, smiled, and said, "You see? All perfect again."

"Thank you so much, Sofia. Remember what you told me earlier about wanting to take care of me?"

"Yes."

"Well, I would like that very much, but I have to insist that you move back home and give up your apartment."

"Okay, I would like that very much and so would Lawrence." She took him back into her arms and kissed him, then looked at me warily. "Is that lady still moving in?"

"You mean Jennifer?"

"Yes, Jennifer."

"Not if you don't want her to, but she will still have to come back and pick up her things."

"That's okay as long as she does not move in."

"And from this moment on, you and Lawrence will be living back home with me."

"Yes, Daddy."

My daughter's speech sounded robotic, programed, with little emotion. I took her by the hand and we walked into the kitchen. I opened the refrigerator and took out a jar of peanut butter and a jar of jelly, then placed them on the table with a loaf of sliced bread.

"And how many can I make you?" I asked.

"Two, thank you."

"And for Lawrence?"

"He's not hungry, but maybe later."

I made two sandwiches for each of us and poured us each a glass of milk. As we ate our meal, I asked her about her time away from home. "What did you usually eat all this time you were on your own?"

"Peanut butter and jelly sandwiches."

"Didn't you ever go out to a restaurant with your friends and order a steak or pasta? What about pizza?"

"No, Daddy, I ate peanut butter and jelly sandwiches all the time."

"Well, it's not like I can argue with that, because God only knows I eat peanut butter and jelly sandwiches all the time too. But now that you are back home I think it would be a good idea if we added a little more variety to our diet. Maybe a steak, once or twice a week, or fish?"

"Is that what the doctor told you to do?"

"Yes, and I think it's time I follow his advice."

"So do I. We will add a lot more variety to our diets because I plan on taking really good care of you."

"Thank you, sweetheart."

I remember a time when the sound of my beautiful daughter's voice brought a smile as wide as a football field to my face, but now it sounded more like a computerized bank message. She finished both her sandwiches, drank her milk, grabbed Lawrence and kissed me on the cheek, then got up from the table.

"I'm going to lie down for a little longer, but if you need me, wake me up."

"I will, angel." She started to walk away and I called after her, "Sofia, I am so happy you're back home. I love you so very much."

She turned, smiled, and for a moment her entire face lit up as though a latent light bulb from years back went off from inside her. "I love you, Daddy."

She walked into her bedroom as I sat back and finished my sandwich. I opened the refrigerator and took out a beer as the phone rang. It was Jennifer, sounding so excited and happy that it felt like she was trying to jump through the phone line. Saint Joseph's Hospital had called and offered her a job in the pediatric oncology department. She had already given her notice to Doc Hollywood and, in a goodwill gesture, he'd given her two weeks of vacation pay and allowed her to leave for good after the day's shift was over.

She jokingly told me that he hired my girlfriend who I bought the chocolates for. Apparently, she and Dr. Souter had a falling out over an examination he wanted to perform on her while taping the whole thing. I nearly choked on my beer as I thought to myself, "That crazy son-of-a-bitch actually tried to go through with that insane idea. Time to get a new doctor, stat."

After regaining control, I had to put a damper on her celebration and tell her about Sofia and her demands. I felt terrible, but, true to form, Jennifer thought it would be the best thing in the world for Sofia to move back home. She only asked to be allowed to pick up her stuff that she left behind in the bedroom and to have one minute with Sofia.

Naturally, I agreed. For a few minutes after hanging up the phone, I marveled at how mature and thoughtful Jennifer was to put Sofia's interests above her own. She didn't even hesitate, and she seemed to understand right away that Sofia's needs had to take priority over our budding relationship. But darker thoughts soon crept in, and I started to think that Jennifer took the news a little *too* well. It wasn't long before I'd convinced myself that Jennifer viewed Sofia's return home as a convenient "get out of jail" card for a new relationship that was moving too fast and that probably wouldn't suit her needs anyway.

Chapter 8

I opened the front door and Jennifer walked in, looking as radiant as ever. She kissed me on the cheek and put my car keys in my hands.

"I really wish we could have gone out tonight to celebrate your new job."

"We will, just not tonight," she replied as we walked toward her bedroom. She glanced into Sofia's room and saw my daughter sitting on her bed, with Lawrence in her arms, staring into nothingness.

I whispered, "Are you sure you want to talk to her?"

She looked at me and smiled. "Surely, you didn't think I came back here just to pick up a hairbrush and a few bits of clothing." She pinched my cheek as she carried her things out of the room in a shopping bag. She placed a restraining hand on me as she knocked softly on Sofia's half-open door.

"Hi Sofia, do you mind if I come in just for moment before I leave?"

"No," Sofia replied in her new robotic tone.

Jennifer entered the room as I watched through the slim space between the door and its frame.

"And what is that handsome bear's name?"

"Lawrence."

"Well, he's quite scholarly looking."

"Yes, like my daddy."

"Quite true, just like your daddy. Do you mind if I just sit down for a minute? I have been on my feet all day."

Sofia looked at Jennifer suspiciously. I was praying that we weren't about to see another meltdown like the one in the study.

"Do you like little children?"

"Yes, I love little children," Sofia replied, sounding a little less robotic.

"Well, I work with little children who are sick, but thankfully many of them get better. Would you like to see some of them?"

"Yes!" Sofia replied, suddenly sounding more enthusiastic than she had in years. Jennifer took out her purse and showed her a picture of a four-year boy, bald from chemotherapy and radiation.

"Is he very sick?" Sofia asked, leaning into the picture, then looking back at Jennifer with worry in her eyes.

"He was, but not anymore." She turned over another photo of the same boy. This time he was dressed in a cowboy outfit, looking completely healthy, with a head full of light brown hair.

Sofia stared at the two pictures and asked, "Is that the same boy?"

"It sure is," Jennifer said. "His name is Jacob. He's one of my favorites. Isn't he adorable? He just turned seven."

"He really is adorable. And he's all healthy now?" A smile crossed my daughter's face — the same smile that for years had made me feel like the most blessed man in the world.

Jennifer nodded and turned to another photo of a little girl who, like Jacob, had lost her hair and looked very weak and ill. "This is Catherine. When this photo was taken she was four years old." She turned to a later photo of Catherine sporting a full head of curly blond hair and wearing a princess outfit. Her wide smile produced a pair of dimples that could light up a room.

"My God, she is so beautiful," Sofia said, staring at the photo as though transfixed. "And she's all healthy?"

"All healthy and a whole six years old. I called her my little Shirley Temple. Do you know who Shirley Temple is?"

"Yes, Daddy and I watched all her movies, but I think Catherine is even more beautiful. Do you?"

"Absolutely. She's also a wonderful dancer and likes to play basketball. If you like, you can come with me and visit some of the children. I know they would just love you. Would you like that?"

"Yes, I would love that."

"Great! We'll make it a date and you can come along with me. Just let me know when you want to come. I'll go now. I don't want to take up any more of your time. It was very nice talking to you, Sofia."

Jennifer got up to leave but before she could take one step toward the door my daughter yelled out, "No! Please don't go. Please don't leave us."

"Are you sure?"

"Yes — please don't leave us. Can I see more pictures?"

"Of course." Jennifer sat back down next to Sofia, but this time there was no distance between them. Sofia was literally leaning over her as she showed her picture after picture.

If I didn't already believe in miracles, I would have immediately been converted. I could not help but think that my beautiful mommy was looking down at us this very moment and smiling. Surely, she must have put in a good word with Saint Joseph.

I walked into the kitchen, opened the refrigerator and grabbed a Budweiser. From Sofia's room I heard laughter — laughter! — and like a Sinatra song, it brought tears to my eyes.

I was tempted to bring Jennifer a glass of wine, but I held off. The last thing I wanted to do was interrupt the rapport between my beautiful daughter and the perfect lady from Kentucky. Instead I sat at the kitchen table and drank my beer and soaked in the mirth that had been absent from this house for so long until I met Jennifer.

After about an hour, I peeped into the room and they were still talking, laughing, and looking at pictures.

After another hour things seemed to get awfully quiet. I crept down the hall and peered into the room again, only to find my lovely daughter asleep with her arms around Lawrence and Jennifer asleep with her arms around Sofia.

Chapter 9

It was nearly ten o'clock when the two sleeping beauties walked into the living room. I was sitting on the couch watching reruns of *I Love Lucy* when my daughter kissed me on the cheek and asked, "How are you feeling, Daddy?"

"Wonderful, sweetheart."

"Great. I have really good news. Jennifer is moving in with us. That's okay, right?"

"Outside of you telling me that you were moving back, that is the second-best news I have heard today."

She kissed me again and then nearly jumped into Jennifer's arms. "I told you he would be happy!"

Jennifer wrapped her arms around her and remarked, "Yes, you did." Jennifer bent down and kissed Sofia on the top of the head.

I ordered pizza and we ate on the couch while watching reruns of *I Love Lucy*. I had hoped to get Jennifer alone for a moment to thank her and make sure she was fine, but the ladies were inseparable. At around midnight I called it a night and went off to bed, leaving them on the couch planning out tomorrow's agenda.

I lay in bed and stared at the ceiling. The window was open and shadows danced across the surface. The day had started off beautifully, then deteriorated rapidly, and finally ended as perfectly as any day could possibly end. I thanked Saint Joseph and my mom, and then begged that it continue.

Chapter 10

I woke up at my usual time, and for the second morning in a row, there was music coming from the kitchen. I put on my running gear and walked out of my room to find Jennifer and Sofia dancing in their pajamas to The Crystals' rendition of "Then He Kissed Me." They might not have been Fred and Ginger, but my God, they were wonderful.

Jennifer handed Sofia off to me and I twirled and whirled my laughing daughter around, and I swear I could have danced all morning long. Singing to the music, Jennifer tossed pancakes in the air and placed a stack on the table with syrup and a glass of milk, then nodded to me to sit down as she went back to dancing with my daughter. I felt so happy that I had to seriously stop myself from crying.

The pancakes were delicious, and after finishing them and drinking my glass of milk, I blew both girls a kiss and went out for my run, feeling a little bloated but still eager for a sweat. I turned on my iPod, and by an amazing coincidence the first song to pop up was The Crystals' rendition of "Then He Kissed Me." I ran like I was on air, occasionally twirling and whirling as the early morning sun rose higher and greeted me like a heavenly orb. As I passed by the park near my house, a flock of starlings rose off the grass, and I was so filled with happiness that I whispered "I love you" to the world.

The girls had their whole day planned, and were heading out the door as I came back from my run. First they were going out for breakfast, because they "deserved it." Then they were going over to Sofia's apartment to clean out her few belongings and tell the landlord that she was moving out. Later, they would come back and pick me up and we would all go over to Jennifer's apartment to pick up her stuff and move it into the house. She had a lot of stuff and my help would be greatly appreciated, I was told. It wasn't like I had a choice in the matter, or wanted one. I wasn't some kind of macho guy; I had absolutely no problem being ordered around by two beautiful young women.

I jumped into the shower and let the water pour down on me. The bandage from my surgery came loose and fell to the floor and swirled around. I leaned down and picked it up. Except for a dab of blood, there was nothing else to see. I felt around the incision. Except for the few stitches, I felt nothing and had absolutely no pain.

I sat down at my desk and started writing, and like the day before, it came easily. Scene after scene of my latest screenplay flowed as if they were being written by an unseen hand. It was amazing how effortless writing became when my mind was free of guilt and anxiety. Maybe someday I would sit down and write the novel I had been contemplating since graduating from college. But for the moment I would continue writing screenplays, because that's where the money was. *God*, I thought, *you've got to love the movie industry.*

I looked out the window just as Jennifer pulled into the driveway with Sofia. It didn't take Jennifer long to get comfortable driving around in my car, with its air conditioning and SiriusXM radio. Jennifer and Sofia carried two small boxes and some clothes into the house. When I asked if I could help with the rest of Sofia's stuff, Jennifer said, "No, this is all of it. Not all girls are hoarders. Isn't that so, Sofia?"

"Yes," Sofia replied, then looked at me. "How are you feeling today, Daddy?"

"Wonderful," I said. "How else could I feel when looking at the most beautiful girl in the world."

"Thank you, Daddy, but I think that honor goes to Jennifer."

I looked at Jennifer who winked at me and said, "So did you miss us?"

"Of course, I missed the two of you."

"Great, because unlike your gorgeous daughter, who knows how to pack light, I am pretty attached to my stuff and I have a lot of it. Your male prowess will be tested."

"Glad to know I can help," I said.

Jennifer pinched my cheek and said, "He's so adorable."

Something struck them both as funny, and they were still laughing as they walked into Sofia's room carrying the two boxes. It had been so long since I had two women living under the same roof as me that I'd forgotten how strange they could occasionally act.

Chapter 11

Jennifer drove while Sofia sat in the front passenger seat. The hired help, that being me, sat in the back. After picking up some moving supplies, we headed over to Jennifer's apartment, with the girls singing along to the Beatles song "I Need You." It was one of my favorite songs in the entire catalogue, and I sat there in silence, transported back to a time when Sofia and I used to sing it together every time it played. She was about ten at the time, and apparently, she had not forgotten any of the lyrics. She was in heaven.

Jennifer's apartment was a small one-bedroom located in West Hollywood, just below Sunset Boulevard, west of Laurel Canyon. It came pre-furnished and was in a small apartment building built in the 1950s. I couldn't help but feel the mile-wide difference between the spacious, open landscape of Kentucky and this crowded section of West Hollywood. Yet, as I looked at the lovely Kentuckian, it was obvious that she could adapt to any environment. In so many ways, she didn't remind me of a girl from Kentucky or a resident of Los Angeles, but a citizen of the world. When I thought about why I felt that way, I couldn't really explain it. Maybe it was the first stirrings of love. Maybe it was the way she had won over Sofia in a single day. I was suddenly convinced that this girl from Kentucky could do anything.

As advertised, Jennifer's apartment was overflowing with her stuff. Sofia took a look at Jennifer's large book collection and decided that every volume needed to be put in alphabetical order, by author, before going into the boxes. I tried to intervene and tell my lovely daughter that she could do that once we got home, but before I could get a word out, Jennifer stepped in front of me, put her hand on my arm, and said, "Let her do it!"

I stepped back and started working on Jennifer's sizeable collection of framed family photos. Using newspapers that she had lying around, I wrapped up dozens of pictures Jennifer had brought with her of her mother, her patients, doctors, fellow nurses, and custodians back in Kentucky, and started layering them carefully in boxes. As I finished with that, I stopped to look at her desktop computer. It had to be a late 1990s model. The monitor was as big and bulky as an old TV set. "Is this an antique like your car?" I jokingly asked.

She smiled and said, "Not all of us can make millions of dollars just by sitting down in front of a high-tech computer to write blockbuster after blockbuster."

"Sofia, after we have your new best friend moved in, please remind me to go out and buy her a new computer. I'm afraid if she plugs this antique in she might start a fire in our house."

"Yes, Daddy."

"No, Daddy," Jennifer remarked, biting her lower lip, as she glared at me. "After you put it like that, I will never accept a new computer from you. I'll simply save up and buy myself a not-so-high-tech computer."

"No, Jennifer, let him buy you a new computer. My daddy has a lot of money and you will need a new one if you want to safely upload all the pictures of the children we plan on taking."

I so wanted to pinch Jennifer's cheek at that moment, but she still looked mad, so I hung back and whispered, "You heard the child."

Jennifer turned away from me and sat down beside Sofia, "Okay, I'll let him buy me a computer, but I am going to pay your daddy back. Does that sound good to you?"

"No, Jennifer. He has a lot of money."

It was nice to see my lovely daughter taking my side, but it was also a bit unnerving to hear her talking so openly about my wealth. It made me wonder who else she had talked to, and whether I should think about ramping up my home security system. But I decided to push the thought out of my mind. Just yesterday I was worried out of my head about her. I didn't want to say anything to upset her.

Jennifer thought for a moment, then turned to Sofia. "Thank you, sweetie, for helping me see the light." Then she looked at me. "On the advice of your daughter, I will let you buy me a new, top-of-the-line computer as a gift."

"Oh, it's top-of-the-line, now, is it?" I joked. "I think I said 'new,' but okay."

"Daddy!" Sofia protested, as Jennifer poked me in the arm.

It took Jennifer and me about an hour to move her clothes, pictures, and her antique computer into my car. Then it took another three hours for Sofia to arrange Jennifer's books in alphabetical order, by author. During my time alone with Jennifer, I tried to get the lowdown on what she had discovered about my daughter, but she was less than forthcoming. It quickly began to feel like a one-way interrogation.

"What was her apartment like?" I asked. After all, I had never been invited over.

"It was clean and orderly."

"And did you meet any of her roommates?"

"She had no roommates. She lived alone."

"As I suspected," I said. "And what did the two of you talk about at breakfast?"

"Girl stuff."

Her replies were so terse that she almost reminded me of Sofia, and like a coward, I decided not to test the waters any further. At least, not until I had Jennifer living under my roof. I had too much to lose. I had finally found a woman who was so perfect that I still found it hard to believe she had even given me a second look, and on top of that, she connected with my daughter in a way that I could not believe possible. Yes, I had far too much to lose.

Jennifer drove back toward our house while Sofia started using her phone to research the very best computer for her. The help sat in the back, wedged between boxes of books and pictures. Sofia hit upon the perfect computer and at a stoplight she showed a picture of it to Jennifer.

Jennifer asked, "Are you sure?"

"Yes, it's definitely the one," my daughter reassured her as she turned and showed me the picture with the description and the price. *At five thousand dollars it better be the perfect one*, I thought. Then Sofia asked, "Can I have the same one, too?"

I looked into her big brown eyes and said, "Of course, honey."

I couldn't say no to her when she was disobedient and rude. How in the world could I deny her anything when she was being so wonderful? After all, I had plenty of money.

We brought Jennifer's possessions to the house, then drove to Fry's Electronics to buy the computers. Sofia had insisted we go there right away. The store was crowded and as we walked over to the computer section, we must have passed fifty guys who couldn't take their eyes off my daughter. She ignored them all as she barreled toward a young salesman in the computer section. Not surprisingly, even he was taken aback by her beauty and seemed to have a hard time concentrating on the picture on her phone and the words coming out of her mouth.

Finally, he showed us the computer on display, and after Sofia inspected the device and checked with Jennifer to make sure it was what she wanted, she told the young man that she would take two. Before he had time to sell her on all the programs she might like to buy to go with it, she said yes, she wanted all of the software recommended in the description, and she wanted the store to download them for her.

The salesman tallied up the combined totals for the computers and the programs and handed the bill to Sofia. After a quick glance, she handed the bill to me. It totaled sixteen thousand dollars and change, and that included a discount. Jennifer looked at the bill as I handed my American Express Centurion card to the young man.

"Wow!" she whispered into my ear. "It really is nice to have a lot of money."

Sofia leaned over and kissed me on the cheek and said, "Thank you, Daddy."

She then turned her attention back to the computer on display as I turned to Jennifer and whispered, "That alone was worth a million dollars."

Jennifer kissed me on the cheek and said, "Thank you, Joe."

"And that was worth another million," I replied as Jennifer and Sofia looked at the display and talked about all the things they were going to be able do with their new machines.

Chapter 12

Back at home, I ordered two large pizzas for dinner. The girls had two slices each and then disappeared into Sofia's room to play with her computer and then into Jennifer's room to play with hers. I sat at the kitchen table and ate a whole pizza pie, washed down by several ice-cold Budweiser beers, and disappeared down a rabbit hole of introspection. Only a couple of days ago I thought I had lost my daughter to her own reflection, and now I was fairly certain that I had lost her to the Kentucky beauty who I planned on marrying. I was a little lonely at the table by myself, but it was still a win-win situation, no matter how you looked at it.

After putting the few remaining slices into the refrigerator, I sat down on the couch and turned on old reruns of *I Love Lucy*. I fell asleep after watching five episodes, and when I woke up hours later the TV was off and I was covered with a blanket. I walked toward my bedroom and looked in on Sofia, who was asleep holding Lawrence. I then walked into my room and suddenly turned around as I heard crying coming from Jennifer's room.

I rushed to her room and found Jennifer crying hysterically as she held her phone in her hand. I went to her and said, "It's Lou."

"Yes, my mommy's gone." She struggled to stay upright as her body shook violently and tears flowed down her face. I wasn't sure if she even knew I was standing there, trying to hold her. Sofia appeared in the doorway, and without any idea of what was happening, she rushed toward Jennifer and hugged her, burying her face against her breast. Jennifer returned the embrace and they stayed there for a long time, holding each other, with me next to them, laying my hand on Jennifer's shoulder. A few minutes went by and finally Jennifer raised her head and looked at me and said, "I have to make plane reservations. Hopefully I can get an early flight out."

Sofia stepped back from Jennifer and said, "I'm going with you."

"No sweetheart, it's not going to be any fun, but I appreciate the offer." Jennifer ran her hands lovingly through my daughter's long hair as she spoke.

"I'm going. Is that okay, Daddy?" she asked. I was speechless at this request. She turned back to Jennifer and said, "Remember, you said I could always lean on you when things got difficult, and I promised you that you could lean on me when things got difficult."

Amid all the sadness, I never felt prouder of my daughter. A tear rolled down my cheek, which I quickly removed with my hand. Jennifer nodded at me and said to my daughter, "As long as your father agrees."

"Daddy, can I go?"

"Of course, you can go, sweetheart," I said, before turning to Jennifer. "Will you be flying into Lexington?"

"Yes, if we can get a flight into there that would be the best thing."

"And where will you be staying?"

"I have friends that we can stay with who live just outside Lexington and not far from the nursing home."

"I have a better idea. Let me make the reservations. All I need is both of your driver's licenses." Sofia ran off to get her license and Jennifer stood up. Before she could start arguing with me over money, I said, "It's my daughter you're taking with you, and I don't need to worry about the two of you flying around the country for twelve hours just to save money when you could get there in four."

Jennifer backed down and fished her license out of her purse just as Sofia came running back with hers. I purchased two first class tickets, round trip directly into Lexington. I then booked a suite for them at the Hilton Lexington for the ten days they were going to be gone.

Chapter 13

I skipped my early morning run to help Jennifer and Sofia get ready for their trip. Grief hung over the house like a rain cloud. It was a feeling I knew well from growing up in a family with fifteen aunts and uncles on my mother's side. Most of them were gone now, and I had attended my share of funerals.

I asked Sofia to get her purse, and then I sat down next to her at the kitchen table and took her hand. "Remember what you promised me a few days ago? That you were going to take care of me?"

She looked at me as she ran her hand nervously through her hair. "Yes. Are you mad at me because I am going with Jennifer?"

"No, angel. I have never been prouder of you. But if you truly mean what you said about taking care of me, I need you to promise to call me every day, and when I call you, I expect you to answer. That way I don't have to worry. Can you remember that?"

"Yes, Daddy."

I reached into my pocket and pulled out a credit card with her name on it. "I want you to use this card anytime you need something, or if Jennifer needs something and doesn't want to spend the money. If that happens, I want you to use this card and buy her what she needs. If she complains, I want you to tell her that you are only following your father's wishes, which you promised you would do." I put the card in the side pocket of her purse. Then I took out five hundred dollars from my pocket, peeled off five twenty-dollar bills, and tucked them into her purse. "Remember what I told you about always carrying some cash around with you? God forbid someone ever tries to mug you, but if it does happen, you just hand over your purse."

"Okay," she replied as I handed her the other four hundred dollars and told her to put it into her carry-on luggage. She walked over to her luggage by the front door as I looked up and across at Jennifer, who was looking directly at me. Her eyes were bloodshot from crying, but I had a feeling, for a moment at least, that there was something else on her mind besides her mother.

I walked over to her and said, "I know what you're thinking."

"Is that so. And what might that be?"

"That if I spoiled my daughter any more than I already do, it would be truly amazing."

"No, that's not what I was thinking. I was thinking how beautiful it is that you love your daughter so much." She started to cry as I took her into my arms and stroked the back of her hair.

Chapter 14

I drove the girls to the airport, and as I watched them pass through the security gates, I could not help feeling anxious, alone.

I walked into the house and was greeted with a repulsive quiet. A quiet I had lived with for a long time, yet the last few days with Jennifer and Sofia were a reminder of what I so desperately missed — the sounds and laughter of family and friends. One often presumes that a writer cherishes quiet more than anything else, and for some writers that may be true. But for others like me it's comradeship and the company of others that is indispensible to our craft. I still remember when Sofia was just a few weeks old and asleep in her crib almost all the time. Her crib had wheels on it and everywhere I would go in the house I would roll her up beside me, then just keep doing what I needed to do.

Many times I would be in my study writing intently, on a real roll, and suddenly my lovely baby would start crying. After an initial sigh of frustration, I would look down at her and whatever I was writing became meaningless; all that mattered was her. If she needed changing, I would change her, and if she just needed a little holding I would pick her up and walk around the house singing John Lennon's "Beautiful Boy" to her, substituting the word "Girl" for "Boy." I don't think Mr. Lennon would have objected.

I opened the refrigerator and took out the leftover pizza from last night and, you guessed it, an ice-cold Budweiser. I had given up the idea of working the moment I walked into the house.

The pizza was as delicious cold as it was hot, and the Budweiser tasted so good that there was no way I was only going to have one, like that was even a possibility. I finished the pizza and walked into Sofia's room. The once-empty bookcase was now filled with Jennifer's books, arranged, naturally, in alphabetical order by author. I could only hope that this was another indication of Jennifer's influence on my child, and hopefully my Sofia would become an avid reader, even if it were only to impress her new best friend.

I looked at all her stuffed animals arranged beautifully across her bed — each boy animal sitting beside a girl animal of the same species. The only one without a girlfriend was Lawrence, and that was because he was Sofia's boyfriend. He was not on the bed or anywhere in the room. I was pretty sure he was on the airplane, sitting in first class, between Sofia and Jennifer.

As I walked by Jennifer's room I stopped, took a few steps back, and entered her room. I picked up the first thing that caught my eye on her desk: a framed picture of an adorable little boy dressed in a sailor's uniform. He had a huge smile on his face and was holding a hand-written poster board that read, "Cancer Free." There were stars and smiley faces in all four corners of the sign, and the boy's father and mother stood on either side of him, beaming. I tried to jump into his parents' shoes and imagine how they must have felt at that moment, but I knew I was only grazing the surface of the overwhelming joy and relief that they must have experienced after learning that their son would live.

My eyes welled up, and as I went to put the picture down, a stash of other photos behind it fell to the floor. I picked them up, and as I was putting them back into a neat pile, I looked down at one image of a little girl in bed. She was bald from the chemotherapy and radiation, but she was still managing to smile. I turned the photo over and read what Jennifer had written. "Holly came to us about a year ago. She had such an infectious personality, and the most gorgeous smile. Her locks of golden hair were so soft and beautiful that it was hard to believe they were real. Holly, age six, died this morning, shortly after I came on duty. I held her hand as she took her last, labored breaths. If there is a God, he is apparently losing the battle with the devil. No all-loving God could allow innocent little children to suffer like Holly did. Only an evil force could unleash such cruelty."

Then my eye caught another picture of a teenage girl. She was sitting up in a hospital bed, her head bald and her face wan and ashen, but like Holly, she was managing to smile for the camera. I turned the picture over and strained to read a big block of text in tiny, cramped handwriting. It began, "Sarah, who we fondly called 'Ginger,' came to us over a year ago. All she could talk about was her prom. She had every intention of being there, and she planned to dance all night long. She had a large tumor just above her right kneecap. After a month of chemotherapy, they were able to shrink the tumor, and then they operated. They removed the tumor but were fairly certain that some of the cancer cells had spread to other parts of her leg. They had to amputate her whole leg, and suddenly the girl who wanted to dance all night was missing a leg. It took months of therapy and counseling and finally she was fitted with a prosthetic leg and miraculously she went to her prom and danced all night long.

"Six months went by and she was re-admitted. The cancer had spread to her lower abdomen and despite all efforts to control the disease, it spread rapidly through the rest of her body. She passed away early this morning, next to framed pictures of her prom night when she danced all night long, like Ms. Ginger Rogers.

"I have stopped going to church and don't waste my time praying anymore. There is too much evil and cruelty in this world for there to be any semblance of a loving and caring deity."

I turned over four other photos and found stories that were just as devastating as Holly's and Sarah's, each one ending with the same argument against a just and caring deity. I put all the photos back behind the framed photo of the little boy in the sailor suit and looked down at the antique computer that Jennifer had placed directly below her new computer. I knew there hadn't been much time to dispose of the old computer before she and Sofia left for Kentucky, but I wondered whether Jennifer would be able to bring herself to get rid of it at all. It seemed possible that the old clunker held too much sentimental value for her, as the probable container for many more photographs of children from the cancer centers where she had worked. I resolved to help her transfer every last picture over to the new system when she got home, and I marveled at how much I still had to learn about this complicated person who I had invited into my life.

I sat down on the edge of the bed and was suddenly sure that I could detect the scent of her perfume. It filled my nostrils and was more intoxicating than twenty beers. I laid my head back on her pillow and looked up at the ceiling, and suddenly one of the things that Jennifer had said to me came back with striking clarity. She had warned me against marrying her because, as she put it, the other men in her life who were serious about marrying her had been "scared off" once they got to know her. In fact, I really *didn't* know her. Working at Doc Hollywood's office is a lot different than working a twelve-hour shift in a pediatric oncology ward. She might come home a totally different person than the one who left in the morning. She might be a female Jekyll and Hyde. Thankfully, I'm an old hand when it comes to dealing with a female Jekyll and Hyde. Before Jennifer's intervention, that's exactly what my lovely daughter was like for the last five years. Hey, they might actually neutralize each other, which could be a win, win, win … or possibly not.

I turned on my side and looked, once again, at the little boy holding the "Cancer Free" poster. I remember Jennifer telling me that the vast majority of children with cancer are cured, but I couldn't help feeling that that wasn't any relief to the parents who lost a child to this horrific disease. I could easily see how one could lose all faith in a loving and caring God.

I looked across at other pictures of Jennifer smiling with children still going through treatment and the ones who looked cured. It was the same lovely smile, the only smile she has ever shown to me, and at that moment I felt so proud of the woman I hoped to marry.

Hemingway, in *For Whom the Bell Tolls,* asks why we exist, if not to help one another, and I cannot think of another person I have known who epitomizes that statement more than Jennifer. If she comes home in a depressed and sour mood, who was I to complain? She has a job where she makes a major difference in the quality and health of the most vulnerable among us, whereas I write bullshit and make millions.

I got up from the bed, grabbed another beer, and walked into my study. I picked up a piece of paper from my desk that Jennifer left behind for me. It read:

Joe,

Thank you for everything. I do not know what I would have done without you and Sofia. Since I doubt I will ever be able to pay you back, I promise, instead, not to make fun of your beloved but terrible New York Knicks … at least for a couple of months.

Love you,
Jennifer

I folded the piece of paper, opened the bottom drawer of my desk where I kept my most cherished correspondences with my parents, and placed it beside them. Sometimes a few simple sentences, from the right person, can have more meaning than the loveliest poem by the great Lord Byron.

I walked out of the study as my phone rang. I looked at the display to see who was calling and didn't recognize the name or area they were calling from. I nevertheless answered and it was none other than the famous Nick Jones. He was quite drunk and I could hear the sound of women's voices in the background. It sounded like a party.

I asked, "Where are you?"

"Tahiti, I think. All these islands down here look the same. The girls are beautiful and every fucking drink tastes like it has been mixed with pineapple."

"What are you doing there?"

"I'm on my honeymoon. I would have invited you to the wedding but I didn't know I was getting married until a couple of days ago. Besides, you never leave that stupid house of yours. Do you even have a valid passport?"

"Do you even know who you married?"

"What type of stupid question is that? Of course, I know who I married. I just can't recall her name at the moment. But she's young, dark skinned, speaks French, English, and some native dialect that I can't pronounce and has these dark blue eyes that are mesmerizing. Never seen a girl down this way with those types of eyes. Personally, I think the bitch is wearing contacts but who gives a shit. I make a wonderful living creating illusions, so why not be fooled by one?"

"I don't know what to say. Congratulations. Hopefully, this one works out for you."

"Thanks Joe and fuck yeah it's going to work out as long as I stay drunk. Have you started on the script yet?"

"Yeah, it's moving along nicely."

"Great! Well, don't break your hump. I'm in no rush to get back to work. I got to go, honeymoon business I need to take care of. You do understand?"

"Yes, I get the picture quite clearly."

He hung up as I wondered if he was a modern-day John Huston or Howard Hughes or if he was a new species of genius that had yet to fully evolve.

I owed my career to that man. Yes, I wrote the scripts and the sequels to all our hits, but in the hands of any other director there most likely would never have been even one hit, and he always made sure I got a percentage of the movies' net profit. One and a half percent might not sound like a lot, but all our movies combined grossed nearly ten billion worldwide, with a net profit of just less than five billion.

Film is a director's medium, and without the director working in tandem with the cinematographer, cameraperson, editor, sound people, special effects personnel and the actors, there would be no movies. Yes, I provide the embryo, but the director fertilizes it, and the rest of the crew brings it to term. Without all these other people and many more I never would have seen any of my dreams come true. Nick Jones took my words and my stories and created magic that I never even considered possible.

I was fairly sure that this was his seventh marriage, and he was only a few years older than me. At this rate, by the age of fifty he could easily be in the double digits for divorces, and that's without any repeat marriages. Once the man was done with a wife, he was done with her for good, except for the alimony.

I thought about Nick's track record with the ladies, and I had to admit that it was hard to defend. The gorgeous young women who floated down the aisle with him had no idea what they were getting themselves into. He was a serial monogamist, obsessed with the *idea* of matrimony but unable to make it stick. I was starting to feel bad about enabling the guy. Then a saving thought occurred to me: At least he's not as bad as Dr. Souter. That guy was unhinged. I still couldn't believe that I'd been receiving medical care all these years from a guy who thought it was fine to force his secretary to perform in a sleazy sex video as part of a revenge fantasy against his wife.

I grabbed another beer and sat down on the couch and turned on the classic TV show *The Honeymooners*. A little Jackie Gleason, Audrey Meadows and Art Carney were exactly what the occasion called for. "Bang, zoom … You're going to the moon!" I fell asleep after a few episodes. I was dead tired and woke up hours later to my phone ringing. It was Sofia. She and Jennifer had arrived safely and were now at the funeral home where Jennifer was in a separate room viewing her mother's body, while Sofia was sitting in the lobby with Lawrence.

Sofia wanted to go with Jennifer to view her mother's body, but Jennifer insisted that it was not necessary and that she stay in the lobby. Sofia was anxious that she had done something to upset her, but I assured her that it was only natural that Jennifer wanted to be alone with her mommy. I asked her about the flight, and she said, "It was wonderful. It was the first time Jennifer flew first class. She told me that you made her feel like a movie star. I told her that you always made me feel like a movie star."

"And that's because you *are* a star. The brightest in the universe."

I could feel Sofia grinning across the miles. "And so is Jennifer, right?"

"Yes, so is Jennifer. But no one is more precious to me than you. I love you so much."

"Thank you, Daddy. I love you with all my heart. I lied to you about taking acting classes. Please don't hate me."

She had changed the subject so abruptly that at first I didn't know how to respond, and she repeated, "Please don't hate me."

"What? No! I could never hate you, Sofia. Never! I don't care about any silly acting classes. When you're ready, I will put you in one of my films and write you the best scenes in the whole world."

"I don't want to act. I want to help Jennifer with the sick children. I want to help them get better."

"That's even better. I would be so proud of you if you did that. Much prouder than if you ever became an actress."

"I lied to you about having roommates. I never had any roommates. I wanted to have some, but I didn't know if I could put up with them."

"That's okay, sweetheart. I'm so happy you're telling me all this. Sometime when you're ready to talk about it, I'd love to know *why* you felt you needed to lie about those things. But for right now I don't even care. I just need you to know that I love you like crazy, and that that will *never* change. You will always be the number one person in my life."

"I'm never going to lie again. I've been praying to Grandma and Grandpa and asking them to forgive me for being so mean. Do you think they will forgive me and love me?"

"I'm certain they never stopped loving you, and I have no doubt they have forgiven you…"

"Jennifer is back. I promise to call later."

She hung up and I started to cry.

Chapter 15

It was times like this when my remedy of one Budweiser after another needed a little boost. I poured myself two shots of Jack Daniels Old No. 7, then chased that with a third shot, and suddenly everything was perfectly clear.

Sure, it was strange that my beautiful, eighteen-year-old daughter had a stuffed animal as a boyfriend, but on the plus side, Lawrence was handsome and scholarly, well-dressed, and always there for my daughter. In a sense, he was the perfect boyfriend. All my life I worried about perverts, like Dr. Souter, hitting on my daughter and her falling for the wrong guy, but with Lawrence I didn't have to worry about that. Quite possibly, one of my best decisions concerning my child's health was choosing a different doctor than Dr. Souter for her primary care physician. I reached for the bottle of Jack and poured myself a fourth shot. Just the thought of the man was frightening.

Being an optimist, I concluded that my daughter telling me that she had been lying to me for the last month was a good thing. It showed a level of maturity that I was proud of, and besides, I was happy that she wasn't actually pursuing a career in show business. I didn't want her hanging around with a bunch of egoistic, conniving, back-stabbing actors. Not that long ago, I was convinced that my daughter was so in love with herself that it was only a matter of time before some doctor pegged her as a clinical narcissist. Now she wanted to devote her life to helping sick children. And it was all thanks to Jennifer's positive influence. I just couldn't believe the difference this one perfect lady was already making in my daughter's life and my own.

I kept going over and over the conversation I had just had with Sofia. It was the first time she displayed remorse over the way she treated her grandparents, and it was a sweet sound to hear her seeking their forgiveness. I wondered if she really had any doubt that her grandparents would forgive her. They loved her no matter what she said or did to them, and I was pretty sure they were smiling down on her this very moment.

I have to admit I was fairly proud of myself. It wasn't easy coming to such sound and lucid conclusions about all the complexities I was suddenly faced with — not to mention trying to make sense of the conversation I had with Nick. Now, all I had to do was remember why I was so proud and happy. I stumbled over to the couch and turned on *The Honeymooners*. "Bang, zoom ... You're going to the moon."

I fell asleep and, once again, the ringing of my phone woke me up. Once again, it was Sofia. She was quick to remind me that she promised to call me back. Amazing, how the fulfillment of a simple promise could bring so much happiness to a father who was still feeling the effects of the four shots of Old No. 7 and ten beers.

She kept repeating that she had promised and I kept reassuring her of how proud I was of her for keeping her promises. After a while I wasn't quite sure if I was awake or still asleep and dreaming. She was always in the habit of repeating herself, but this went quite a few steps further. Finally, Jennifer got on the phone. Right away, she started complaining about the suite being far too large for just her and Sofia. I cut her off, saying, "Just tell me now, once we get married are you still going to complain about me spoiling you?"

She laughed that wonderful, infectious laugh that could brighten up the worst day, and asked, "Have you been down to Casa Vega without me?"

"No, I would be too embarrassed to step foot in Margaritaville without you, especially if it wasn't happy hour and I had to pay full price for a drink."

"Wow! Once again, making fun of a girl because she was raised to spend her money wisely. I'll be sure to cross that little tidbit of wisdom off my list after we walk down the aisle. So if you weren't at Casa Vega, where did you go after dropping us off at the airport?"

"Straight home. I haven't been outside once, not even to sit by the pool."

"Really? So you been at home all day getting drunk by yourself, or did you have your little girlfriend who you bought the chocolates for come over and keep you company?"

"Jealous, are you?"

"Of course I'm jealous. It's not every day I have a man promise me the moon and beyond."

Sofia took the phone from Jennifer and said, "Don't believe her, Daddy. Every guy we talked to today fell in love with her and the waiter at the restaurant even left her his phone number."

"Really, every guy you talked to, and exactly how many guys was that?"

"A bunch, Daddy. A bunch."

Jennifer took back the phone and remarked, "The only reason they were talking to me was because of the gorgeous young lady I was traveling with."

"And the waiter?" I asked.

"Okay, he did leave me his phone number, but that was only because he was much too old for someone like Sofia. He was at least your age, wouldn't you say sweetheart?"

"Yes, he was at least your age, Daddy," I could hear Sofia reply.

"Wow! Talk about making a guy feel old."

"But he wasn't nearly as cute as you and, God knows, he definitely doesn't have your money, so I wouldn't lose any sleep over him."

"So it *is* about the money?"

"What else would it be about? A girl needs to secure her future before the wrinkles settle in. Isn't that so, Sofia?"

"Yes, a girl needs to secure her future before the wrinkles settle in." I could hear Sofia repeat the phrase word for word.

The tone suddenly changed as I could hear Jennifer going quiet on the other end of the line. All at once I felt like a jerk for not asking about her mother. I lowered my voice to a whisper and asked, "How are you holding up, Jennifer?" I could hear her struggling to hold back the tears.

"I would be doing a lot worse if I didn't have Sofia to lean on. I can't thank you enough for letting her be a part of my life."

"I don't think I had much to do about that. You're the one who won her over." I paused, as it was my time to struggle with my emotions. "You won her over, the same way you won me over … by being the most compassionate, caring, and loving person I have ever met. It is Sofia and I who are the ones who are truly thankful that you have allowed us into your life."

I remained on the couch for a long time after I finished talking to Jennifer and my daughter. Her mom was going to be buried tomorrow, following a short graveside service. Sofia would stand beside the grieving child, a pillar of support. The irony was baffling. Just a few days ago, I could not imagine my daughter coming to the aid of another human being under any circumstance, and now I could easily visualize my beautiful daughter, dressed in black, in high heel shoes, her dark hair blowing in the wind, as she gazed across at the preacher while Jennifer held onto my daughter for comfort.

I walked into my bathroom and washed my hands and face. I looked at my refection in the mirror. At times, coming to terms with who you are might be the most difficult choice you have to make in your entire life. I felt like I was on the cusp of understanding some things that had escaped my notice, probably for many years. But I wasn't close enough to these discoveries to know what they were. I could sense the evolution in my thinking without being able to see it.

I lay down on my bed and looked up at the ceiling. I didn't bother to turn off the light. Tonight, I would fall asleep with the light on like I used to do when I was a child.

Chapter 16

At three-thirty in the morning my phone rang and woke me up. It was Sofia. She was quick to remind me that she had promised to call and to always take care of me. I don't think my daughter realized that there was a three-hour time difference between Lexington, Kentucky and Los Angeles, and I wasn't about to tell her. Every opportunity I got to talk with her was a gift, and after losing that gift for a month, I wasn't about to let that happen again. I was so intent on keeping her at home that I was more than willing to give my blessing to her and Lawrence if they decided to get married. As far as I was concerned, there was not a guy out there who was good enough for my daughter. Lawrence wasn't much of a talker, but as far as I was concerned he treated my daughter like a princess, and what more could a father hope for?

Jennifer was taking a shower and so I didn't get to talk to her, but Sofia filled in the gap. She was concerned about her grandparents. Despite praying to them and asking them to forgive her, she wasn't sure if they even loved her anymore. And if they didn't love her, she wanted to know, would they ever be willing to forgive her?

I asked her if she thought it was an accident that Jennifer was suddenly in her life. She didn't answer, and I could sense that she was confused. So I asked, "Do you think it's a blessing that Jennifer is now part of your life?"

"Yes, I love Jennifer."

"And don't you think it is a little unusual that a girl from Kentucky, a place neither of us have been, would suddenly enter our lives like a guardian angel?"

"Yes."

"Well, I think she showed up because Grandma and Grandpa wanted someone in our lives who would love us both and make us both happy. She is their gift to you. She wouldn't be in our lives if Grandma and Grandpa didn't forgive you and love you."

"You're right, Daddy. Jennifer is proof that they have forgiven me and still love me. I am so happy. Thank you, Daddy."

Deep inside, that is what I honestly believed. The intelligentsia would laugh at me, but I found it hard to believe that my parents' abundant love and caring for both my daughter and me would suddenly dissipate because they were no longer visible to us. I could hear their voices in my head all the time, and my dreams were filled with images of my mother and father from all stages of our lives together.

I walked out of my room and paused before Jennifer's room. I stepped into the room and picked up the photo of the little boy dressed in the sailor's uniform, holding the "Cancer Free" sign. I took out the hidden photos from the back of the picture frame and looked down at the photo of Sarah, playfully called Ginger, who had her leg amputated, yet still managed to dance all night long at her prom.

I could hear birds chirping as they welcomed a new day filled with promise and hope — things that Sarah would have been waking up to, had she lived. Yet she was robbed of these pleasures, and denied her place in the world. I could not think of any crime more inhumane than the theft of a child's future. And yet there was no one to blame for this horrible outcome. I was beginning to see that Jennifer blamed a cruel God for these thefts, but I was not ready to assign blame to a Creator who I had been raised to love.

I changed into my running gear, left my iPod at home, and ran and ran toward the rising sun, across shadows of doubt, the voices of generations ringing in my ears like an unchained melody.

Chapter 17

By the time I got home, it was already after nine o'clock. I picked up my phone and looked down at a text message from Doc Hollywood's office. The results from the biopsy were back. Everything looked great, but he would like to see me for a quick consultation and to take another sample of blood to make sure all my numbers were back to normal. The text ended with a bunch of smiley face emojis.

I called back and got my girlfriend, the ex-receptionist, Caroline, who I gave the chocolates to way back when, even though it was less than a week. She was excited to hear from me and got me in at eleven o'clock. I had forgotten that she took over for Jennifer when Jennifer quit. Suddenly, the thought of seeing her was scarier than the thought of seeing my biopsy results.

I entered Doc Hollywood's office and was greeted by Caroline, dressed in a sexy nurse's uniform exactly like the one Jennifer wore. I have to admit, it was hard not to look, but I did my best. She put her hand out for me to take and I pretended not to see it as I asked her how she liked her new job.

She looked at me knowingly, and said, "Anything is better than working for that pervert."

I nodded appreciatively, and she went on to give me a minute-by-minute account of how Dr. Souter tried to seduce her, or rather, "how he tried to rape me."

"He actually asked if he could tape the whole thing, and he asked me if I could pretend to be having the time of my life."

I looked at her, my mouth open in amazement. "What was he thinking?"

"Can you imagine such a thing?" she continued. "I might be a wonderful actress, but I doubt if even Meryl Streep could pull off *that* performance. Just the thought of having that beast touching me is enough to turn me into a lesbian, and believe me, I have never thought seriously about ever being with another woman, especially when there are such gorgeous men in the world like you."

That was the first time in my life that I was called a gorgeous man. Not even my loving mother could stretch the truth that far. I was flattered all the same. "So how did you get away from him?" I asked.

"I kicked his erect penis so hard that I'm surprised it didn't break in half and then I stuck a needle in that nasty looking butt of his."

I cringed at the thought of the whole thing, especially about striking his erect penis so hard that it could actually break in half.

"He screamed like a wild beast. Hopefully, he got that on tape."

She sat across from me as the phlebotomist took a sample of my blood. She reassured me that it was just a precaution and that the doctor just wanted to be sure that my blood count was back to normal. She crossed and uncrossed her legs at least twenty times in the short time it took to take my blood, and I couldn't help thinking that if that "pervert" had promised her a part in a movie he might not be in the mess he was currently in. Then again, it would take a whole different reality to even imagine that sicko as a gorgeous man, so she might not have been susceptible to him under any circumstances.

Caroline escorted me to Doc Hollywood's office and told me that the doctor would be in shortly to see me. She winked at me as she closed the door. I sat in a chair and went through a stack of golf magazines, mainly because there was nothing else to read. Personally, I could never understand the fascination so many people held with a sport that never even caused you to break a sweat. Then again, after having a few drinks in the clubhouse I might have a whole different perspective on the game.

After a half-hour, Dr. Casey finally entered the room. I stood up and shook his hand and he apologized for taking so long. He wanted to look at the blood work first and after reviewing it he was happy to say that it looked really good. The biopsy also came back totally clean without any traces of cancer or any of the half-dozen other infections and viruses that he'd decided to test for, just in case. He touched the area around the biopsy and told me that the nurse would be in shortly to clean the incision site and put a new bandage over it. He shook my hand, told me how thankful he was that everything came back clean, and as he walked toward the door he turned and asked, "You don't play golf, do you?"

"No," I replied.

"Well, if you know anyone who does play, please let them know I'm looking for a new partner — preferably someone with money who enjoys a little wager now and then."

He closed the door, and instead of feeling a great sense of relief at the diagnoses, I suddenly felt incredibly sad. They say a picture is worth a thousand words, and all I could see was the picture of that young girl Sarah, sitting up in bed, attempting to smile, her head bald and the promise of dancing all night long and into the future, gone — gone like a fucking golf ball landing in a pond and aimlessly dropping to the bottom with a few hundred other balls.

Chapter 18

I left Doc Hollywood's office and pressed the button for the elevator. The image of the young girl was cemented in my consciousness as I stepped onto the elevator, and I was suddenly aware of feeling a little lightheaded. On the way down to the lobby, the elevator stopped at the second floor. The door opened and two hands reached in, grabbed me, and pulled me out and into another universe.

Dr. Souter stood in front of me, disheveled and smelling like a dead rodent. He shoved me up against the wall of the hallway just outside his office. His eyes were ragged little pools of desperation, and he was begging me for help. "Joe, thank God. You got to help me, Joe. You can't let them take me. Please, Joe, don't let them take me."

I suddenly thought about the scene from *Casablanca* where Peter Lorre's character is begging Rick, played by Humphrey Bogart, to protect him against the Nazis, and Rick just says, "I don't stick my neck out for anyone."

I knew I should be pulling a Rick in this situation, but I'd always had trouble saying "no" to anyone, especially someone who was standing right there, begging like a pathetic fool. Dr. Souter opened the door to his office and ushered me in. The office was empty and I asked, "Where is everyone?"

"Gone! They abandoned me like rats deserting a sinking ship."

I couldn't help noticing the parody in his statement. After all, he was the one who smelled and behaved like a rat — a perverted, psychotic rat.

"Who's after you?" I asked.

"They're all after me. Don't you watch the news? The police, FBI, IRS, and for all I know the CIA."

"Why?"

"For everything. Rape, attempted rape, laundering money, not paying my taxes, illegal dealings with foreign governments."

For a second there I thought he was delusional and was mistaking himself for our president. I asked, "Who did you rape?"

"My wife."

"I didn't know you could even be accused of raping your wife?"

"Of course you can, especially when you are legally separated. Her and her girlfriend."

"You raped both of them?"

"You bet I did. I've got the proof right here." He proudly pulled out a videotape marked "The Avenging Angel."

"Jesus, Doc, you taped yourself committing a crime?"

"I had to."

"Why, in God's name?"

"I couldn't just let her do what she did and get away with it!"

"Right, I mean, I guess not, but you do realize that you've incriminated yourself totally with this tape, don't you?"

"How else was I going to prove to the world that the bitch got what was coming to her?"

"I don't know, Doc. I don't know what you should have done, but I think it might be a good idea to destroy the evidence."

"Too late. I mailed a copy to both of them, and left my mark inside both bitches. Would you like to look at the tape? It's very high quality and I have a machine in my office."

"Not right now, but maybe some other time," I replied.

"You could learn a thing or two."

"I'm sure I could, but not right now."

Over the next twenty minutes I heard the whole story, down to the grisliest details. The sick son-of-a-bitch invited himself over to his wife and her lover's apartment for dinner. He assured them that he had accepted the fact that they were in love and was going to grant his wife the divorce she wanted, and that this was just his way of putting to rest all of the bad feelings that had accumulated over the last couple of months. He brought over two expensive bottles of wine that he had injected, through the corks, with large doses of tranquilizes. As he put it, "Enough tranquilizers to knock out an elephant."

His wife, knowing that he was a scotch drinker, didn't suspect anything when he didn't have any wine. She prepared his favorite dinner, turkey with gravy, stuffing, and cranberry. They were having a grand old time and then about halfway through dinner both ladies stopped laughing as they both fell face down into their plates of food, unconscious. Like a true gentleman, he lifted their faces out of their plates and cleaned them off. He then dragged both ladies into the living room, took off their clothes, and laid them on the floor side by side. He went out to his car, and took out his video camera and some other equipment. Then he set up his tripod and camera and positioned them so that his sexual prowess would be captured in all its grandeur.

He then raped both ladies, ejaculating first in his wife, and after a few hours had passed, during which he finished off his meal and had a few more glasses of scotch, he raped them again, this time ejaculating in his wife's girlfriend, leaving his mark in both of them.

Of course, he never would have done any of this if it weren't for that bitch Caroline, Dr. Souter explained. If only she had allowed him to have sex with her and tape the whole thing, that would have satisfied his desire for revenge against his faithless, back-stabbing wife. He would have sent her the video with a note saying, "You see, I've moved on too, and am not sharing."

Caroline had also pressed charges against him, accusing the good doctor of harassment and attempted rape.

As I listened to Dr. Souter drone on about his crimes and all the other people who were to blame for his actions apart from him, I glanced around for an escape, but there was no getting away from the cretin. He kept grabbing me by the shoulders and begging me to help him. It was suddenly obvious to me that I needed to be retrained in the art of assertiveness, both in order to get out of situations like this one (which were thankfully rare) and in order to keep my place at home. In less than a week I would have two women living with me — one who had been walking all over me since before she was able to walk, and another who I was ready to do cartwheels for in the hope that she wouldn't change her mind about marrying me.

I asked the pervert about the IRS and he told me that he had every intention of paying his taxes — after all he was a patriot — but he owed so much money to Doc Hollywood from their golf wagers that he felt more obligated to pay his colleague than the IRS agents who could have him arrested and put behind bars.

He was just getting ready to tell me about the money laundering when there was a sudden banging on the door of the office, then a gruff male voice saying, "LAPD, open up immediately."

"No! You can't let them take me, Joe. Please! Distract them as long as you can while I plan my escape." He locked himself in the room at the end of the hallway as I walked to the front door and opened it.

Immediately, six members of the LAPD pushed their way in, pinned me against the wall, and asked, "Joshua Souter?"

"No! God forbid," I said, hoping it wouldn't take much to convince them. "The pervert is in the last room on the right. I'm just a patient."

One officer stayed with me as five others gathered around the room at the end of the hall with their guns drawn. As they banged on the door, I could hear the doctor's cries and pleas of innocence and then suddenly one loud declaration: "You'll never take me alive!"

After another moment I heard the deafening sounds of glass crashing. The cops knocked the door down and I could just hear their distant voices repeating, "He's jumped! He's jumped!"

It would have been a lot more spectacular if the drop from the second floor to the ground weren't only thirty feet, but then everything can't be as exciting as in the movies. The cops pulled him out of a plush boxwood hedge that sustained more damage than he did. Then they arrested the pervert and threw him into the back of a police car where he cried like a baby.

I gave my statement to the officer and he asked if I had ever been molested by the doctor.

"No," I replied. "Why would you ask that?"

"Because he's also been accused by male patients of sexual assault."

"You got to be kidding."

"No, I guess you just weren't his type. Lucky you."

After the police released me, I got into my car and drove to the nearest 7-Eleven and bought a six-pack of Budweiser. I was so shaky that I would have killed to be able to open a Budweiser in my car, but I wasn't going down that road — literally. Instead I tucked the brown bag behind the driver's seat and started driving, gripping the leather steering wheel tightly. I drove down Riverside Drive and turned left onto Lakeside Drive. I stopped at a red light and looked up at a Warner Bros. billboard, adorned with pictures of Bugs Bunny, Duffy Duck, Porky Pig, and all the great Warner Bros. cartoon characters. This familiar sight started to calm me down, but I couldn't stop thinking about that sick bastard, Dr. Souter. What a psychopath. And to think he was my doctor for over twenty years. I suddenly felt clueless for having put up with him for two visits, let alone two decades.

I shook my head and turned on the radio just in time to hear the opening strains of Terry Jacks' "Seasons in the Sun." Just like that, all thoughts of the pervert floated away on a sea of familiar melodies, and all I could see was Sarah dancing all night long at her prom with her prosthetic leg and soon after dying in her hospital bed. For some reason I couldn't stop thinking about the fact that she died next to those framed pictures of herself at the dance. My hands started shaking again, and a wave of nausea overtook me, until I had to force down the vomit that was trying to escape my mouth.

The light changed and I drove pass Warner Bros. Studio and the famous Smoke House Restaurant. I turned left and drove through the gates of Forest Lawn cemetery where many famous movie stars, gangsters, producers, and directors were buried. I drove to the very top of the cemetery and parked beside the Memorial Court of Honor where large murals of the Revolutionary War, World War II, Abraham Lincoln, facsimiles of da Vinci's paintings and Michelangelo's *Sistene Chapel* and sculptures of American heroes adorned the area along with water fountains, a museum, and a replica of an eighteenth-century church.

The Court was a hidden treasure in a town famous for its history and legends. Whenever I felt down, or for that matter happy, I came up here with a few beers and sat on a stone bench for hours contemplating the beauty of the place. Occasionally, I would bring Sofia up here and wheel her around in her baby carriage, or walk through the displays with her when she was a little older, before her big change.

I took the six-pack out of the car and sat on a bench facing the Lincoln mural. I opened a beer, took a long drink, and stared at Abe's stovetop hat, but it was like my eyes weren't even working; all I could see was a mental image of Sarah dancing and laughing as her future ebbed away. I could see her doing her best to enjoy life, but the fact that her future was about to be stolen from her turned her dancing and laughter into a kind of desperate pantomime. Maybe it was survivor's guilt. I was spared and allowed to live, but I was no more deserving of this life than she was. Meanwhile, she was denied what no child should be denied: the chance to become an adult. I couldn't get my head around any of it.

My phone rang and it was Jennifer. She asked me if I was celebrating. She apparently knew the results of the biopsy before I did.

"Celebrating? No. Happy with the result, yes. But I'm sad because I know the pain and grief you are going through."

"I'm doing okay; after all, I have Sofia to lean on. The service was beautiful and the preacher said some very nice things about my mommy." There was a long silence as she tried to get control over her emotions. "Where are you?" she asked.

"At Forest Lawn cemetery."

"Why? Did someone you know pass away?"

"No!" I replied as I told her about the beautiful Memorial Court of Honor. She said she would love to see it and asked if I could take her there one day.

"Of course, I'd love nothing more," I said. Then she suddenly changed the subject and asked me about my girlfriend, Caroline.

"No, I didn't bring her any chocolates."

"How did she look in the sexy nurse's uniform?"

"Great!"

"Really," she said with a heavy sigh. "And did you look really hard at the most revealing parts of her outfit?"

"Yes, Jennifer. It's kind of hard not to look when an attractive lady like her is wearing such a skimpy outfit."

She apparently turned to Sofia who was standing right beside her and said, "Of course, he looked. Just like a man!"

A few seconds later I heard my daughter repeat, "Just like a man!"

Just when I thought the day couldn't get any stranger after my run-in with Dr. Souter, I couldn't help but feel that Jennifer and my daughter were playing some type of mind game with me.

"Why don't you seem happier about the results from the biopsy?" Jennifer asked. "Is there something you are hiding from me?"

"No, Jennifer, I am not hiding anything from you. Everything is great," I said, as I looked across at the mural of President Lincoln, a man who was reportedly compassionate and loving, and who lived without malice. Then I thought about how important it is to lay down a strong foundation of truth in any new relationship, and I decided to let her in on my thoughts about Sarah.

"On the day that you and Sofia left, I wandered into your room and picked up the picture of the little boy, dressed in the sailor's uniform, holding the "Cancer Free" sign. I was putting it back when the pictures you had placed behind the photo dropped to the floor."

Jennifer went quiet, then said, "I'm listening."

"I found the picture of Sarah and I read what you wrote on the back. Today, when the doctor was giving me the wonderful news about my results, I suddenly thought about Sarah and felt terrible. I'm sitting here trying to figure out why, and all I can come up with is that I'm suffering from survivor's guilt."

Jennifer wasn't saying anything, so I kept talking. "I couldn't stand the thought of that sweet child never having another chance to dance. It just isn't right."

There was a palpable and significant silence on her end, and I couldn't help but feel that I had crossed a line I had no right to cross.

"And do you know why you feel that way?" Jennifer asked, obviously choking up. "Because you are a really good person. Goodbye Joe. I have to go." She hung up before I had a chance to respond.

I opened another beer and drank it quickly. I called back and Sofia answered. I asked, "Where's Jennifer?"

"In the bedroom. You made her cry. Just like a man!" She hung up without saying another word. I lay down on the bench and stared up at the blue sky, surrounded by thousands of tombstones and the secrets and desires buried beneath them.

Chapter 19

Back at home, I put the four remaining beers from the cemetery in the refrigerator and took out a cold one. I walked into the living room, sat down on the couch, and turned on the evening news. Of course, the first image to jump out at me was Dr. Souter's fat face. He was being handcuffed, and was crying like a two-year-old as a small army of cops escorted him to a patrol car and one of them lowered him into the back seat. What a pathetic, sick pervert. I still couldn't believe that for nearly twenty years I had that man examining my body and I had never once suspected anything.

I turned off the news and put on reruns of the *I Love Lucy* show. If ever I needed a dose of comforting entertainment it was now, and what better group of individuals than Lucy, Ricky, Fred and Ethel to return me to planet earth.

After about an hour the phone rang. It was Jennifer. She was so excited that at first I couldn't understand a word she was saying. She seemed to be speaking a foreign language and then I suddenly realized she was speaking "southern." It didn't take her long to revert back to her native language, and I had to admit that I found it sexy.

I told her to begin from the beginning, and after she had calmed down, she said, "I have great news! Our daughter has given us her blessing to get married as soon as possible."

The words seemed to thud to the ground at my feet. *Our daughter?* When exactly she had become *our daughter* I wasn't quite sure, but I knew right away that I could live with that. Besides myself and Lawrence, I never really remembered my lovely Sofia communicating with anybody for at least a few years. The way she got along with Jennifer was something of a miracle.

"I wasn't aware that we were waiting for … our daughter's blessing to get married," I said.

"Surely, you didn't think I would ever marry you without getting Sofia's okay first?"

"Honestly, I never really thought of it."

She turned to Sofia and remarked, "Amazing! He thought I was going to marry him without first getting your blessing."

"Just like a man!" I could hear my daughter reply.

"Just like a man!" I could hear Jennifer repeat as she turned her attention back to me and asked, "So, if you really want to go through with this crazy plan to marry me, I'm all in and ready to say I do as soon as you want. Preferably before I start my new job."

I replied, "Well, why don't you give me some time to think about it?" and I hung up — "Just like a man!" Just under a minute later, and just like a wimp, I called her back and told her that nothing in the world would make me happier than to marry her as soon as possible.

She asked, "Did you just hang up on me?"

"No!" I lied, just like a man. "It's just a bad connection."

I didn't have much work to do to convince myself that marrying Jennifer was the right thing to do. From the moment she'd changed out of her sexy nurse's outfit and walked into my life, I knew she was the one. Sure, she had her quirks, but they only made her more appealing to me. She was the most compassionate, loving, and kind person I had ever met, and if I ever had any doubts about that, all I had to do was remember what she wrote on the back of the photos of the poor children who died from the terrible disease she chose to confront and combat. On top of all that, she'd effectively given me back my child, become my daughter's best friend, and in a short time, she would become the mother Sofia never had.

She was acting a little strange lately, but then what loving child wouldn't be, after losing her mother — her last blood connection in the world.

The girls, even before getting my consent, had already started planning the wedding — *just like women!* Jennifer preferred a small ceremony and naturally Sofia agreed. My daughter never felt comfortable around a lot of people, and that was kind of strange considering how beautiful she was and all the attention she garnered from adoring men. It was one of the reasons I stopped going to premieres and parties. The anxiety she exhibited at these events was so intense that it felt like I was torturing her, and since she was the only date I would consider taking, I just stopped going altogether.

Jennifer chose "our daughter" to be her maid of honor, and since she didn't really have any friends in Los Angeles, she was happy with just Sofia and no other guests on her part. I had friends, but figured why bother complicating things, so I decided not to invite any of them. If Nick was available and not on his seventh honeymoon in Tahiti, I would have asked him to be my Best Man. No one was happier than Sofia that it would be just the three of us.

After listening to the two ladies discussing all the details of a simple wedding for an hour, I decided it was time to call it a day. I told them that whatever they came up with would be great with me, not that my opinion mattered.

I walked toward my bedroom and stopped and looked into Jennifer's room. It was like some unseen force was pulling me toward the photo of Sarah, a child I had never met, but who seemed to have captured a piece of my soul, my consciousness, and refused to let go. It was like she was reaching out from beyond the grave and trying to tell me something, to enlighten me — not to scare or warn me, but to disclose a universal truth.

I closed my eyes and fought back the urge to look at her photo. I walked into my room and did something I rarely do: I closed the door to my bedroom.

I sat down on my bed and methodically went over the events of the day. On a day where I was told that I did not have a disease that could possibly end my life, it barely registered. How crazy is that?

I lay my head down on the pillow, closed my eyes, and in the distance I could hear Pink Floyd's "Learning to Fly." Pillows of heavenly clouds enclosed me, and in the distance, I could see a woman and a man dancing atop the billowing white and gray forms. As I moved closer, the image of the man and the young lady became clearer. It was Fred Astaire dancing effortlessly, gracefully, with a radiant and beautiful Sarah. Sarah with both her legs, dressed in a lovely white gown, her long, dark hair glimmering in the reflected light as Mr. Astaire twirled her round and round and into the arms of Gene Kelly.

They waltzed across the clouds until suddenly Mr. Kelly and Sarah separated and Mr. Kelly extended his hand to pull Sarah back to him. They galloped across the clouds, circling back and forth, laughing and laughing, and then, in a flash, I was dancing with the young lady, which was strange because I really wasn't much of a dancer.

"Sarah?" I asked.

"Yes, Joe. Why do you seem so surprised? Surely, you didn't think closing your bedroom door would keep me out?"

"No, that wasn't my intention."

She smiled knowingly as her eyes sparkled, and it was as though I was looking into the face of God. I danced effortlessly, as though I had stepped into the shoes of Mr. Astaire or Mr. Kelly. We were moving together in perfect time until the clouds suddenly closed in on us. It was as if a blanket had been thrown over our heads. I held onto Sarah's hands as we continued to dance through the blinding vapors. Her laughter, like the song of sirens, was both intoxicating and reassuring.

When the vapors finally cleared, we were dancing across the full-court basketball court I grew up on in the Bronx. The court was empty, except for the two of us dancing across it like Fred and Ginger — Sarah radiant in her gown, and me looking sharp in a top hat and a tuxedo.

"Smile, Joe. This is your happy place."

"I don't understand. What are we doing here?"

"Of course you understand. You have always understood. Just close your eyes and try to remember."

I closed my eyes. It wasn't like I had a choice. She was my guide, my Beatrice, beckoning to me before the pearly gates, and who was I not to obey? I entered and I suddenly found myself in the middle of a full-court basketball game with all the friends that I had grown up with on this very court. Thankfully, I was no longer wearing a top hat and a tuxedo. I was also no longer a middle-aged man but a teenager,

Sarah's age. I was dressed like everyone else in dungarees and a T-shirt, my feet smartly encased in a pair of black Converse sneakers. I was dribbling the ball up court and saw a hole in the defense and dribbled straight to the basket and hit a back-handed layup. I heard clapping and looked over to see Sarah. She walked directly toward me, onto the court, and all the action stopped as everyone looked at her. She stopped before me and threw her arms around my neck and said, "Don't tell Jennifer, but I have never kissed a boy and this might be the only chance I get." She pressed her lips against mine and we kissed. I can't tell you what I was thinking or feeling in the moment. All I sensed was a sort of trembling that started on my left side and spread through my whole body. Sarah stepped back, releasing her hold on me, smiled and said, "Thank you, Joe. It was even better than I imagined." I watched as she waved goodbye, slowly disappearing into a swirl of clouds.

My phone rang and I woke up. It was three-thirty in the morning and I didn't even have to look at the display to know who it was. "Good morning my sweet and beautiful daughter."

"Good morning, Daddy."

Chapter 20

Sofia was very concerned that she might not be a very good maid of honor, and the last thing she wanted to do was disappoint Jennifer. I tried to reassure her that there was no need to worry, but she had been up half the night on her computer researching the many responsibilities of a maid of honor. Suddenly she was worried about coming up with a fun theme for a bridal shower, ordering crudités and party favors, managing the bridal party that didn't, and wouldn't, exist, and writing a moving but funny speech to deliver at the reception.

I had always sensed that my daughter was different, but over the last week or so it had hit home with astonishing clarity. It was as though she saw the world simply in terms of black and white. She had difficulty detecting the emotional nuances that make up so much of all our social relationships. She didn't pick up on the fact that a change in a person's voice might indicate that they were upset or joking, or know that someone gently touching your hand was a reassuring gesture or a sign that they liked you.

It took me over half an hour to explain to her that everything she had read about the duties of a maid of honor did not apply to our wedding — that the ceremony at the church would be less than ten minutes and that there would be no speeches or entertainment afterward. Her only responsibility was to stand beside her best friend while Jennifer and I recited our wedding vows. She finally acknowledged that she understood and said she felt a lot better.

And then for some inexplicable reason I asked, "How is Lawrence?"

She hesitated for a long moment and then replied, "He's wonderful. He's always wonderful."

"Does he like Kentucky?"

"Yes, Daddy. He would make such a wonderful professor at the University of Kentucky but he would never leave me."

"Of course not. He has always been your best buddy."

She didn't say anything and I could sense a rising level of anxiety overtaking her, so I quickly asked, "And how do you like Kentucky?"

"It is very pretty but I like where we live better."

"The weather is a lot nicer where we live," I said, like a hack writer incapable of coming up with an original idea.

"It's definitely better where we live," she agreed.

"How do you think Jennifer is holding up?"

"Holding up? Oh." Sofia thought about this and said, "She seems happy and sad. I think she feels better today."

I was so impressed by this simple description of grief that I burst into tears, which I tried to keep very quiet.

"I love you so much, Sofia," I said. "And I'm so proud of you for being there and helping Jennifer get through this hard time."

As tears rolled down my face, I felt an overwhelming desire to reach across the two thousand miles that separated us and hug her tightly while softly singing a Beatles song to her as I used to do when she was just a baby. A smile crept onto my face as I remembered singing "Michelle, ma belle" to her so often that she once asked me if her real name was Michelle.

"I love you too, Daddy. I am so happy that you are going to marry Jennifer and that she is going to live with us forever."

"Me too, honey," I said. "And you are going to make the most beautiful maid of honor." As the words came out of my mouth, it crossed my mind that my lovely daughter might never know the pleasure of kissing a boy for the first time.

I could hear Jennifer enter the room and suddenly her voice rang cheerfully through the phone. "Good morning, honey."

"Good morning, sweetheart. You sound awfully chipper for so early in the morning."

"And why wouldn't I? I know my mother is looking down upon me, fully cognizant and aware … and happy, that her daughter is marrying the most wonderful man in the whole world and adopting the loveliest daughter anyone could imagine. You haven't changed your mind?"

Sofia screamed "No!" before I could say anything, then called out, "He loves you so much, Jennifer."

"I guess that answers *that* inane question," I told my bride-to-be. "I just wish we didn't have to wait nearly two weeks to get married."

"Well, Sofia and I have talked about cutting our trip short. I thought I would have so much more to do concerning my mother's estate, but when you don't have anything to your name except a few knickknacks, pictures, and a copy of the Bible, it really doesn't take long to settle things."

"I'm sorry, sweetheart."

"It's okay. We had many wonderful years together and it's those years and the memories we made together that no one can ever take from me."

"That's right, honey. God, you're so … balanced and mature."

Jennifer sounded surprised. "Thank you, sweetie. It's really nice to hear that you value those things."

"I do."

"*I do*," she said. "I like the sound of those words."

"Me too."

"So, can we come home early? Is it going to cost a fortune to change the tickets? We'd like to head back there in three days if it all works out."

"In three days?" I repeated.

"Yes, unless of course you made other plans and our coming home interferes with them."

"No, besides making lunch plans today with Caroline and dinner plans with her for tomorrow night, I should be free to pick you girls up in three days."

She laughed that infectious laugh that made everything seem wonderful. "For the record, I still have that really good-looking waiter's number and I imagine my lovely daughter can get a date with a rich, cute university student quicker than you can buy a box of chocolates."

I laughed and said, "I'll change the plane tickets and the hotel reservations. You girls go have a wonderful time and I don't want to hear about any waiters or university students."

The girls had the next two days completely planned out, and it wasn't difficult to conclude that even if I'd said I couldn't change their tickets they had every intention of coming back home in three days. After all, God only knows how many times my daughter reminded Jennifer that I had a lot of money. She loved to repeat things, and telling my bride-to-be that I "had a lot of money" was one of her favorite sayings.

The first thing on their agenda was to visit a friend of Jennifer's who owned a horse farm. Sofia was excited that she was going to get to feed a horse an apple or two or three. Who knew they liked apples? Certainly not me, a boy raised in the Bronx and living the last twenty-two years in Los Angeles, entirely horse free.

After that, they were going to go visit the last hospital Jennifer worked in before moving to Los Angeles, to catch up with friends and colleagues. Then the remainder of their time would be spent visiting all of the children that Jennifer helped take care of and who were currently living at home or being treated as outpatients, as well as some others who were in remission and cancer free. Jennifer kept in touch with all of her patients, and I was quite certain that she also kept in touch with the parents whose children did not make it, such as Sarah.

I changed into my running gear and walked outside. It was still dark out. Not even the birds were up yet. For a moment I felt like I was alone in an ever-expanding universe. I started to run as I replayed the dream I had of Sarah as billows of clouds raced through my consciousness. I wasn't sure what was happening, but I felt like I was on the verge of taking in some new truth, or at least some new information that I needed. I tried to run a little faster to catch it, but whatever it was stayed ahead of me in the wind, disappearing around every corner.

Chapter 21

I sat down at my desk and wrote for hours. Despite what Nick told me about not rushing, I knew that any day he might call, divorced once again, and suddenly be ready to get to work. The phone rang and it was the bank that issued the credit card I gave to Sofia. She, or possibly someone who had got hold of her card, had apparently made quite a few expensive purchases, and the total was way over the limit.

I immediately called Jennifer and could hear the laughter of children in the background. I asked Jennifer if Sofia was on some type of spending spree. She hesitated before saying, "She wouldn't listen to me and insisted on buying all the children we visited new computers and games they could play on their new devices. I sent you a bunch of pictures."

I opened the file on my computer and found a dozen pictures of Sofia in a dozen different states of joy. One of the pictures showed her smiling and laughing as she fed a horse an apple. In others, she was happily attending to children in the hospital, the outpatient children, and those in remission as she helped them set up their new devices and install the games. I couldn't remember the last time I'd seen her like this.

Jennifer sounded a little worried as she asked, "Should I take the card away from her?"

"No," I said. "I am going to put a lot more money on the card. I can't think of a better way to spend money. Please don't mention our conversation to her. Let her buy the children whatever they want." I waited for her to make a sly remark about how nice it must be to have a lot of money, but she didn't say a word.

And so I tried to egg her on, saying, "What, no sarcastic remark?"

"And why would I make a sarcastic remark about how generous, giving, and caring our daughter is, or about her dad, who obviously taught her how to be that way?"

"I like it that you call her 'our' daughter."

"Why wouldn't I? Surely, you don't think I would be marrying you if she wasn't included in the deal." She laughed, and in that moment I fell even more in love with her than I thought possible. Any more of this and my heart was going to burst.

"You really are perfect," I said.

"She's the one who is perfect," Jennifer replied. "And you're not so bad for an old man."

I laughed and said the only thing I could think of: that I loved her, and would marry her today if she was standing in front of me.

She was quiet, and I could feel her smiling as she said, "I love you, too."

I hung up and clicked through the pictures again, marveling at the sight of my loving, caring, and joyful daughter. Never did I imagine that she could make me so happy.

Chapter 22

I arrived at the airport early, eager to see my girls and to start our new lives together. I had a thing about airports. Years ago, before Sofia was born, I would purposely get there hours before my flights were scheduled to take off. I used to love sitting in the airport bars and talking to people who were coming and going from different parts of the country and the world. Occasionally, I would voluntarily give up my seat if my flight was overbooked and I didn't have to be at my destination at a particular time or day. They would usually book me on the next flight out and give me a free ticket on a future flight, but I didn't do it for the free tickets. I was just having such a good time meeting people at the bar that I didn't want it to end. This usually occurred around the holidays when I went home to visit my parents for a couple of weeks. Today, though, it was all about the girls.

I waited by the baggage area. Ever since 9/11, many of the airports around Los Angeles relocated their bars to areas where only ticketed passengers were allowed. So, sitting at a bar and conversing and having a few cold beers were out of the question.

I spotted the girls coming down the walkway toward the baggage claim and for the first time in my life I was faced with the quandary of which beautiful girl I would kiss and hug first. While lost in contemplation, I suddenly found myself with both girls in my arms, hugging and kissing me. I felt like I was the envy of every man in the baggage area.

As I expected, Jennifer sat behind the wheel of my car and drove home with my daughter beside her. The houseboy sat in the back.

During the drive home, I leaned forward between the two front seats and talked about the plans I had made for our wedding. I had talked to the preacher at The Little Brown Church on Coldwater

Canyon and he said he would be happy to marry us in four days at ten o'clock in the morning. The church was Christian and was probably no bigger than my living room. The few times I had been in the church I could not help but think that this tiny place of worship, with its simple wooden pews and wooden frame, was the perfect symbol of what Jesus represented and preached. It also seemed like the ideal place to start my new life with Jennifer. I figured that if we could do without surface trappings of so many other churches, including gold chalices, marble alters, and crystal ceilings, then we would stand a better chance of always telling each other the simple, unvarnished truth.

Before making the arrangements, I asked Jennifer if she would be happy getting married in The Little Brown Church. I described it to her, and said I thought it was the perfect compromise for a marriage between a woman raised Protestant and a man raised Catholic. I also hoped that the church would appeal to her beliefs about modesty and her distaste for the flaunting of wealth. She replied that as far as she was concerned we could just as well get married at city hall, but if it made Sofia and me happy, she would love to get married in a church.

I told her that it would make Sofia and me very happy if we got married in a church, and that it would be an affront to my late parents if we didn't. As progressive as my parents were in many areas, they remained staunchly loyal to the Catholic Church, and there was no denying that the Catholic faith was the foundation of my own world views and beliefs about morality.

During the rest of the drive home, Sofia was busy on her phone arranging her calendar right up to the wedding and directly after the wedding. Before entering anything into her calendar she checked with Jennifer to make sure it was all right. Apparently, she didn't think my input mattered. We should leave for the church at 9:40, and arrive at 9:45. At 10:00 the ceremony should begin and be over no later than 10:15. After all the paperwork was signed and made official by the preacher, we should arrive back home by 11:00.

"And what are our plans after we arrive home?"

Jennifer looked at me and said, "Really Joe, you want to go into those lurid details with our daughter right in front of us?"

I shook my head, as the comment seemed to go way beyond my eighteen-year-old daughter's comprehension.

"I was thinking about renting a limo, going out for a lovely, celebratory dinner, and then taking a nice ride up the coast."

Jennifer shook her head, looked at Sofia, and replied, "I would much rather stay at home and celebrate with the two people I love most in this world. What do you think, Sofia?"

"I like your plan very much."

"We'll be married by then, so there won't be any need to flaunt your money or try to impress me." She looked at Sofia and said, "Just like a man!"

"Just like a man!" Sofia naturally repeated.

"But that was very thoughtful of you, sweetheart."

"Very thoughtful, Daddy."

I wasn't quite sure if this echo chamber was some kind of game they were playing with me, or if this was Jennifer giving in to every wish of my daughter, or if this was Jennifer grieving over her mother.

I couldn't figure it out, so I decided to turn my attention to practical details. "We still need to go to the courthouse and apply for a marriage license."

"Okay," Jennifer said.

This reminder seemed to send Sofia into a panic. "You should do that right now!" she said. Her tone of voice made it sound like a matter of life or death.

Jennifer looked at her and said very softly and reassuringly, "It's okay if we wait until tomorrow. It won't speed up the process and it's not like we can get married any sooner."

"What time will you be going tomorrow?"

"Ten o'clock, sweetheart, before it gets too crowded," I replied and Sofia typed the time and date into the calendar on her phone.

Chapter 23

Once we got all of the luggage into the house, I went to the kitchen and grabbed myself an ice-cold beer. The ride home from the airport had been bizarre. At least, that was my perception of it, or maybe I was just so happy they were home that I just wasn't thinking straight. Maybe I was just imagining things. Either way, I needed some relief.

I downed the beer and grabbed another as Jennifer walked into the kitchen, followed by her shadow … my lovely daughter. "Would you like a glass of wine, my beautiful wife-to-be? I bought a couple of bottles of your favorite." I pulled out a chilled bottle of Far Niente chardonnay and was fully expecting her to object with a round of, "Oh, you shouldn't have. No need to buy such expensive wine … throwing your money around just to impress me. Just like a man!"

Instead she smiled and kissed me on the cheek and replied, "Oh, how sweet. Please pour me a large glass."

I opened the bottle as both ladies looked at me as though I was some type of alien specimen. Strange, because I was starting to believe that they were both aliens. I handed Jennifer a large glass of wine as Sofia reached into the refrigerator and took out a bottle of water. They walked into the living room and sat down on the couch, as I took out a bottle of Jack Daniels from the cabinet. I took a large gulp straight from the bottle as Jennifer called out, "Aren't you going to join us?" followed by Sofia calling out, "Yes, Daddy, aren't you going to join us?"

I took another gulp from the bottle and put it back in the cabinet. I grabbed another beer and walked into the living room, thinking that I might cuddle next to my fiancée, but instead I found Sofia stretched out across the couch with her head resting on my fiancée's lap. I pretended that all was normal as I sat across from them in a chair and watched as Jennifer softly stroked my daughter's hair.

"How is the wine?"

"Simply wonderful, thank you so much." She stretched out her hand and pointed to a ring on her finger. "How do you like it?"

I got up from my chair and looked down at the ring, "It's lovely," I replied, not knowing a damn thing about rings.

"It's my mother's ring. I move it over one finger and it becomes my wedding ring, if you have no objections?"

"Of course not. If that's what you want, then I definitely have no objections."

"It's definitely what I want. You see, it's costing you nothing to marry me."

"Yes, Daddy, it's costing you nothing to marry her. You should be so thankful."

I looked down at my daughter and couldn't help thinking, *This from the girl who charged over fifteen thousand dollars to my credit card over two days, without blinking an eye.* Then I reminded myself that it was all for a good cause.

I looked at Jennifer's glass and it was nearly empty. "Let me get you some more wine."

"Yes, please," she replied as she finished the little remaining wine in her glass and handed it to me.

I walked back to the kitchen and poured Jennifer another large glass of wine, setting the bottle on the counter. I looked up at the cabinet that housed the Jack Daniels and asked myself, "Should I or should I not?" I opened the cabinet, grabbed the bottle, and took a large gulp. Surely, it couldn't hurt.

I walked back into the living room and handed Jennifer her glass of wine. "Thank you, sweetheart." She looked down at my daughter and asked, "Isn't he simply wonderful?"

"Yes, he's simply wonderful," Sofia repeated. I started to wonder if my daughter had taken on the personality of a parrot.

"We're so lucky to have such a loving man in our life," Jennifer said. Before my daughter had a chance to repeat my fiancée's remark, I put my hand in front of Jennifer's face and pointed to my father's ring that I had been wearing since his death. "Is it okay if I use my father's ring as my wedding ring?"

"Of course, sweetheart, but on our wedding day you are going to have to move it over a finger. I don't want any other women to get the crazy idea that you're available."

"He would be crazy to even look at another woman when he'll be married to the most beautiful woman in the whole world."

"He's a man, angel, and 'just like a man,' he can't help looking at any scantily clad woman that passes him by."

I sat down in my designated chair and knew damn well that Jennifer's last statement was an allusion to Caroline. I thought Jennifer was above silly jealousies, but apparently I was wrong. There was the "Me Too" movement, and apparently my fiancée and daughter were starting their own crusade called the "Just Like a Man" movement.

I had so much I needed to talk to Jennifer about, but with my daughter glued to her I couldn't get her alone and I wasn't about to have my daughter privy to intimate conversations, especially since she was now in the habit of repeating everything that Jennifer said.

"And how is the new screenplay coming along?" Jennifer asked.

"Wonderful! I could easily have the first draft finished in a couple of days but apparently Nick is in no rush to get back to work. He just married a girl he met a few days ago in Tahiti and they're on their honeymoon."

"Is this his first marriage?"

I started to laugh. "Surely you're joking. He's almost as famous for all his marriages and divorces as he is for his movies. This is like his eighth marriage, and he's only like forty-six years old."

"Is he trying to set a record?"

"Maybe. Don't you ever read any of the gossip magazines on the racks in all the supermarkets, or look at any of the five hundred entertainment shows on TV?"

"No! I have more important things to do with my time than to be concerned with the lives of overpaid, misogynist pigs."

I held my tongue for about a second before setting her straight. "That misogynist pig, as you call him, is one of the main reasons I have been able to provide my daughter with such a comfortable life.

He's also the main reason that I was able to give my very deserving parents some luxuries that they greatly enjoyed but never would have been able to afford."

"I didn't mean it like that," she said apologetically.

"No, Jennifer, you meant it exactly like that, and if you have such a problem with the way I make my money and the way I live my life, then maybe we should seriously reconsider the idea of getting married."

Sofia sat up like a rocket and looked alarmingly at Jennifer. "It's okay sweetheart, just a little disagreement. I apologize for offending you, Joe."

"She apologizes, Daddy."

I walked into the kitchen before I could say anything that I would seriously regret. I looked up at the cabinet holding the Jack Daniels and decided to play it safe. I turned to find Sofia standing right in front of me, wearing a worried expression. "She apologized, Daddy."

"Yes, sweetheart, I know," I replied. As I looked into my daughter's eyes, I could see that this was more than worry. Her expression was one of pure fear … and she wasn't big on facial expressions.

"But, she apologized," she repeated. I gently touched her face. My daughter was always my greatest weakness, and she was so traumatized by this little argument that I would swallow my pride, once again … like I had a choice.

I took my daughter's hand and walked back into the living room. I tapped my fiancée on the shoulder and she turned around. I wiped the tears from her face and said, "I accept your apology and I'm sorry for overreacting." I bent down and kissed my lovely fiancée for a long moment. She threw her arms around my neck and we kissed again, this time for even longer. My daughter clapped.

Chapter 24

The following morning at exactly 9:30, Jennifer and I got into my car and pulled out of the driveway. Finally, I had my fiancée alone. I had a lot of questions, especially about our daughter.

Sofia had decided to stay home. She was never comfortable around crowds, and since neither Jennifer nor I could guarantee that there wouldn't be a lot of people milling around at the courthouse, she decided to play it safe and stay home. We just had to promise her that once we got the license we would call her and that we would try to be home by noon.

Jennifer turned onto Moorpark Street and drove toward the freeway. Just as I was about to ask her about Sofia she jumped in and said, "I have something very important to tell you."

"Okay," I replied as I braced myself for some terrible news about my daughter.

"I can't have children," she remarked.

"What?" I asked, not quite sure I'd heard her correctly.

"I can't have children," she repeated as she gripped the steering wheel very tightly.

"Is that the reason the guys who were supposed to marry you all backed out? That was the big, bad thing they found out about you that had them running away?"

"Yes. I couldn't really blame them. What newlywed couple doesn't want to have children?"

"Yeah, I agree. What's the use of getting married if the woman can't have children?"

She looked at me as though all the blood had been drained from her body and asked, "Should I just turn around and go home?"

"What the hell have you been smokin' this morning?" I asked. "I thank the good Lord in Heaven that those clowns who were supposed to marry you backed out. Their loss is my gain. Honestly, I have not even thought about children ... the thought hasn't crossed my mind once. Wow! Just think about all the money we are going to save not having to buy birth control devices, and I know how important that is to you."

"Very funny!"

"I can't even handle the one child I have," I continued. "What in the world would make you think I wanted more?"

"She's perfect, and don't you ever forget that."

"If you say so. After all, if anyone would know, it's you, right, Ms. Perfect?"

"And what is that supposed to mean?" she asked as she stopped at a red light.

I reached over and ran my hand through her hair and said, "Despite your aversion to money, you are the most perfect individual I have ever met. I've told you that numerous times. Your beauty is undeniable, but it's what is inside that makes you so special. In a city filled with pretenders, I have never once doubted your sincerity, caring, and compassion. In just a short time, you have been able to connect with my daughter in a way I have never been able to."

"Don't kid yourself, Joe. That child loves you more than is humanly possible. She might have a difficult time expressing herself, but never question her love."

"When I see her with you I can't help but wonder how much she would have benefited from having a loving mother to confide in."

"Was there ever a time you weren't there for her?"

"Of course not, but there have been so many times that it felt like my daughter and I were living in different worlds. Her behavior toward her grandparents will forever dumbfound me."

The light turned green as I looked out the passenger-side window and remarked, "A couple of times when the two of you were away, she confided to me over the phone that she had been praying to her grandparents to forgive her and to try to love her again. She said she wasn't sure that they were listening. I told her of course they were listening, and that you were the proof of that. It might sound a little crazy, but she and I both believe that they sent you to us to make us happy. How else can we explain your sudden appearance in our lives?"

I turned and looked at Jennifer as tears rolled down her cheeks. "Is this the reason they pay you the big bucks? Because you can make girls cry so easily and make them feel like they are the most loved creatures in the world?"

"No, just the opposite … it's because I can make girls laugh and forget their problems for a few hours." I handed her a tissue.

"So that's the secret?"

"I would hope so. I would hate to think that I was responsible for creating even more tears in a world filled with far too much sorrow."

"Not all tears are expressions of sadness."

"Of course not, but I will always prefer laughter over tears." I looked across at the beautiful girl a couple of feet away from me and I couldn't help but feel like I was the luckiest man in the world and beyond.

We parked across from the courthouse and I took my fiancée's hand as we walked up the front steps. The line for marriage applications was relatively short, which really wasn't much of a surprise since on any giving day in the city of Los Angeles the number of divorce fillings had to vastly outnumber marriage applications. We showed our identification, paid the fee, and while we were filling out the application I couldn't help but notice that Jennifer's date of birth was June 4th, 1988. Today was her birthday.

We walked out of the courthouse and before walking down the stairs I took her aside and pulled her to me by the waist. "Happy birthday, beautiful lady! When were you planning on telling me?"

"Never," she replied, and laughed. "Surely, you don't expect a lady to advertise her thirtieth birthday?"

"Surely not," I repeated as I reached further around her waist and kissed her for a long moment. "We need to celebrate."

"And what might you have in mind?"

"Champagne, of course. French champagne. Cristal. You do like champagne?"

"Which lady doesn't?"

"And no complaining about any prices?"

"Absolutely not! I decided as I was signing the marriage application that if it was your desire to spoil me, who was I to complain? I deserve it."

"Wow! I see my daughter has had some influence on you."

She laughed and laughed and in between laughs I managed to get one more amazing kiss.

Jennifer called Sofia once she was over her giggling spell and informed her that everything went according to plan. As a sound effect, she crinkled the copy of the marriage license she was holding in her hand. I could hear my daughter happily screaming and then hear her remind her soon-to-be-stepmother that she promised to be home by noon. Jennifer took a picture of the marriage license and texted the photo to Sofia. She then took my hand and we walked down the stairs and down two blocks to a liquor store.

The store owner placed four bottles of Cristal champagne on the counter as my fiancée browsed the wine selection. She picked out two bottles of Far Niente chardonnay, two bottles of Far Niente cabernet, and two bottles of Brunello chianti and placed them on the counter.

The store owner remarked, "The señorita has excellent taste."

"Gracias, señor," Jennifer replied as she kissed me on the cheek. I paid the gentleman eighteen hundred dollars, and without so much as a smirk from my fiancée.

We walked out of the liquor store and I asked, "And do you like caviar?"

"Of course, but I don't feast on endangered species. I do feast on oysters and shrimp … and Godiva chocolates, which are also a favorite of Sofia's."

"Yes, that's one of the five food groups my daughter chooses from, along with peanut butter and jelly sandwiches, pizza, plain pasta with butter, and cereal with chocolate milk."

"If I'm not mistaken, at least three of her favorites are also your favorites," she said with a laugh.

"I didn't say she didn't have wonderful taste, but she doesn't even allow herself a little wiggle room. She is exceptionally picky and certain food smells will have her running for the door."

We stepped into a seafood market and bought thirty jumbo shrimp and two dozen oysters. Since I was quite certain my lovely daughter wouldn't taste either, we walked into a confectionery store next and bought four boxes of Godiva chocolates as a treat for her. I was quite certain that Sofia would have no problem eating the chocolates, possibly with two slices of pizza or two peanut butter and jelly sandwiches.

Chapter 25

We pulled into the driveway of the house at 11:50 a.m. ... a full ten minutes before we would have turned into pumpkins. Sofia was sitting on the couch, with Lawrence, watching *The Honeymooners*. Like I said, she did have wonderful taste. She was quick to remind us that we were a whole ten minutes early, but she was so very happy ... especially when Jennifer showed her the actual copy of the marriage license. She read it so carefully that she reminded me of a lawyer.

Jennifer opened a box of the chocolates and the two girls in my life sat on the couch laughing, talking about how wonderful everything was, and eating one piece of chocolate after another. There was nothing that could compare with the laughter of children, but the merriment and joy of women, especially the two glorious women I loved so much, was an elixir that could pour sunshine down on a rainy day.

I put the white wine, champagne, and seafood into the refrigerator and left the four bottles of red wine on the counter. Suddenly, everything went quiet for a minute and when I turned around my daughter threw her arms around me and hugged me tightly and repeated over and over again, "I love you so much, Daddy, I love you so much." In a day filled with magical moments, no moment was more magical than the tight and loving hug from my daughter.

Chapter 26

After harvesting every joyful moment of my daughter's hug, I whispered into her ear that it was Jennifer's birthday. She looked shocked and said, "I didn't buy her a gift."

I gently caressed her arm and replied, "That's because she didn't tell anyone. I found out by mistake."

"But I need to get her gift," my daughter insisted as Jennifer walked into the kitchen and overheard her.

Jennifer gently took Sofia's hands in hers and said, "But you have already given me the best gift any girl could want on her birthday. Do you know what that is?"

Sofia shook her head and Jennifer replied, "You and your daddy have allowed me to be part of your lives, and I can't imagine any gift being better than that ... knowing that every day I wake up I'll have the pleasure of knowing that both of you are there for me."

She gently ran her hand across Sofia's face, "You understand, my lovely angel?"

"Yes," Sofia said as Jennifer planted a bunch of kisses all over her forehead and looked across at me and asked, "How about opening a bottle of that wonderful champagne?"

"Yes, my beautiful." I took out a couple of champagne flutes and opened a bottle as Jennifer asked Sofia, "And would you like a little? It's all bubbly and tastes a little bit like ginger ale." Sofia looked up at me and as usual I could not say no to our lovely angel.

I took down one more flute and poured the champagne. I handed Jennifer the first flute but she waited to taste the bubbly as I made a toast. "To the girl who is going to make the loveliest bride, happy birthday, and to our beautiful daughter who is going to make the most beautiful maid of honor."

Jennifer and I drank up as Sofia sniffed the flute, took a taste, and then drank the remainder of the champagne in her glass. She exclaimed, "It *is* bubbly! Can I please have some more?"

I looked at Jennifer for guidance and she remarked, "Just a little bit more, sweetheart. We don't want you to get drunk, fall asleep, and miss all the celebrating."

I poured a little more into her glass and she simply drank it down like it was ginger ale. Jennifer took her hand and said, "Time to finish off that box of chocolates." They walked back into the living room as I refilled Jennifer's glass and grabbed Sofia a bottle of water. I handed the ladies their beverages and sat down next to my daughter with my glass of champagne. Sofia was talkative, bubbly, somewhat incoherent, but smiling the whole time until she passed out with her head planted firmly on Jennifer's lap.

"I think we might have given her a little too much champagne," Jennifer remarked as she lovingly and gently ran her hand through Sofia's hair.

"Quite possibly, but she certainly seemed to enjoy the bubbly. The child has wonderful taste."

"She sure does. You have done a wonderful job of spoiling her."

"Thank you. Hopefully I'll have the same success with you."

"I'm all in on the spoiling," Jennifer said with a laugh as she tapped her empty glass. "A refill, please."

I took her glass and walked into the kitchen and refilled both our glasses with champagne. I handed Jennifer her glass as I looked down at our daughter for a pensive moment.

"And what might you be thinking?" Jennifer asked as she took a sip of champagne.

"How little she has changed since she was a child — the same face, an unblemished complexion, that beautiful olive skin and those lovely eyelashes. I used to look at her for hours when she was asleep, hugging Lawrence, surrounded by all those stuffed animals. I couldn't believe how such a perfect creature could be my child, my offspring. I used to imagine her dreaming about places and people as wonderful as her … and now I can't even begin to imagine what she is dreaming about."

"Why would you say such a thing?" Jennifer asked with a sharp intonation in her voice. "She's still dreaming of those wonderful places and people, except that now there is a handsome prince in her dreams … one not worthy of her."

I didn't dare say a word. I knew better. She had always stood up for Sofia, even after meeting the rude and obnoxious Sofia that first night when she cooked dinner, but now it was elevated to a whole new level. She was acting like an overprotective mother, which was absolutely great. After all, it wasn't that long ago that I thought I was going to lose my darling fiancée because of Sofia. One had to put things in perspective, and from where I was standing I could not have imagined that things would work out so perfectly.

I sat down next to my passed out daughter and lifted my glass for another toast. "To our lovely daughter." Jennifer and I clinked flutes over our daughter's laid out body, and cheerfully drank up.

Chapter 27

Finally, the big day arrived. The day I would be marrying a Kentucky-bred beauty so far out of my league that the only way I could figure out such good fortune was that my mother and father had engineered it from above.

Naturally, my daughter was punctual, as always. As planned, she had us out the door and into the car at exactly 9:40. We arrived at The Little Brown Church at exactly at 9:45. Jennifer was dressed in a simple but lovely white dress with her hair done up perfectly. Her maid of honor was dressed in a very similar white dress with her hair done up exactly like Jennifer's hair.

I had suggested a couple of days earlier that I hire the gentleman who did all our location scouting for our movies to take pictures at the ceremony. He was the best photographer I knew, and I figured he could use the money because he had been out of work since our last movie. My daughter vetoed the idea and Jennifer naturally agreed with her. Sofia did not like people she did not know taking her picture. But neither did she like the idea of taking work away from the photographer, so she came up with an idea to make sure he was compensated. Since I had so much money, she said, it would be nice if I sent the out-of-work photographer the money I was going to give him for taking the pictures. It would be a very kind gesture.

I did not argue. It was far too late in the game to upset the ladies, so I did as my daughter suggested and sent the photographer two thousand dollars for not showing up.

The way I saw it, it was the bottom of the ninth and I was up ten runs, with two outs, and the great Mariano Rivera was on the mound. The preacher performed the simple ceremony, we said our vows and exchanged rings, and the preacher pronounced us husband and wife and told me, "You may kiss the bride." We moved closer together and we kissed, for maybe a tenth of a second, before my daughter rudely interrupted and told us we were running late and needed to get going.

I turned away from my wife and looked at my daughter and, in what should have been one of the happiest moments of life, I had to use every effort at self control not to pick her up, put her over my lap, and spank her silly. I could swear that nothing my daughter did even registered with her. Jennifer grabbed me by hand and led me into the preacher's quarters where we signed the necessary papers. I whispered to Jennifer to take Sofia outside and that I would be out in minute. I reached into my pocket and handed the preacher and the organist five hundred dollars each and thanked them.

I started to walk out of the church as the preacher reached out and touched my arm. "You just married a beautiful woman who is madly in love with you. Don't let a little mishap by your loving daughter ruin the day. You will have many opportunities to kiss your bride." I shook the preacher's hand and thanked him. I walked out into the parking lot and looked at the two ladies conversing happily by the car. I could see the anxious look on Jennifer's face as I approached. I kissed my lovely daughter and told her she was the most perfect maid of honor one could ever hope for and that I was very proud of her. I then kissed my bride and the thought of kissing this woman every day for the rest of my life made everything perfect.

We got into the car and drove home, and as luck would have it we got home at 10:45, exactly like my daughter calculated. She was very happy about that, and there we were, the entire bridal party — my wife, daughter, and Lawrence who sat in a pew at the church and witnessed the entire ceremony. I couldn't help but wonder, once again, whether one day Lawrence would be my son-in-law. I tapped the little professor on the head and whispered, "You have my blessing. Good luck with her."

Within a few minutes of arriving home, the girls were sitting on the couch eating chocolates. I don't know why that seemed so bizarre to me. It was like I was expecting something different on my wedding day, such as sitting next to my beautiful wife, smooching and kissing, taking photos to one day place in our wedding album, and drinking champagne.

I walked into the kitchen, undid my tie and the top button of my shirt, and grabbed a beer. I placed my head against one of the cabinets and slowly drank the beer as I listened to the girls in the living room. And then suddenly like a bolt of lighting I heard Sofia exclaim, "Thank you for becoming my mommy!"

I slid down the side of the cabinet, covered my head with my hands, and started to cry.

Chapter 28

Cries from the living room called for "champagne" and so I took out three chilled flutes from the refrigerator, a bottle of Cristal, and a bottle of ginger ale. Sofia decided against trying any more champagne for a while, but since she didn't want to miss out on any of the festivities, she remembered Jennifer saying that champagne tasted like ginger ale, and so she had me buy her a big bottle of the soda. I filled two of the flutes with the champagne and a third with ginger ale.

I handed Sofia her flute with ginger ale and Jennifer her flute with the real thing. Sofia insisted on making the first toast. After collecting herself she raised her glass and said, "To my mommy and daddy. I love you both so much." We all drank from our glasses and then it was Jennifer's turn to run off and have a good cry.

Sofia looked at me and asked, "Did I say something wrong?"

"No, my beautiful angel, what you said was perfect. Sometimes we cry when we are overcome with happiness." I took my daughter by her hand and kissed her on the forehead. "I love you so much."

Jennifer, smiling, came back after a few minutes and remarked, "Just a little emotional … just like a woman!"

"Why were you crying? Did I do something wrong?" Sofia asked.

"No, my sweet darling, you didn't do anything wrong. You are so perfect and I love you so much." She handed me her empty glass and, before going into the kitchen, I snuck a quick kiss … still very much in shock that I was actually married to this woman.

I refilled her glass as I grabbed myself a beer. Sure, I liked champagne, but beer was my drink. I took out a platter of shrimp, crab, and oysters with three cocktail forks, lemons, and cocktail sauce.

I walked back into the living room and handed Jennifer her glass of champagne and laid down the platter on the table. Sofia gagged and ran off in a panic into her room, closing the door behind.

"What just happened?" Jennifer asked as she started to walk toward Sofia's room, only to have me stop her.

"She can't stand the smell of certain foods."

"But…?"

"She was passed out drunk when we had the seafood a couple of days ago. Eat as much as you can and I will bring the rest over to the church. I think it's looking like a celebration with pizza as the entrée. Is that okay?"

"Pizza sounds perfect," Mrs. Perfect replied as I walked into Sofia's room. Our daughter was on the bed, under the blankets with Lawrence … shielding them both from the repulsive odor of the seafood. I closed the door.

"Oh Sofia, I know you're under those blankets. I'm sorry. I forgot you don't like the smell of seafood." The blankets moved slightly. "Jennifer didn't want the seafood but I insisted … just like a man!" I heard her giggle. "I'm going to pack it all up and bring it down to the church and tell them you wanted to give it to them as a gift for the lovely service they performed." She lifted the blanket and her face appeared. For moment I was thrown back in time to when she was just a child and I would have to slowly entice her out when she got scared and reassure her that I would never let anything happen to her.

Chapter 29

After quickly stuffing a few shrimps into my mouth and swallowing a few oysters, I packed up all the remaining seafood and drove to the church. The preacher and the organist were still there in the back office and they were overjoyed with the gift from Sofia. I walked out of the office and sat down in a middle pew in the church. I was the only one there. It was cemeteries and churches that I often went to when I felt eternally grateful or when I felt sad. I especially liked them when they were empty. Even though I was raised a devout Catholic and swore I would die a Catholic, I loved being in any place of worship. They reminded me that there was something out there that was much bigger than me and the movie industry I worked for.

I closed my eyes. The last couple of days had been joyful but exhausting. Suddenly, I found myself back with the lovely Sarah atop a pillow of white clouds, dancing. Her body was fully intact, and she wore the same long white gown, while her long hair glistened. "Congratulations, Joe. You have wonderful taste in women … and you don't look so shabby in a suit and tie."

"Thank you. Where are your other dance partners … Mr. Astaire and Mr. Kelly?"

"Oh, I wore those two old men out."

I laughed as I suddenly found myself sitting on a bench outside the basketball court I grew up on. Once again, I was a teenager dressed in dungarees, a T-Shirt, and Converse sneakers. Sarah was Sarah, except for the fact she was no longer in a gown but a Kentucky Wildcats sweatshirt, ripped jeans, and flip flops. Her toenails were painted pink.

"So tell me, Joe, did you like playing more in games with your friends or practicing by yourself late into the night?"

"Strange, you should ask such a question. I loved playing by myself, pretending to be Walt Frazier or Willis Reed and taking the game-winning shot."

"And did you have a girlfriend?"

"No! But I was in love with a girl named Jackie who lived in the same building as ours. She was beautiful, but I was so shy I could barely say 'hello' when we passed in the hallway. My friends assured me that she liked me but I could never tell whether they were joking or not. She died tragically in an accident, but I have never stopped thinking about her."

"Do you ever wish you said 'hello' and eventually went on to marry her?"

"Not since Sofia was born, and especially not now that I am married to Jennifer." I looked at her and noticed her leg was missing like in the picture. "Was it really difficult and painful?"

"Jennifer made it a lot easier than it ever should have been."

"She has a way of doing that," I said as I looked up from Sarah's missing leg and into her eyes.

"Kiss me, Joe. I know I'm not perfect like Jennifer, but…"

I reached in and kissed her like I would kiss Jennifer, and when I pulled back she was bald and her face was sullen. I reached in and kissed her again and said, "You're perfect, as perfect as anyone."

"And does that mean you still want me to visit you?"

"Yes, forever and ever."

My phone rang and I woke up. It was Sofia calling to tell me that the pizza had arrived. I got up and as I walked toward the door I turned and looked back at the empty, unsullied church and whispered, "Thank you."

Chapter 30

I opened the door to the house and could immediately smell the freshly baked pizza, and suddenly the smell of oysters and shrimp gave me the willies. I was greeted by my wife at the door. She had changed out of her dress and into a Kentucky Wildcats sweatshirt and matching sweatpants. She threw her arms around me and kissed me.

"We thought you ran off."

"And why would I do that?"

"I don't know, maybe you bumped into a runaway bride at the door of the church and decided to flee town with her."

"Only if she was a New York Knicks fan, and there aren't many of them left." She laughed as I looked across at my daughter who was now dressed in the same outfit as my wife.

"You changed teams on your father?"

"Your team sucks!" Sofia remarked.

"They didn't always suck," I said.

"In her lifetime, they have always sucked," Jennifer said as she led me into the kitchen.

"You know, that's why they write history books, so unbelievers like you two can go back and get the whole story."

"Is that so? I always thought they wrote history books about significant events in time, not about the one or two good years your team had in an otherwise lackluster history."

She shoved a piece of pizza in my mouth and opened a beer for me. "What, no champagne for the groom?" She laughed as she sat down next to me, crossed her legs, and sipped her champagne. A second later, my daughter sat down, crossed her legs and sipped her ginger ale.

"Okay, what's going on?" I asked as both ladies simply stared at me.

"Nothing, it's just that we missed you," Jennifer said with a smirk.

"I wasn't gone that long."

"Maybe not, but it's our wedding day and every second away from you feels like an eternity. Isn't that right, Sofia?"

"Yes, you should be ashamed of yourself. It takes ten minutes to get to the church and back, and five minutes to give the preacher the food. You should have been back in twenty minutes; whereas you were gone for an hour and thirty-two minutes."

"Apparently, you two couldn't have been that worried. It didn't stop you from eating."

"We were hungry," Sofia replied as she put her hand under her chin like Jennifer.

"Yes, we were famished," Jennifer said as Sofia jumped up and walked into her room. Jennifer edged closer, her big blue eyes relentlessly focused on me like a prosecutor about to bounce on a witness.

"So, where did you really go?"

"After dropping the food off, I went back in the church and sat down. I talked to my parents and said prayers for Lou. I promised your mom that I would always take care of you and that I was the luckiest man in the world to be married to her daughter."

Jennifer's eyes grew moist as she lowered her head. I placed my hand under her chin and lifted her head back up. "I then fell asleep. I felt exhausted ... exhausted by an abundance of happiness, if such a thing is possible."

Jennifer laughed as I wiped the tears away from her cheeks. I couldn't tell her about my dream and my dalliances with a girl I never met but to whom I felt intimately connected. Bizarre, but I felt guilty as though I was actually cheating on my wife ... but then feeling guilty was quickly becoming a natural state of existence for me.

"I love you so much," Jennifer said. We kissed passionately, and then suddenly there was a flash, a blinding light that at first I thought was God's wrath cast down upon my infidel soul before realizing that it was just my daughter taking a picture of her parents with the fifteen-hundred-dollar camera I bought her six years ago during her brief but intense interest in photography.

I shook my head as Sofia started scolding me about not kissing my lovely bride. She needed fifty pictures of us kissing for the wedding album she was putting together and at the rate we were going she would never meet her goal by tonight's deadline of midnight. How she came up with fifty pictures I had no idea but it was a goal I had every intention of meeting and surpassing.

The child was dictatorial, like Nick on the set of one of our movies. Naturally, Jennifer was laughing and enjoying every moment as our daughter started yelling out directions meant exclusively for me … "Bend her this way, that way, be careful you don't drop her, can't you kiss the most beautiful bride in the world a little more passionately, a little more enthusiasm, Daddy…" Flash! Flash! Flash! Kiss! Kiss!

I was exhausted by the time Sofia was finished, and immediately after she and Jennifer disappeared into her room to download the photos onto her computer, but not before giving me permission to have a beer.

I had a number of beers and a few more slices of pizza. I then finally realized that I was the only member of the wedding party, besides Lawrence, who was still dressed up. I walked into my room and took off my suit. I was so tempted to put on one of my twenty New York Knicks sweatshirts, but then I realized that would just subject me to more ridicule from my wife and my treasonous daughter. To save myself the grief, I put on one of my twenty New York Yankees sweatshirts … the Yankees, winners of twenty-seven championships and over forty World Series appearances, would be less likely to come in for abuse.

I walked into Sofia's room and the girls were busy deciding which pictures came out the best. I asked, "So how did they come out?"

"Wonderful!" Jennifer replied as she looked at me and started to laugh. "Seriously, a New York Yankees sweatshirt?"

And then it was my daughter's turn, "Seriously, Daddy, everybody loves the Yankees. They win all the time."

I was so tempted to remind them that the Yankees hadn't won a championship in nine years, but that would be playing right into their hands. I walked back into my room, defeated, taunted by the laughter of the two ladies in my life. I changed into a simple red sweatshirt and walked back into Sofia's room. I looked down at the pictures and I have to honestly admit that my lovely daughter took some amazing photos. She was always a very visual person and would notice things when we looked at a film or simply went for a walk — things that never even registered with me, despite the numerous times I had seen the film or walked through a certain neighborhood.

I stood behind my wife, and gently played with her hair while softly kissing her on the neck and behind her ears. She turned and threw her arms around me and we kissed passionately. Thankfully, our daughter didn't decide to take a picture because I think the flash, at that short distance, might have blinded me.

In keeping with the theme of simplicity, we had peanut butter and jelly sandwiches for dinner. After all, what goes better with wedded bliss and Cristal champagne than a couple of peanut butter and jelly sandwiches for the entrée? Sofia insisted on making all the sandwiches while keeping a watchful eye on both parents.

After dinner, we located to the couch and Sofia put on *The Honeymooners*. It had already been an exhausting day, yet my wife who was now on her third bottle champagne and my daughter who was now on the equivalent amount of ginger ale, showed no signs of slowing down. If anything Sofia seemed more excitable than ever, and as the evening progressed toward midnight, and despite numerous hints that her father might want some alone time with his bride, nothing I did seemed to register with her. Even more worrisome, my wife made no effort at all to disengage from our daughter. In fact, it was Sofia and Jennifer who were sitting together, and the groom who was cast off to the side.

I couldn't help but think that I was going to be spending my honeymoon night the same way I had spend the last twenty years, sleeping alone. You see, that's what happens when you expect too much. Less than a month ago I could not imagine being married to a woman as beautiful and brilliant as Jennifer, and after a series of passionate kisses I simply got carried away actually thinking that we would be sleeping together after getting married. It was starting to feel like a faulty assumption.

I got up off the couch and went toward the kitchen for another beer, and on my way toward that haven of solace, my wife called out and asked if I could pour her some more champagne and my daughter, not to be outdone, asked if I could bring her some more ginger ale. I took out two freshly chilled champagne flutes from the refrigerator and poured champagne into one and, as God was my witness, I was tempted to spike my daughter's ginger ale with some champagne, until I realized that if she had some type of negative reaction and got sick, I would have no choice but to kill myself. I love her so much. So like always I gave my daughter whatever she wanted, even if it prevented me from enjoying some real honeymoon bliss.

I handed the girls their drinks, finished the beer I was drinking, faked a yawn and declared that it was time for this old man to go to bed. I kissed my wife on the forehead and she replied by saying that she would be in shortly. I kept my fingers crossed with the expectation that shortly might mean tomorrow morning. I then kissed Sofia and she responded by hugging me tightly and declaring how much she loved me. This from the girl who, before Jennifer entered our lives, had a difficult time expressing any type of emotion, especially the physical type.

I walked into my bedroom and closed the door. I stood before the bathroom mirror and contemplated what I should wear to bed; pajamas that I had not worn to bed in a couple of decades or the sweatpants and sweatshirt that I already had on and that I would usually wear to bed. I compromised and changed into a different pair of sweatpants and a sweatshirt. I lay down on the bed, closed my eyes for a second, and quickly opened them as I sensed someone else in the room. It was Sarah sitting on the edge of the bed and dressed in very revealing lingerie.

"Sarah, what are you doing here?"

"What are you talking about, Joe? You opened the door and let me in."

"I did?"

"Yes, Joe, don't you remember you told me I could visit anytime I wanted."

"Yes, you're right but not necessarily on my wedding night, especially dressed the way you are."

"Are we suddenly changing the rules, is that it?"

"Of course not, what type of man do you think I am?"

"I think you're a wonderful guy. Do you think I look sexy?"

"Of course you look sexy, but you're also sixteen years old and I'm an old man."

"No, Joe, you're sixteen years old, just like me."

"I am? How did I pull that one off?"

"Easy, every time you think about me or look at those pictures you are looking at me as a sixteen year old. Do you like my new hairdo?"

"Yes, it's the same hairstyle that my teenage crush, Jackie, used to wear."

"I know, I hope you don't mind but I took the liberty of looking her up on the Internet. She was quite beautiful, but not as pretty as Jennifer."

She edged closer as she ran her hands through her hair, revealing a little too much of herself. "I was thinking about what you told me earlier today about how you enjoyed playing basketball by yourself more than playing in games with your friends. Was that because there were fewer barriers between you and the goal when there was only you on the court?"

I closed my eyes, hoping that this vision of youth and beauty might vanish, but no such luck.

"I'm still here, Joe."

"Yes, I can see that. How is it that a girl so young could be so perceptive and knowledgeable?"

"Because when death is knocking on your door at such an early age you seem to mature quicker and see things differently than other kids your age."

She slipped the lingerie off and started to kiss me as I tried to force her off of me, yelling, "Sarah! No, Sarah!"

I felt shaking, intense shaking, and my name being called over and over again and when I woke up it was Jennifer standing over me. "You were having a nightmare," she said. I looked at her and smiled, and then I shut my eyes and shook my head and slowly opened my eyes to make sure it was Jennifer before me. At this point, I wasn't sure of anything. For all I knew, Sarah might be a shape-shifter.

"I surely hope your nightmare didn't have anything to do with me?" Jennifer said, sounding a little worried.

"Why would you say that?" I asked, suspicious that my wife might know about Sarah and me.

"I don't know, maybe you were having second thoughts about how it might not have been the wisest thing to marry me."

"That's insane. I have been in love with you since you changed out of that ridiculous nurse's outfit. Never once I have doubted that you were the best thing to come into my life since Sofia, and never once did I even question, for a split second, my desire and wish to marry you. You are so perfect that even now as I sit here I can't believe how blessed I am to have you as my wife."

"Wow! You keep talking like that and you might even get lucky." She laughed as she sat down and we started to kiss passionately, and if I felt like the luckiest man before that point, I soon felt like I was in a totally different stratosphere. Life was grand!

Chapter 31

I woke up my usual time and when I looked over at my beautiful wife it was still hard for me to fathom that for the rest of my life, I would be waking up next to this amazing woman. She was out cold and I tried to make as little noise as possible as I changed into my running gear. I kissed her on the forehead and whispered, "I love you so much."

I opened the door to the room and quietly closed it behind me. I turned and looked across at Sofia who was sitting in the hallway opposite our bedroom. I asked, "Sofia, what are you doing out here?"

"Waiting for Jennifer."

"Sweetheart, Jennifer is asleep and I don't think she will be getting up for quite a while. She's exhausted."

I reached down and grabbed her by the hands and lifted her up. "Remember what you told me? That you wanted to take care of me?"

"Yes, I've been trying very hard."

"I know and I'm so proud of you. But you know what would make me really happy? If you went for a run with me."

"I don't run very well and I fall all the time."

"We can walk instead. That way I can concentrate solely on you."

We walked out of the house just as it was getting light outside. She immediately started talking about Jennifer, nonstop, pointing out all the wonderful things about her. She was kind, and always happy, except for when her mommy died. That was very sad. She always listened to what Sofia had to say and told Sofia how smart she was all the time. She was interested in the same things Sofia was interested in, and she was the best mommy in the world, and she was so much fun.

I asked her if she might be interested in doing what Jennifer does for a living, taking care of sick children and helping them get better.

Sofia replied, "That is exactly what I want to do, Daddy. I love the little children and I want to help them feel better and be happy. Jennifer is going to help me get a job and if I do really well, I can work toward becoming a nurse like Jennifer."

I asked, "And why do you think you like working with children so much?"

She thought about that for what seemed like a while. "I just like them. It's easy to talk to them, and I can help them."

"Do you think maybe it's nice to be with kids because they like you for who you are?"

"Yes!" This seemed to strike a chord. "They like me for who I am."

"And they never pass judgment, like some people your age and older?"

"They never pass judgment."

We walked in silence for a bit as the sun rose a little higher, revealing brighter shades of green in the lawns and trees around our neighborhood. I put my arm around Sofia's narrow shoulders and pulled her to me as we walked. "I hope you know that I have *always* loved you for who you are and would never pass judgment."

"I know, Daddy, and that's why I love you more than anyone."

When Sofia got a little tired, we stopped and sat down on a curb and watched as the sun rose behind a sign for Universal Studios. She placed her head against my shoulder and we remained quiet for a long time before Sofia asked, "Daddy, are you mad at me?"

"No, sweetheart, why would you even say such a thing?"

"Because you wanted me to become an actress and be in your movies."

I looked down at her face against my shoulder and could immediately recognize that this issue was very troublesome to her. "I'm sorry, angel, if I ever gave you that impression. Naturally, if you wanted to be in one of my movies that would be great, but what you want to do is so much more important than ever being an actress. I can't think of anything more important than working with and helping sick children and I am so very proud of you, as proud as any parent could ever be."

She reached up and kissed me on the cheek. "Thank you, Daddy."

Chapter 32

Jennifer was up when we returned from our walk. We found her in the kitchen, cooking a big breakfast of French toast for the family. She figured that if I occasionally ate French toast for breakfast, Sofia must like it too.

Sofia greeted Jennifer with a near-perfect recounting of our walk and conversations. I couldn't help but laugh at the realization that everything I told Sofia would automatically be retold to my wife, practically verbatim. They were already behaving like an inseparable mother and daughter pair, and I knew there would be no secrets between them.

We sat around the kitchen table and ate breakfast just like a normal family. Anyone happening upon us would think that we had been doing this for years. I volunteered to clean the dishes and I didn't get a word of dissent from either lady, but I did receive a kiss from each of them, which more than repaid my minimal labors. Besides, I reminded myself, Jennifer had made the French toast. I wondered if we would settle into a routine, with one or two of us doing the cooking and the other, or others, doing the dishes, like families everywhere. The thought of such a normal state of affairs was so comforting that my eyes welled up for a moment as I wiped the counters and lay the last dish in the rack.

I thought about how Jennifer and I would manage to have time to ourselves. It helped that we had our own bedroom, and that Sofia had no expectation of being in there with us! Besides the obvious benefit of sharing the same bed with my lovely wife, it also gave us time to talk about certain things that we didn't want to discuss in front of our daughter. It was no exaggeration when I say that Sofia was literally glued to Jennifer the rest of the time, and I could already tell that I would come to view our bedroom as a sanctuary, and my time with Jennifer there as a precious resource.

Yes, it was obvious that I would have to compete with my daughter to secure enough quality time with my wife. And I wasn't the only man in the house who was in danger of feeling neglected. Poor Lawrence had it worse than I did. After all those years of unconditional commitment from Sofia, here he was, stuck in her room by himself, waiting for her to return. I couldn't help but feel sorry for the poor guy. Like me, he only got to spend time alone with his true love when they went to bed.

Later that day, Jennifer and I retreated to the bedroom for a rest while Sofia spent some time exploring the capabilities of her new computer. As we lay on the bed, I asked Jennifer about Sofia's plan to work with the children. It was no surprise to learn that my wife had it all figured out. Once she got comfortable at her new job, she would ask permission to have Sofia come in as a volunteer. They were always looking for volunteers to help with the children who were admitted for long spans of time, and since Sofia's hours were so flexible, she would even be more valuable. At first, she would only have our daughter volunteer on days when she worked. She would be working three twelve-hour shifts a week, and would most likely be asked to work a fourth day that she would never refuse unless she definitely had no other choice. I figured that was a not-so-subtle hint that I'd better get used to the fact that she would work as many extra days as they asked her to. I knew within a few hours of meeting her that she took her job exceptionally seriously. She might have moved out here in order to make more money to help her mom, but now that Lou had passed away, money wasn't going to be much of an issue. I didn't dare, even in jest, to bring up the fact that I had a lot of money and that she didn't have to work extra days.

My wife's work was more like a crusade, an undeniable part of her identity, and the consequences of her work, after she finished her shifts and came home, were still very much a mystery to me ... a mystery that would be unfolding before my very eyes in just a few days.

I asked her about the concerns I had about Sofia and the difficulties she might have seeing little children so sick and in the worse cases possibly dying. She had never been around anything remotely similar to what she would be seeing on a daily basis. Jennifer assured me that she would shield Sofia from the worse cases, even though the children admitted on a long-term basis usually looked relatively healthy at first, then went through a very difficult time during treatment and surgeries, before slowly returning to their former selves. She had no doubt that Sofia would do wonderfully during all the stages. She had a natural rapport with children and that would make her a special champion in the fight against this dastardly disease.

"There is no greater feeling than seeing a child who has been diagnosed with cancer go through surgery and chemotherapy, and then walk out of the hospital in full remission. It's incredible to see them returning week after week as the blood work comes back normal again and again. You get to see the spark returning to their eyes. Sofia is going to be a part of that whole process. She'll be contributing to the recovery of these beautiful children, and she'll also be helping their parents and siblings feel a lot less stressed. She is going to do great things."

I wrapped my arms around my wife and tried to mirror her optimism, but I couldn't help but feel anxious. "You need to promise me, Jennifer, that you will not push Sofia too hard. She doesn't handle stress very well."

"Of course!" she said. "Sofia is my top priority. I will never let anything happen to her. I feel so blessed that you have allowed me to be such an important part of her life."

I had little doubt that my wife knew more about Sofia and her peculiarities than I did, but I couldn't help feeling that her compassion and zeal for her patients might blind her to Sofia's needs.

I could feel the tension in my limbs and guilt ratcheting through every neuron in my brain. I backed away from Jennifer as an uneasy silence ricocheted off the walls of the room.

"What's wrong?" Jennifer finally asked.

"I feel like a real louse … putting my own petty concerns about my daughter ahead of the needs of some very sick little children."

"You're her father. There is no such thing as a petty concern when it comes to your child, and never once did I feel that you didn't care greatly for sick children. If you did, I wouldn't be sleeping next to you."

"No, you would be sleeping next to Sofia," I said as she laughed and playfully slapped me. We kissed, and in that moment, everything was perfect.

Chapter 33

And so, the day that I had been dreading finally arrived. The day my wife started her new job. Yes, I was sad. I was so madly in love with her that the idea of not hearing her laugh, or listening to her snappy comebacks, or seeing her radiant face for twelve hours at a time was enough to put me into a state of mild depression. But, I was also a realist. I understood that the days of wives staying home and doing housework and looking at soap operas were long gone. In fact, I don't even remember them. My mom had a job the whole time I was growing up, and it wasn't until my father retired and pressured her to retire that she finally gave up working. He threatened her with the totally unrealistic possibility that if she didn't want to quit her job and spend time with him that he would just have to go out and find himself a girlfriend on the side. My poor mom succumbed to his demand, fully aware that the chances of her husband finding a girlfriend were about as good as him being recruited to play shortstop for the New York Yankees.

But the real reason for me dreading this day wasn't because I would be separated from my better half for more than half a day, three to four days a week. I was more concerned about my daughter being unglued from *her* better half. What would she do all day? How would she cope?

The night before she went back to work, Jennifer had to spend hours repeating all of the reasons why our daughter could not go to work with her. Sofia could not understand why she couldn't just show up with my wife and start volunteering without being vetted first or given a position. She even offered to pay the hospital if they would allow her to work there with Jennifer. After all, her daddy had "a lot of money," and what father wouldn't be happy to pay her employer money so his daughter could work there as a volunteer? As I listened to her argue the point, I thought, *My God, I've spoiled my daughter to the point of no return — as any decent Italian father should.*

After displays of patience so exquisite that they would have impressed Job, Jennifer finally got through to our daughter. She then turned in early in order to be ready for her shift the next day. I figured that working in pediatric oncology required a lot of patience, but I couldn't imagine anyone having the patience that Jennifer exhibited with Sofia. I was starting to believe that she wasn't joking when she said she would never have married me without Sofia's approval. The idea that my daughter was the driving force behind Jennifer's decision to marry me struck me as almost funny. For most of her young life, Sofia had alternated between showing no emotion at all and displaying an excess of intense, irrational emotion. And here she was, the person who secured my happiness by delivering Jennifer into my life.

Jennifer rolled out of bed at four o'clock in the morning and shortly after I rolled out of bed. Her shift was from 6:00 a.m. to 6:00 p.m., but she needed to be at work an hour earlier on her first day to fill out paperwork and visit with human resources. While she was in the bathroom getting ready, I opened the door to our room and nearly fell over my daughter who was sitting right outside our room.

"Sofia, what are you doing out here?" I asked, despite knowing the horrifying answer beforehand.

"Waiting for Jennifer," she replied as I reached down and helped her to her feet.

"She's in the bathroom getting ready, but you might be able to go in and keep her company. Just knock first."

"Thank you, Daddy," she replied as she kissed me on the cheek and hurried into the room, nearly tripping over herself. In my entire life, I don't know if I ever knew a clumsier girl. Maybe, it was a good thing she had no interest in modeling. She was the most beautiful creature in my universe, but the idea of her walking down a runway and falling over herself was something I did not need to see. It hurt just to imagine it.

I walked into the kitchen, sliced open a bagel, toasted both halves, and spread cream cheese across it. I put it on a plate with a large glass of orange juice and placed them on the kitchen table. Jennifer and Sofia had gone out the night before and bought a bunch of power bars, deli meat, and rolls. Jennifer insisted on bringing her own lunch to work, along with power bars to munch on when she had a little break. I knew hospital food wasn't the best, but there were a number of nice restaurants right next to the hospital that specialized in getting customers in and out in under half an hour. I asked her jokingly if she was bringing her own coffee to work and she replied that there was always a pot of coffee brewing in the nurses' lounge. I didn't pursue the topic any further, but made a mental note to keep chipping away at her frugality until she was willing to buy lunch at least once a week. She had a long way to go to be in a class with my spoiled daughter, but then I had a long time to work on her. I could already see a few cracks in her armor.

Jennifer walked into the kitchen, followed by her shadow, and squealed when she saw her breakfast already laid out for her on the table. She threw her arms around me and planted a big kiss on my face. "Do I not have the best husband in the world?" she asked Sofia.

"Yes, and I have the best mommy and daddy in the whole world."

The girls sat down at the table and I put a bowl of cereal mixed with chocolate milk in front of Sofia, then poured the same for myself. No bagels for us. We knew what we liked.

As she ate her breakfast, Jennifer carefully went over a typed list of suggestions for Sofia. Everything on the list was designed to help Sofia get through the day and eventually help her when it came to working with children. There was nothing on the list that was mandatory. "They're only suggestions," Jennifer repeated several times. "I won't be judging or grading you on any of this." Sofia looked at the list for a long time and finally Jennifer reached over and took it out of her hand and folded the paper and handed it back to her. "They are only suggestions," she said. "It's nothing to get nervous about."

"Okay," Sofia replied meekly. Jennifer reached over and gently touched her face and said, "I love you so much and there is nothing in this world that is ever going to change that."

"And I love you so much," Sofia replied as she looked down at the folded paper with her big brown eyes full of anxious affection.

I cleaned the dishes as Jennifer did one last check to make sure she had everything she would need. I handed her the bag with her lunch and her power bars in it, and she asked, "Have you seen my car keys?"

"You mean the ones that go with that classic you have parked in our driveway?" I replied as I asked Sofia, "Have you seen Jennifer's car keys?"

"No!"

"This is no time to joke, Joe."

I reached into my pocket and handed her the keys to my car. "Remember the promise you made to me on the steps of the courthouse? That I could spoil you as I saw fit because you deserve it? Well, as your husband I am not going to have you driving around in a car with no air-conditioning on a day that it's going to be over ninety degrees."

"That's the same excuse you have used every time I want to drive my classic."

"And if you don't stop being thick-headed about driving that car, Sofia and I will gladly turn that little classic in and buy you a brand new car. I imagine we could easily get a hundred or two hundred in the exchange."

She shook her head and then kissed me and said, "Thank you for taking such good care of me."

Sofia quickly added, "You can have my car if you like."

"Thank you, sweetheart, but for now I think your father's car will suit me just fine."

We followed Jennifer outside. It was still dark out as we watched her drive off to her new job. I turned and looked at Sofia who was standing in the doorway. Tears were pouring down her cheeks as she turned and ran into the house. Instead of running after her, I took a moment to look up at the sky, notice the dimming of the stars, and welcome the advent of another day. I knew I would need all of the patience I could muster in order to get through this first day without Jennifer by Sofia's side, and if I had to pull that patience out of the glimmering sky, that's what I would do.

I walked into the house, closing the door behind me, and slowly and deliberately walked toward my daughter's room. Her door was open and she was lying on the bed, hugging Lawrence and crying. I pulled up a chair beside her and asked, "Is there anything I can do?" She tried to speak but got all choked up. I took the folded paper that Jennifer left with her and asked if I could look at it. When Sofia nodded her approval, I unfolded the paper to read my wife's first suggestion, which was more a reminder. "When you get frustrated, remember that your father and mother love you more than anything in this world and are so proud of you." This was followed by a suggestion to look through the pamphlets she left on Sofia's desk about volunteering, childcare, and procedures that one has to follow when dealing with sick children in a hospital.

She suggested that Sofia spend no more than thirty minutes at a time reading and studying the pamphlets. The note specified that before she started looking at the material, she should set her clock to ring in thirty minutes. Once it rang, Sofia was to put the material down and go do something else, such as watching TV, listening to music, sleeping, taking a walk, or helping her daddy write. This line item included a starred comment that said, "I'm quite sure he would welcome any suggestions you have to offer." Thank God I had very little ego left, otherwise I could have read this as an unflattering remark on my ability. Another item on the list said, "Don't forget to eat lunch. You could even show your father what a wonderful daughter you are by whipping him up two peanut butter and jelly sandwiches. But, let him do the dishes. We don't want to spoil him too much."

I looked across at my daughter and wiped the tears from her face. She looked like she was on the verge of falling asleep and I told her that I thought it would be wise for both of us to take a nap. After all, that was one of Jennifer's suggestions. And once we were fully awake, she could help me with my work and I could help her work through Jennifer's list. And if none of that worked for her, I said we could do whatever she pleased, because just being around her was more precious to me than anything in the world.

I walked into my room, kicked my sneakers off, and lay down on the bed. I must have fallen asleep instantly, because suddenly I was sitting on a bench across from the basketball court I grew up on. It was a lovely, sunny day with just a little bit of a breeze … certainly not enough to affect one's shot. I found it strange that no one was playing. My basketball sat next to me, unused. I noticed Sarah walking toward me. She picked up the basketball and put it under the bench.

"Hello, Joseph."

"Hi, Sarah. Is everything okay?"

"I guess. It's not easy to be rejected by the boy you want to spend the rest of your life with, but I'll get over it."

"Sarah, what is it that you don't understand? I'm old enough to be your father."

"Oh please, go tell that story to someone else. What do I have to do to make you believe that you're sixteen? Here, take a look in my mirror." She took out a small compact mirror from her purse and handed it to me. I looked into it, and by God, the reflection that stared back at me was me at sixteen.

"Is this some type of trick?"

"No, it's not some type of trick. For a boy who wants to grow up to be a great writer you seriously lack imagination. I just don't know how you could ever succeed, unless you change your way of thinking."

I looked at myself in the mirror again and the reflection was the same.

"You can look at it a million times and it's not going to change. You're sixteen, Joe, sixteen. Why can't you accept that?"

She lay her head down on my lap and asked, "Would you like me better as a blond?"

"No, I love the color of your hair. It's beautiful, just like you." I ran my hand through her dark, glistening hair as she looked up at me and smiled.

"How about as a redhead?"

"No, definitely not. That's the color of my mother's hair. Every time I kiss you it'll remind me of my mother and that's just a little too freaky."

"But you like my nails painted red." She lifted her hand up to my face to show me her painted nails.

"Yes, but they're a totally different shade of red that looks great when painted on your nails but wouldn't look too natural as a hair color."

"How about if I put some highlights in my hair?"

"Why do you want to change the color of your hair so much? I love your hair. It's natural and beautiful, just like you."

"That's what you say now, but if a girl doesn't mix things up and keep things interesting, it gives the boy an excuse to explore other possibilities and adventures."

"How do you know about this stuff?"

"I read my mother's Cosmopolitan."

"That's a girl's magazine?"

"Yes, Joseph, a girl's magazine that alerts girls to the warning signs that their boyfriend might be thinking of other girls besides them. Such as when your boyfriend pushes you away when she is giving you every indication that she is willing to give herself to you."

"I would never cheat on you," I said as I looked down into her eyes that were filled with affection and hope.

"Of course not, cutie," she replied with a giggle. "That's what they all say."

"Is that what they say in that magazine?"

"Not exactly, but what am I to believe when the boy that I love, want to marry, and have a family with rejects my offer to be intimate?"

"Maybe you should think that it's because I respect you."

She lifted her head off my lap, threw her arms around my neck, and kissed me. "I love you so much."

"I love you," I replied as she got up and started to walk away and I asked, "Where are you going?"

"To my dance class. Would you like to come?" She put out her hand and motioned for me to join her.

"You know I can't dance," I replied.

"I don't understand. When you're playing basketball you twist and turn like Mikhail Baryshnikov, yet you can't dance?"

"That's because when I play basketball I don't think about what I'm doing. It's just instinctual."

"Oh, it's that, is it? Well, maybe when dancing you should try not to think. You seem to be really good at that." She laughed and laughed and then continued, "If you think that lame excuse is going to get you out of dancing with me at our wedding, you really are crazy." She laughed again, and then disappeared into a swirling cloud while the sound of her laughter lingered in my ears.

I reached under the bench and grabbed my basketball. I threw the ball over the twelve-foot chain link fence and climbed over it and onto the court. I flipped the ball in front of me, bounced it between my legs, twirled like Pistol Pete Maravich and laid the ball in. I then dribbled up court, like Walt Clyde Frazier, as I heard the legendary voice of New York Knicks announcer Marv Albert announcing my every move, or should I say Clyde's every move.

"And Frazier crosses the half-court line and West (Jerry West that is) picks him up. Talk about a classic match-up. Frazier dribbles toward the foul line … five seconds showing on the game clock. He fakes as West, trying not to foul, leaps past him. Clyde jumps, shoots, and scores and the New York Knicks win! The Knicks win!"

I take the ball and fling it high up into air as I scream, "Yes, the Knicks win! The Knicks win! The Knicks…"

I felt someone shaking me and I woke up and looked into the face of my lovely daughter. She asked, "Are you okay?"

"Yes, sweetheart. I was just dreaming."

"I guess so. You were screaming, 'The Knicks win! The Knicks win!' And as we all know, the Knicks never win."

"I thought I raised you to love all the New York teams, regardless of whether they have a losing season or not. A true fan never changes teams because they are going through a little losing streak."

"I understand that, Daddy. But I never remember the Knicks ever having a winning season."

"So now you're a Kentucky fan like your mommy?"

"It's only fair that I root for at least one of her teams, and they win all the time like the Yankees. Are we going for a walk?"

I shook my head as I looked down at my daughter's untied Nike sneakers. "Maybe the reason you're always tripping over yourself is because you don't tie your sneakers?" I reached down and tied her laces like I used to do when she was a little girl. I then got up, put on my sneakers, took her hand, and we walked out of the house.

Chapter 34

After watching Jennifer's interaction with Sofia over the last couple of weeks, I started to copy her approach. After all, my wife had more success building a loving relationship with Sofia than anybody I'd known in the last five years ... except of course for me, who spoiled her silly. Jennifer listened to Sofia intently and didn't interrupt, even when my daughter for no apparent reason changed subjects. Jennifer would slowly lead her back to the original topic, without a hint of condescension. It was obvious that my wife had "the patience of a saint," as they used to say in the old country known as the Bronx, when it came to her darling Sofia.

I also had great patience when it came to Sofia. I also had difficulty saying "no" to her, even when deep down I didn't think her decisions were very wise, such as when she decided to move out and share an apartment with her imaginary friends who all belonged to an illusory theater group. If ever a child was unprepared to live on her own, it was Sofia, but I felt I had no choice. She was eighteen, after all, and she was in full rebellion when she moved out. She had stopped coming out of her room except to eat, never talked on the phone, even with the one or two friends I knew she had, and I could swear she went days without taking a shower. She literally smelled, and there were times I felt like throwing her into the pool.

Sofia's beauty had always blinded me to the real possibility that she was different from other people. I blamed her, calling her a spoiled, rich child with an attitude problem, for the despicable way she treated her grandparents. I labeled her a narcissist. But what if this was always just a convenient way to explain her behavior? I sensed that Jennifer knew something about Sofia that I didn't, but what was it? I was afraid to ask, but I would try to work up the courage to ask Jennifer to share her theories. For right now, though, I was just happy to have Sofia near me. She was back in my care, and I could protect her like I had since the day her unloving mother left her with me, like a used coat dumped at the Salvation Army store. I had promised Sofia that I would always be there for her, and I had every intention of making good on that pledge.

The sun had just started coming up over beautiful Studio City as Sofia and I started our walk. We had just cleared the driveway when Sofia asked, "Do you think Grandma and Grandpa are still mad at me?" It was the first time she had brought up her grandparents since that phone call from Kentucky.

"What makes you ask that?"

"Because Jennifer has been taken away from me, and you said that Jennifer was proof that Grandpa and Grandma still loved me."

"Jennifer hasn't been taken away from you, honey," I said. "She'll be back home tonight."

"Do you really believe that?"

"Yes, my beautiful angel, I definitely believe that, just like I know that your grandparents love you and will always look after you." I looked into her big brown eyes and could see a troubling sense of uncertainty.

"Jennifer is at work helping the children," I said. "You know how important that is."

"Yes, Daddy, that is the most important thing, and she will be home after work," she said, as though trying to convince herself.

"Yes, she will unquestionably be home after work," I said, hoping that a little repetition, of the kind that had always seemed soothing to Sofia, might help it sink in. "She isn't going anywhere, and will always be there for us."

"She isn't going anywhere, and will always be there for us," she repeated.

We stopped and sat on a curb again to watch as the sun rose behind the Universal Studios Sign. She placed her head on my shoulder and we sat there and didn't speak.

After returning home from our walk, I sat with Sofia at her desk, and for exactly thirty minutes we each read pamphlets on volunteering, each taking notes and exchanging ideas. We then sat on the couch in the living room and watched *The Honeymooners* for a couple of hours. "Bang, zoom … You're going to the moon!" We laughed as though it was the first time we were viewing the shows.

We then went into my study and Sofia started reading the new screenplay I was writing, making suggestions in the margins as I continued to work. In the back of my mind, I was expecting Nick to call at any moment and tell me he was getting divorced and needed to bury his head in this new film.

One hour after this thought crossed my mind, he called. He was drunk but coherent and still somewhere in French Polynesia. Naturally, he was "divorcing the bitch" he married less than three weeks ago. "She turned out to be just like all the others, blissfully happy for about a week and then nothing but bitching and more bitching. It was a worldwide conspiracy among all women to make men miserable." Thankfully, the divorce was going smoothly and all she was asking for was fifty thousand American dollars and a new "hut" for her family.

I told him I was very close to finishing the script and that Sofia was sitting beside me reading it over and making suggestions. He insisted on speaking to her and so I put the phone on speaker. "Hello, beautiful Sofia," he said, making an effort to sound sober.

"Hello, Nick," Sofia said. "I love you and miss you." As mechanical as the words sounded, I knew that the sentiment was genuine. She really did love Nick.

"I love you too, you beautiful, beautiful child. So, what do you think of your dad's script?"

"It's wonderful," she said.

"Are you just saying that because your father is sitting next to you?"

"No, it's wonderful."

"Are you in it?"

"No!"

"Then how wonderful could it be if your father didn't write a nice juicy part for the most beautiful girl in the world. Don't forget, that when you make your film debut it will be in one of my movies so I can take credit for discovering the next Sophia Loren."

I could see Sofia getting anxious so I picked up the phone, but not before Sofia said "Love you" again. I clicked over from speaker and said, "At the moment, Sofia is concentrating on much more important matters, and I am so proud of her."

"More important things than making films? Surely, you've got to be kidding?" I heard him ordering another drink, at which point he laughed and then just hung up.

I looked at Sofia as she anxiously clutched her hands together. "A strange man," I said. "A very strange man. Aren't you happy you decided not to become an actress?"

"He wants me to act in his movies," she said, as though a judge had sentenced her to death.

"Sweetheart, what director wouldn't want the most beautiful girl in the world to be in his movies? But you have nothing to worry about. Nick loves you so much that he would never force you to be in one of his movies, or do anything you didn't want to do. In fact, he'll be overjoyed, once he sobers up, to hear that you want to work with sick children instead of acting."

"Then why did he say he wanted me to act in his movies?"

"He has been telling you that since you were a little girl. That's his way of telling you how much he loves you."

Sofia's phone rang and it was Jennifer. Suddenly, all thoughts of Nick vanished as she cheerfully chatted with her mommy. After about ten minutes she hung up and I didn't even get a chance to say "Hi" or "I love you" or "How's the job?"

Taking advantage of the change in Sofia's good mood, I immediately took her by the hand and led her straight out of the study and into the kitchen. She insisted on making our lunch, which consisted of two peanut butter and jelly sandwiches each, and two glasses of chocolate milk. She talked non-stop about Jennifer, and after we finished our lunch, I was left with doing the dishes. After all, one didn't want to spoil me too much.

She then took me by the hand, and led me into her bedroom. She sat me down beside her, set the clock for exactly thirty minutes, and we read more pamphlets, took more notes, and exchanged more ideas. The clock rang, and we relocated to the couch in the living room with Mr. Lawrence, and turned on the television and watched *The Honeymooners.* "Bang, zoom ... You're going to the moon!" Despite my initial doubts, it turned out to be the best day I could have ever imagined ... just my daughter and me.

Jennifer called at 6:00 p.m. and told me that she was going to be late and that we should just go ahead and eat dinner. It wasn't much of a surprise, especially since it was her first day at a new job. I tried to explain this to Sofia, but it didn't sink in. She burst into tears at the news, grabbed Lawrence, and ran into her room. A few minutes later, despite my wife warning her repeatedly against calling her at work unless it was an emergency, I heard her talking on her phone to Jennifer. The child just couldn't help herself. She was like a drug addict ... addicted to Jennifer, her newly minted mother. I grabbed myself a cold beer and headed toward her room with every intention of grabbing her phone and hiding it from her, if not smashing it into a thousand pieces. Thankfully, she had hung up before I reached her room. She looked at me and said, "Jennifer said she would be home at eight o'clock and we should go ahead and order a pizza half an hour before."

She walked past me, still gripping Lawrence tightly, and curled herself into a ball on the couch. I couldn't help but feel that it was a stroke of luck that I married Jennifer before she started her new job. I grabbed another beer and sat down beside my daughter. The beneficial effect of a few beers can never be overrated. I patiently reminded Sofia that she wasn't supposed to call Jennifer at work, unless it was an emergency, and that getting her dinner order did not qualify as an emergency. She replied a little haughtily that Jennifer was very happy to hear from her and couldn't wait to get home to see her.

I decided not to pursue the subject any further. I would leave that to Jennifer. She would know better than me how to get the message across to Sofia about boundaries, and about when it was, and wasn't, appropriate to call her at work.

At exactly seven thirty my daughter ordered the pizza. At five minutes to eight the pizza arrived and Sofia placed the pie on the table with three paper plates. At eight o'clock the headlights from my car flashed through the front windows of the house. A moment later, Sofia greeted Jennifer at the door. There was no way that I was going to be allowed to be the one to greet her, but I stood behind Sofia to lend support. Jennifer looked totally exhausted, but after a long embrace from each of us my wife seemed to perk up as she looked across at me and smiled.

I poured Jennifer a large glass of white wine and handed Sofia a glass of ginger ale. We sat down, a family, and ate pizza and garlic sticks. We asked Jennifer about her day, and she answered simply, saying it was "fine," and that she liked her co-workers, and that she was beginning to meet some of the patients, but that she had a long way to go before she was on top of the caseload.

"They're going to love you just as much as the children in Kentucky loved you," Sofia said, and I almost choked on my pizza. Six months ago, an unprompted show of empathy like that would have been unthinkable. I briefly wondered if aliens had stolen my daughter and replaced her with a convincing Sofia clone.

Jennifer beamed at her and said, "Thank you so much, sweetheart. You know what? You're right. It'll all be just fine."

After dinner Jennifer, followed by her shadow, walked into our bedroom. She "desperately" needed a shower. I was left with cleaning up and the memory of having dinners just like this with my parents. It was never the grandiose moments that left the biggest impressions on my life, but the simple, life-affirming moments, like sitting around the kitchen table eating dinner with your loved ones and discussing each other's day.

I opened a bottle of champagne and poured a glass. I walked into our bedroom, knocked on the bathroom door, and walked in. Sofia was sitting on top of the toilet, with her legs crossed, talking a mile a minute while Jennifer was taking a shower, occasionally sticking her head out through the curtain when Sofia said something especially interesting. I handed Jennifer the glass of champagne and she replied,

"Wow! You really know how to spoil a girl." She reached around the shower curtain; her lovely face dripping wet, and kissed me. "Isn't he the best?" she said, and Sofia naturally agreed.

I walked back into the kitchen and grabbed another beer. The idea that the beautiful, caring, and loving creature in the shower was my wife was still hard for me to fathom. I watched as Jennifer, dressed in her pajamas, and Sofia walked across the hall and into Sofia's room. Suddenly, Jennifer walked back out, tapped her empty champagne glass, and asked, "A little more champagne, please?"

I poured her another glass of champagne, in exchange for another kiss, and then left the girls alone to discuss girl stuff. I sat on a chair in the living room and looked out at the pool and the reflection of the trees swaying across the water. After a little while the sound of the girls' voices went silent and I walked back toward Sofia's room and looked in. Sofia was asleep on the bed, with Lawrence in her arms, and Jennifer, also asleep on the bed, was hugging Sofia. And I was back to sleeping alone and for some reason that all seemed perfectly normal.

Chapter 35

I opened my eyes, barely awake, and saw the image of a beautiful woman flash by and walk into the bathroom. Before I could blink, the same image flashed by in the opposite direction. "Hey, what's the rush?"

She turned, my lovely wife, and smiled as she sat down beside me on the bed. "Work, sleepy head. I didn't want to wake you."

"Did you have breakfast?"

"Yes, prepared perfectly by our lovely daughter."

"And did she also make you lunch?"

"Yes, two perfect peanut butter and jelly sandwiches."

"That's my girl," I said.

"She told me what a lovely day she had with her daddy yesterday. I would suggest, if you're not too busy, to try to repeat yesterday's performance."

"You know, it's not easy trying to live up to the high standards you have set."

"I know, it's a challenge being me," she said, laughing as I reached up and kissed her. "You be a good boy today, and you might get a really special treat tonight."

"Like you spending the night in this bed?"

"Well, I can't promise that, but I might be able to sneak in for a little while." She laughed as she stood up and walked out of the room. I laid my head back down on the pillow and listened as she started up the car and drove off to work. As much as Sofia and I needed and loved Jennifer, it was apparent that Jennifer also needed and loved us. As I lay there on the bed, I started thinking about what it means to have a family.

The rest of the day unfolded just like the day before, except there was no phone call from Nick. Jennifer got home two hours late, we ate pizza for dinner, and my wife spent the entire night in our daughter's room. As for that special treat she sort of promised, it never materialized, but then it was selfish of me to expect treats from a woman who spent fifteen hours on her feet, helping innocent children cursed with a dastardly disease that I wouldn't wish on my worst enemy.

Chapter 36

The next morning I woke up at my usual time of 5:30. The house was unusually quiet. Jennifer had the next two days off, and as I passed my daughter's room, I looked in on the two sleeping beauties and I could swear that they had not moved since I checked on them before going to bed. I opened the front door of the house, took a deep breath, and ran off into the promise of a new day.

When I arrived back home an hour and a half later, the quiet had erupted into the magical sound of the Beatles singing their rendition of "Twist and Shout." My wife was multitasking, dancing with our daughter and flipping pancakes with a spatula that doubled as a microphone. I swear, Sofia was the most ungainly child, but with Jennifer leading and orchestrating each move she could have passed for Ginger Rogers.

Pancakes were served on the kitchen table, along with a glass of orange juice for Jennifer and two glasses of chocolate milk for Sofia and me. The girls had already made plans to take a ride down to the beach and have lunch at one of the seaside cafés. I couldn't help but wonder if any of those cafés served peanut butter and jelly sandwiches or if Sofia would have to resort to another of her favorites, noodles with butter. After all, every eatery served noodles, and butter was always in abundance. I was invited, but I decided not to go. I sensed that Nick was close to sobering up, and with his latest divorce all but finalized, he would be itching to get back to work. That process always began with his reading the first draft of the script, so I had to be ready. Even though we had discussed this latest project in great detail before he left on his latest adventure, there was a good chance, with all the commotion going on in his life, that he had forgotten much of what we discussed.

The project had already been green-lighted by the studio, at a budget of nearly two hundred million. Nick was a proven commodity, and he had made a lot of useless, half-witted executives a ton of money. So, when he went to them about our latest project, with the general idea for the project scrawled on a torn, dirty sheet of paper, they simply said yes. They didn't even ask for a script, which wasn't so unusual because there was a really good chance they didn't know how to read.

Nick made a lot of money on every project, and before even directing our next one, he was guaranteed twenty million dollars plus five percent of the total net profits. To put that in perspective, a number of our projects had grossed nearly two billion dollars worldwide, with net profits in the range of 1.2 billion. In short, on top of the twenty million he was guaranteed, he netted an additional sixty million, and that didn't account for the action figures we created, held the patents on, and which were marketed by the studio and sold in stores and online throughout the world. The marketing and sale of those action figures alone, and our eventual cut of the profit over the years, was usually more than we made on all our films. We split our percentage of the merchandizing profits straight down the middle, fifty-fifty.

Nick's father was an accountant for one of the biggest banks in Australia and he had taught his son well. Nick cut out all the middlemen, or leeches, as he was fond of calling them, including agents, lawyers and managers, and instead did his and my negotiations on all our projects. As he told me once we started collaborating, why give twenty-five percent of your hard-earned money to a manager, lawyer and agent when he could read and negotiate a contract better than any of them, and he wasn't joking. He held all the cards, and if the studio we were affiliated with balked at his demands he made it perfectly clear to them that he had no qualms about taking his project to another studio that would welcome him and his team with open arms. Loyalty was a word often used in Hollywood, but seldom practiced. Studios loved you as long as you were making money for them, but once you had back-to-back flops, they wouldn't even bother taking your call.

It's impossible to say how much Nick was worth. He would take the studio for every penny he could get out of them, but when it came to living life he would spend as freely as any person I knew. During hiatuses between films, you could just as easily find him walking along a beach in Malibu on Monday, partying on the French Riviera on Wednesday, visiting cathedrals and galleries in Rome on Friday, and on Sunday sitting in a Dublin bar getting shit-faced. He loved women, whether Italian, American, Greek, Latino, Black, Scandinavian or, most recently, Tahitian. He did not discriminate. The only women he would not date or marry were actresses, even though they loved working with him. "They whine and bitch," he would say, "and what they all need is a dose of reality and maybe a year or two working as a secretary, or a teacher, or a nurse."

Why he continued to get married was a puzzle for his psychiatrist, should he ever decide to avail himself of one. But why he continued to get divorced was no secret: once they started "bitching," it was all over … whether that took one month, six months, or a year. He was never married long enough for any of his ex-wives to make a convincing case that they played any significant role in his success, and he never had any children. So the alimony payouts were rarely more than a few million per rejected bride, and once the divorce papers were signed, he never had to see them again.

The only girl I knew of who he genuinely loved over a long period of time was my daughter, Sofia. He had adored her from the time she was a toddler. It was as though when he looked at her and played with her, he was looking at something pure and pristine, something he had lost and could not recover.

He was Sofia's godfather, and despite whatever insanity was going on in his life, he never forgot her birthday, the day of her baptism, and of course, Christmas. When she turned thirteen, he stopped sending her material presents and instead started sending her insane amounts of money … ten thousand dollars at a time. When I asked him about the 'wisdom' of sending a young girl that type of money he just said, "What do I care about wisdom? I'm only interested in spoiling her."

During Sofia's irrational period I expressed my concern to him and he remarked, "She's a teenage girl! If she wasn't acting irrational then you would have reasons to worry."

With Jennifer and Sofia at the beach and the house to myself, I was able to sit down at my desk and finish the first draft of the script in about an hour and a half. A few minutes later, just as I had sensed, Nick called and asked about the script. He was already back in Los Angeles, at one of his homes in Malibu; Tahiti, his eighth ex-wife, and her family were a distant memory. I emailed him the script, expecting it back in four to five hours with fifty to one hundred suggestions. This would start a process that would go on for months, with revision, after revision, after revision. Nick and I worked exclusively on each script and nobody got to read it until we both agreed that it was perfect. Actors, like the studio executives, only received a synopsis. Our advance scouting team got detailed descriptions of the type of locations Nick was looking for, and throughout the process Nick and I would receive thousands of photos of possible locations and their availability. Nick's personal life might have been topsy-turvy, but when it came to work, he moved in a straight line, never deviating from his goal. If a problem arrived on set, he resolved the issue quickly, and if it had to do with an actor or actress who was not a lead player, he or she was simply replaced. Nick was not averse to hearing other peoples' opinions, especially if they were coming from the cinematographer, the cameraman, sound or lighting crews, but he despised showboating, and if he suspected it from any of the crew, the consequences were not pretty.

I closed my eyes, dreading the revision process. The best part of writing a script, for me, was the first draft, when I was in complete control of the characters, the story, and the pacing. Once I handed it over to Nick, the intimacy I had developed with the story and characters vanished. It was like a divorce and the story and characters became pieces on a majestic chessboard with each move calculated and analyzed and the spontaneity stripped bare. By the fifth revision, the first draft was a distant memory ... poor me.

I opened my eyes and looked out the window at Jennifer's 1974 Dodge Dart. The irony was insane: on this one movie project I would make more money than Jennifer would make in forty years, and she helped save the lives of children, beating back a mutant foe whose ability to replicate and reproduce was unparalleled in the history of medicine. Yes, poor me ... the idea of sitting at my desk and doing revision after revision.

I dropped my eyes and noticed a piece of paper that I must have accidently shoved off my desk in my rush to finish the script. I picked up the paper and it was a note from Jennifer.

Hi Honey,
I know that I said you can spoil me all you want and I wouldn't complain, but I can't help feeling terrible about you serving me Cristal champagne every night and buying me expensive wines to drink. I do so appreciate it but I would much rather save those for special occasions. Please, oh please, don't be mad at me. Your love and Sofia's love are more than I could ever have hoped for.
Love you so much,
Jennifer

I folded the note and placed it into the top drawer of my desk. It suddenly occurred to me that I didn't even tell Nick that I got married. You would think that was the first thing you would tell your best friend. Maybe, it was because he treated marriage like a sacrilegious temptation, the apple in the Garden of Eden. It was something that he couldn't resist, but knew in the end he would regret.

I watched as Jennifer and Sofia pulled into the driveway of the house. What Nick possibly saw as a trivial institution, which he could discard with a flick of the wrist, I saw as a blessing that not only enhanced my life but also made it complete.

I met the girls at the front door and helped them carry in a bunch of shopping bags. They had stopped at a thrift store and had gone to town, as the saying goes. I imagine that was the first time Sofia was in such an alien place, but then if it was good enough for Jennifer, it was good enough for her. I came up behind my wife who was rearranging clothes in our bedroom closet. I put my arms around her waist and kissed her softly on her neck and said, "Thank you for loving Sofia and me so much."

Chapter 37

The next two weeks felt like a mixed blessing. Thankfully, my wife was not asked to work any extra days, so three days a week I got to spend extra time with my daughter (a blessing) and at night I got to sleep alone (not a blessing). Jennifer was exhausted after her shifts, which were more like fifteen-hour shifts than twelve-hour shifts, and how she had the energy to deal with Sofia afterwards was a mystery. From the moment she got home, Sofia was in her face while she ate dinner (pizza at least three times a week, guaranteed), while she took a shower (Sofia's favorite perch was on the toilet seat), and after she changed into her pajamas. Sofia would kidnap Jennifer to her room where they talked about the children, looked at pictures, and discussed when Sofia would finally start as a volunteer. I was lucky to get in a kiss with each glass of wine I brought to Jennifer, which was usually three. About half an hour after that last glass was delivered, it would get strangely silent, and when I looked in on them, they would be sound asleep. Sofia would be hugging Lawrence, and Jennifer would be hugging Sofia, while the husband and father was left to clean up the dirty glasses and plates.

It was like I was in a competition with my daughter over Jennifer's affection. As in all other areas, when it came to Sofia, I simply surrendered to her wishes. In truth, the idea that they were getting along so well was still shocking to me. I knew that Jennifer would get along with Sofia, but Sofia getting along so well with Jennifer was still a surprise. It was the first time in years that I had seen my daughter truly connect, socialize, and show love for another human being besides me.

The other four days a week were great. Despite every conceivable attempt by Sofia, she could not drag my lovely wife with her when she had to use the bathroom or take a shower. Jennifer drew the line at that and so if I timed it correctly that gave me around forty-five minutes to spend alone with her during the day, and at night I got to sleep with my darling wife and discuss matters that married couples need to discuss away from the child.

The one time I got up the courage to ask Jennifer if she found Sofia's behavior intrusive, she was not hearing any of it. "How could I possibly think that Sofia was in any way intruding upon my space or privacy? I only wish I could spend more time with her. How ludicrous to even suggest such a thing."

One night, while standing in the doorway of our bathroom, I watched as Jennifer meticulously flossed her teeth, dressed in her pajamas. Earlier in the evening, Jennifer and Sofia had spent a long time filling out an application for Sofia to be a volunteer in the hospital. I didn't pay much attention to anything they were discussing, especially since they were doing it in the privacy of Sofia's room. I naturally had my concerns, but I had total faith in Jennifer's judgment and confidence that Sofia would do great working with seriously ill children. I often went back to what Sofia said to me during one of our walks, when she explained that children "like me for who I am and don't pass judgment." In a strange sense her remark made me want to protect her even more, but deep down I knew she needed to get out and work and be productive and that she would never find a better mentor than my wife.

Jennifer rinsed out her mouth and asked, "And now that you have watched me go through the ritual of cleaning my teeth, did you at least learn something?"

"Yes, I learned that even while you are gurgling, spitting, and making strange noises you are nevertheless as beautiful as ever."

"Liar," she shot back with a laugh. She came over and threw her arms around me and we kissed. "But it sure makes kissing me a lot more pleasant."

"You could go without brushing your teeth for a week and kissing you would still be the most pleasant thing in the world." I looked down at her pajamas and couldn't help laughing.

"What's so funny?"

"You, and your pajamas. Have you always worn pajamas to bed?"

"Yes. Why? Would you rather I wear sexy lingerie?"

"God no. I like looking at women dressed in sexy outfits as much as the next guy, but I could never stop thinking about how uncomfortable such outfits must be."

"Amazing what women will do to get a man's attention. You see, it worked for me … if it wasn't for that sexy nurse's outfit you probably wouldn't have given me a second thought, nevertheless asked me out to lunch."

"It's when you got out of that stupid outfit that I fell in love with you."

"But not before you went for the bait."

I laughed and remarked, "You don't see me complaining."

"Me neither, which reminds me — a couple of days ago at work I was looking at the large plaque in the lobby listing all the major donors and I saw a familiar name on the board with the same name as you."

"Spelled the same? You know how Italian last names can be a little deceiving when you first look at them."

"No, I'm quite certain it was the same name. So why didn't you tell me that you were a major donor to Saint Joseph's Hospital?"

"Well, let me see … because you would have accused me of pulling strings to get you in."

"I would never do such a thing."

I looked at her really hard and she started to blush, "Okay, maybe. But just, maybe."

I continued to look at her really hard. "Really, just maybe??"

"Okay, I would have … but you didn't, did you?"

"No, I didn't. Your honor is still intact."

"Why Saint Joseph's and not some other hospital or charity?"

"Oh, there are other charities, but Saint Joseph's is the only hospital."

"Because Saint Joseph was your mother's favorite saint?"

"Yes, and because they are a wonderful hospital and Sofia was born there."

"Can we use you as a reference on Sofia's application?"

"Of course. Why would you even ask that … unless what you really want is for me to make a call on Sofia's behalf?"

"Yes, that is exactly what I want you to do. You probably think that they would welcome as many volunteers as possible and that is usually the case, except when it comes to children being treated for cancer, then you have an abundance of people wanting to volunteer. I would never ask…"

I placed my finger gently against Jennifer's mouth. "Consider it done. I would do anything for Sofia, and I am eternally thankful knowing that you would too." I kissed my wife and her breath was fresh and clean. I might have been idealizing her, but I felt like her breath would have been the same with or without all the care she took with flossing and brushing. Jennifer was a breath of fresh air, inside and out. She was unsoiled by the pollutants around us, providing a canister of oxygen to all those in need.

Chapter 38

The following morning I made a call to the director of the hospital. After only a few minutes on the phone, he guaranteed me that Sofia would be a welcome addition and said she could start as a volunteer in the pediatric oncology unit of the hospital whenever she was ready. He even offered to give her a personal tour of the unit, but I said that wasn't necessary because her mother was a nurse working in that unit. He asked me if there was a particular reason why she wanted to be a volunteer in that unit, besides the fact that her mother was working there. I thought about it for moment and then replied, "Because she gets along really well with children and she hopes to make a positive difference in their lives."

"She sounds like an amazing young lady," the director said, and I couldn't help agreeing with him.

After we hung up, I took Jennifer aside and told her that Sofia could start in two weeks and that the director was overjoyed to help. She hugged and kissed me as I wiped away tears rolling down her face. She laughed and said, "Happy tears."

"I know," I said. She disappeared into our daughter's room and I went into my study to work on the revisions Nick had sent, but I ended up just sitting there, thinking about what a fantastic job Sofia would do with the children in the cancer unit. I had just helped my daughter get a job as a volunteer and, like Jennifer, I was busting with complex joy. Tears of happiness rolled down my face like rain nourishing a budding flower … the flower of my life, my daughter Sofia.

The following two weeks flew by as Nick bombarded me with more and more suggestions and ideas and the revisions started piling up on my hard drive. After working with this flamboyant genius for nearly two decades, I knew we were getting close, and that before long we would have a viable shooting script. Then, the storyboarding would begin and every imagined shot in the movie, thousands of shots, would be illustrated in block after block after block, like in an enlarged comic strip, until the entire film from the first to the last shot was staring back at Nick and to a lesser degree at me.

At times, it was like there were two Nick Joneses. The first one was a meticulous, bankable visionary whose dictatorial style on the set of his films was legendary. It was said that Alfred Hitchcock was so prepared, and his notes and directions for the next day's shoot were so detailed, that his second director could easily have filled in for him, follow the instructions, and achieved the same results as Hitchcock himself.

Well, Nick was very much like Hitchcock, but the idea of having someone else sit in his director's chair, besides Sofia when she was just a toddler, was out of the question. It was his movie, his baby, and like a great conductor, he didn't miss any element of the composition — the rhythm, melody or harmony. He saw the entire landscape, every shadow, prop, and every expression on the actors' faces. Once the shoot was over, he supervised every aspect of the editing process, and when the movie was finally completed, he invited a diverse group of friends, call girls, drunks, critics, bartenders, waiters, school teachers, to a private screening while sitting in the back row. He watched their reactions, and if their responses were overwhelmingly positive, his job was over and everyone in the audience was invited back to one of his Malibu's homes for a grand old party, where the other Nick would appear.

Shortly after the party, he would disappear and except for me he kept in contact with nobody even remotely related to Hollywood. He refused to go to any red carpet premieres, and insisted that his godchild never be allowed to attend such events. When I asked him why he didn't go to any premieres he replied, "I prefer those overpaid prima donnas, with their fake smiles and tight-ass designer gowns, to steal the spot light. After all, it's not like any of them deserved the money they got paid, so it's only fair that they do some free publicity." Except for me, Nick never let on to anyone his utter disdain for actors. They were like freeloaders to him, paid millions of dollars for what amounted to three or four weeks of work.

Today was Sofia's first day of work as a volunteer at the hospital. Jennifer was off and was going to be with her the entire time. By the time I got back from my early morning run, the girls were already up and Jennifer was helping her get dressed. I knew my daughter was nervous because whenever she was anxious she would open and close her hands with the rapidity of a humming bird flapping its wings, and this morning her hands were seriously moving. She looked straight ahead, her large brown eyes, barely blinking as Jennifer combed her long, dark, glistening hair back and tied it into a ponytail. She had the most beautiful face of any girl I have ever seen and when her hair was tied back and away from her face she looked like the Angel/Beatrice character, Paola, in Fellini's *La Dolce Vita*, albeit with darker hair. I bent down in front of her and gently pinched her cheek and asked, "Where did you get that beautiful face from?"

She blinked and smiled and Jennifer replied, "She got that beautiful face from her daddy."

"No, I think only God could have created such a face. Did God give you that face?"

"You and God," Sofia replied.

"Okay, if you insist, I'll take a little credit." I hugged her for a long time and never wanted to let go. "I love you so much, and I want you to promise me that you're not going to suddenly fall in love with some doctor and leave me."

"I would never leave you, Daddy. I love you so much." I kissed her on the forehead and stood up and looked across at my wife who had tears rolling down her face but I didn't bother to ask if they were happy, sad, or simply tears of love.

The girls left for the hospital at 8:30, with Jennifer saying that they would most likely be home in a couple of hours. Sofia carried a shopping bag filled with video games, children's books, and a variety of other games and toys that very young children would like. Jennifer handed me Sofia's credit card that I had given her when she left for Kentucky and said, "She won't need this."

"How do you know?" I said, only half-joking. "She might want to buy all the kids wide-screen TVs."

"She doesn't need to buy expensive gadgets to be liked and adored. She's a natural. And besides, I have credit cards."

"But you also have student loans."

"Don't be such a wiseass. I make very good money, and instead of buying me expensive wines to drink you should have just paid off my loans, honey bun."

"Just give me the information I need, and you will be debt-free by the time you come back home."

"Not a chance, lover. I can pay off my own debts."

I pulled her close to me and kissed her and said, "Thank you for taking care of my little girl."

"She's my little girl, too."

"I know, but thank you all the same." I kissed her again and then I watched as the girls drove off. I closed the door, resisted the desire for a beer, and sat down on the couch and turned on *The Honeymooners*. "Bang, zoom … You're going to the moon."

A couple of hours went by and I didn't hear a word from the girls. A couple of more hours went by and still no word. I was tempted to call Jennifer but decided against that idea. I walked into my study, turned on my computer, and saw a list of suggestions and changes from Nick so long that for the next few hours I was so occupied that I nearly forgot about my absent wife and daughter. Then, I heard a beep from my phone telling me I had a message. It was from Jennifer. She had sent me at least twenty pictures of our beautiful daughter interacting with the children. She looked like an angel … a surreal, caring, comforting and healing messenger from God. The children, almost all bald from chemotherapy treatments and with IV lines running from their chests or their arms, seemed to be having a wonderful time with Sofia as their guide and playmate. Jennifer captioned the pictures with the remark, "Told you she was a natural."

I felt so proud that I forwarded the pictures to Nick with the caption, "Your godchild at work." A few minutes later he responded, "I am so proud of her, so proud. She is the most beautiful creature in the world. I still can't believe that the two of you share the same DNA. There is absolutely no resemblance."

The girls arrived back home at 7:00 p.m., roughly eight hours later than Jennifer's original prediction. I had a pizza pie ready and we sat down to dinner. Sofia could not stop talking about her wonderful day with the kids, repeating herself numerous times, which was her style, as Jennifer and I sat there listening intently with smiles as wide as a football field. My phone rang and it was Nick. He wanted to speak to his godchild and so I handed the phone over to Sofia.

"Hello, Nick," she said, and I could see a tinge of anxiety crease her forehead. Then suddenly her eyes lit up and she sat up and started walking back and forth as she told Nick about her day. Nick's time was precious during this period of intense creativity and the start of a new film, but when it came to Sofia, his time was endless. He always had immense patience with her and he accepted her peculiarities with a grace and beauty that not even the great Willie Mays could emulate on a baseball field.

After Sofia had been talking with Nick for about twenty minutes, Jennifer looked at me and whispered, "Should I try to get her off the phone?"

"No. Nick loves talking to her and she sounds so happy. I'm quite sure he is enjoying every minute of it."

After another ten minutes went by Sofia finally said the magic words, "Love you so much, Nick, and thank you." She handed the phone back to me and Nick remarked, "You did an amazing job raising her. She is your greatest achievement." He hung up and I looked across at my daughter and thought to myself, *Yes, she is.*

"He's so happy for me, Daddy, and he doesn't care that I don't want to be an actress. That's what he said, and he said to tell you that he was transferring ten-thousand dollars into your account and that I should spend it on the children and something for myself, but I don't need anything, so I'll spend it all on the children. Oh, now I have to make a list and see what I should buy."

She looked at Jennifer as if to say "aren't you coming with me" and my wife responded, "I'll be there in a few minutes, angel."

She ran off to her room as I looked across at my wife and asked, "What's wrong?"

"Nothing! I just never realized how close Nick and Sofia were."

"She's his godchild, and since he's never had any children, he has always treated Sofia like she was the most important person in the world. At times, I have felt he understands my child better than I do."

"Is that so," Jennifer remarked in a sharp and cutting tone that felt like she was ready to take a knife to the whole idea of Nick loving our daughter so much.

"Do you Protestants believe in godparents?" I asked.

"Do 'we' Protestants believe in godparents? Is that your question?" she asked with a derisive laugh that was totally unbecoming and out of character.

"Yes, Jennifer, that was my question."

"Some denominations do, but nothing like 'you' Italian Catholics do. Certainly, not enough to make a string of movies about the practice."

"Are you talking about the *Godfather* movies?"

"Yes," she said with a touch of uncertainty that for a moment made her seem childish and endearing.

"You've never seen the movies, have you?"

"No. Should I?"

"My God, you really don't know anything about movies. *The Godfather* and *The Godfather Part II* are considered two of the greatest movies ever made … classics. And the title *The Godfather* is more like a symbol in the movie and has very little to do with the actual practice of being a godfather. The movies are about the Mafia and gangsters."

"I guess I should see them, if you consider them classics."

"Well, I don't know about that. You might see them and suddenly think that Sofia and I … two Italian Catholics … are also in the Mafia."

"Don't be such a wiseass. I would never think that my beautiful Sofia could ever be a gangster." She laughed that infectious laugh, and for a moment everything seemed perfect.

"So why does the idea that Nick and Sofia are so close upset you so much?"

"It's not that. I'm happy to know that he sees at least one girl in his orbit as not being disposable."

"It's the money, isn't it?"

"Yes, it's the money. Okay, I admit it. Sofia is such a natural with the children. I don't want her to suddenly think that she has to buy them all expensive gifts in exchange for their affection."

"She doesn't have to spend all of the money on expensive gifts. She can spread the money out over a long period of time and buy smaller and more appropriate and practical gifts."

"And do you really think that's even possible? In case you haven't noticed, Sofia is a near-perfect clone of her daddy."

"I'll take that as a compliment."

"Of course, you would." She shook her head and continued, "I'll do what I can. After all, I am Miss Practicality."

"Now, that's the Old Kentucky, Waspy spirit I've always heard about."

"Very funny," she remarked as she got up and walked away. A minute later, she returned and dropped a folder in front of me.

"What's this?" I asked as I picked up the folder.

"All the information you need to pay off my student loan and my car payment."

"You have a car payment?"

"Yes, I have a car payment. It's a classic, as you like to say. Now, it's your turn to show me some of that New York, Italian, Catholic spirit I have always heard of." She leaned down and kissed me on the cheek, saying, "Thank you, honey bun." She started to walk away as I grabbed her by the waist and sat her down on my lap.

"Surely, I deserve a little more than a little kiss on the cheek before you disappear into our daughter's room." She laughed and then we kissed long and passionately.

Left to my own devices again, I put the folder on the counter and cleared the table, then put away the leftover pizza and cleaned the dishes. Even without an official announcement, it was clear that I had inherited the job of doing the dishes after every meal. If it was okay for my father, it was certainly okay for his son ... not that either of us had a choice in the matter.

I picked up the folder and went into my study. I turned on my computer and within five minutes I had paid off Jennifer's student loan and the remaining $456.76 on her car loan. She bought the car for $750 from a dealership and had to finance $600 of that, after putting down $150. No wonder she was adamant about going to the Mexican Restaurant and drinking margaritas only during Happy Hour when the drinks were half-price.

I did notice that she didn't put up any more resistance about driving my car. Amazing, how quickly one can get spoiled driving around with air-conditioning and SiriusXM radio. I printed out two receipts for the loans and walked out of the study and into my daughter's room. The ladies of the house were out cold, asleep, accompanied by Mr. Lawrence. I had to admit I was getting awfully jealous of that bear. Stuffed and inanimate as he was, he had all the luck when it came to scoring alone time with my wife and daughter. I placed the two receipts, stamped paid in full, beside Jennifer's head and crept out of the room.

Chapter 39

The following morning I got up at my usual time, put on my running gear, and walked past my daughter's room. The girls and Lawrence were still asleep. I opened the front door, walked a few steps, and then ran off into the early morning darkness.

On my return home, I found my daughter and wife dancing and laughing and my wife singing, "I'm debt-free. I'm debt-free," and pointing at my daughter and asking, "Who's debt-free?" And my daughter replying, "Jennifer is debt-free. Jennifer is debt-free."

They danced toward me and Jennifer kissed me on the lips and asked Sofia, "And why am I debt-free?" And Sofia replied, "Because my daddy paid off your loans!" And then as an extra bonus I got a kiss from my daughter and was treated to French toast and a glass of chocolate milk.

The next couple of weeks went off without so much as a hiccup. Sofia volunteered at the hospital on the same days that Jennifer worked. They left in the morning together and arrived back home fourteen to fifteen hours later. It was as though the sick children had injected into my daughter an overdose of vitality that I never would have thought possible. The children were her friends and even after some of them went into remission and were released she still kept in touch with them. Jennifer was right … our daughter was a natural.

After another tough day of rewrites, I opened a beer and sat down on the couch in the living room and turned on reruns of the *I Love Lucy* show. As I scooted back on the couch, I noticed a business card stuck between the cushions. I picked it up and looked at it. It read: "Dr. Jonathan Moore. Department of Psychiatry at Saint Joseph's Hospital, Burbank, CA."

I twirled the card around in my hand, placed it my pocket, and didn't give it much thought until I finished my fourth beer. I then walked into my study, turned on the computer, and looked up Dr. Jonathan Moore. He graduated from the University of Kentucky Medical School and did his residence at the same hospital that Jennifer worked at as an oncology nurse. He was a native of Kentucky, a handsome man, and about the same age as Jennifer, and started working at Saint Joseph's at about the same time that Jennifer moved out here. This seemed like a strange series of coincidences. Before meeting Jennifer, I had never met anyone from Kentucky besides George Clooney. The only real thing I knew about Kentucky was that it was horse country with millions of acres of manicured farmland and a college basketball team that had won a number of championships and, of course, it was also famous for its bourbon.

A thought crept into my mind and took up residence. What was a beautiful girl like Jennifer doing falling for someone like me, a writer thirteen years older than her, who had never once been mistaken for someone like George Clooney or Brad Pitt? Dr. Moore, on the other hand ... I could certainly see Jennifer falling for someone like him. Actually, if I had to pick someone who perfectly complemented Jennifer's beauty and youth it would be a physical specimen like Dr. Moore. She must have known him back in Kentucky. She knew everybody, and had made a special point of reaching out to colleagues there. If she'd seen him again here, even for long enough to get his new card, why wouldn't she have mentioned him?

Could it be that the girl I thought I married was simply a wonderful actress, a beautiful con artist who has been playing Sofia and me all along, like a couple of puppets? Sure, Dr. Moore made good money, but he was probably still paying off medical school loans, whereas I was a "bank" waiting to be plundered for Jennifer and Dr. Moore's happily ever after.

If this happened to be true, Jennifer was soon to encounter an Italian Catholic from New York who was going to be her worse nightmare.

I shut off the computer and put Dr. Moore's business card back in my pocket. I walked into the kitchen and took out the bottle of Jack

Daniels. I knew at this moment that I wasn't thinking straight, and the only way to start thinking rationally again was to have a few shots of Old No. 7. It worked, and once I was feeling more relaxed, I went back into the living room, sat down on the couch, and turned on *The Honeymooners*. "Bang, zoom ... You're going to the moon."

I naturally dozed off and woke up when my phone rang. It was Jennifer calling to tell me that they were on their way home and asking if I could order pizza. I ordered the pizza, opened a beer, and decided that I was not going to approach the little vixen about Dr. Moore tonight, but would wait to tomorrow. There was too much at stake to do anything irrational. After all, if my suspicions turned out to be valid, this could be disastrous not only for me but also and, more importantly, for my daughter. Sofia idolized Jennifer. The vixen connected with my daughter in a way I didn't think possible ... but then again, that is exactly what a professional con artist does ... look at the mark and exploit their most vulnerable point. Jennifer, if that was her real name, could have been using Sofia to get to me and my piles of movie money.

I placed the pizza on the table, set three plates, and waited for the girls. When they finally arrived, I held my daughter tightly and purposely turned my head away when Jennifer went to kiss me. I got a beer for myself, and a ginger ale for Sofia.

"What, is the honeymoon already over?" Jennifer asked as she stood up and walked over to the refrigerator and took out a bottle of white wine and poured herself a glass.

Feeling guilty, I apologized for my lack of chivalry. I'm such a loser. It's moments like this that I wish I were more like Nick. Jennifer laughed, and I could swear I heard a bit of mockery in her laugh ... the same laugh I thought was so infectious was now coming across as a charade and farce. That being said, I poured her a second glass of wine and then a third, which she took with her as they went into Sofia's room and I was left doing the dishes.

I walked into my study and took a copy of Lord Byron's complete works out from the bookcase. He had always been my favorite poet, and when I was young and had just moved out here and had very little money, I used to go to this wonderful bookstore in Westwood Village, across from the UCLA campus, and sit there for hours and memorize his poems. Since I could not afford to buy the book, it became all the more important to commit as many of his poems to memory as possible. That way I could "read" him wherever I wanted to, regardless of where I was or how poor I was. I could just flip a switch in my brain and a list of my favorite poems by Mr. Byron would appear.

After finally getting a job and receiving my first paycheck, the first thing I did was to walk into that bookstore and buy that book. And for a number of years afterwards, at least once a week I would open it and test my memory. Circumstances could change in a moment … in a blink of an eye … and I didn't want to lose Byron along with everything else.

I closed the book and recited,

"Though the night was made for loving,
And the day returns too soon,
Yet we'll go no more a-roving
By the light of the moon."

I placed the book back in the designated spot on the bookcase and walked out of the study and looked in at Sofia, asleep, hugging Lawrence and Jennifer, asleep, and hugging Sofia. I thought to myself, "No one holds a child that tightly and lovingly who doesn't care about that child more than her own life."

The following night as I watched Jennifer cleaning her teeth, I reached into my pocket and pulled out Dr. Moore's business card. I placed it in front of Jennifer and she looked down at the card and said, "Oh, you can throw that out. I know Jonathan's phone number by heart."

"And where do you know him from?" I asked.

"We worked together in Kentucky."

"Wow! What a coincidence that both of you are now working at Saint Joseph's together."

She stopped cleaning her teeth and looked at me and started to laugh hysterically. "Oh my God, now I know why you have been acting so strange. You think that Jonathan and I are having some type of an affair."

"Are you?" I asked like a real idiot.

"If I didn't love you so much, I would really be angry right now. Yes, I have always found Jonathan very attractive and compassionate, but I'm just not his type. The wrong gender, actually. He's gay and married to a wonderful gentleman, and maybe one night it would be nice to have them over. When I told him I was moving to Los Angeles, he decided that Los Angeles would be the perfect place for him and his husband to relocate to. It's certainly a lot more accepting of their lifestyle than our native Kentucky, and now we're working at the same hospital and it's great."

She finished cleaning her teeth and, once again, started laughing. "My God, I never would have taken you for the jealous type."

"Would you rather I not be jealous?"

"I would rather you not waste valuable brain power on such foolishness. But I must admit, I am kind of flattered."

"You know, it's not very nice to gloat."

"Says who?" She threw her arms around me and we kissed.

"Maybe I should make an appointment with Dr. Moore."

"It couldn't hurt," she said with a laugh. "Sofia likes him a whole bunch."

"You brought Sofia to see him? As a patient or just to introduce her to your friend?"

"A little bit of both … more to verify a suspicion."

"You brought our daughter to see a psychiatrist and you didn't tell me?"

"She didn't want you to know."

"And why wouldn't she want me to know?"

"Because you have always told her how perfect she is, and she was afraid that if you found out she went to see a psychiatrist you wouldn't think she was so perfect anymore."

I lowered my eyes as images of my lovely daughter ran through my mind like an endless, edited version of a homemade movie and I smiled.

"She *is* perfect," I said.

"Yes, she is perfect and Jonathan thought she was an amazing young lady."

I looked into Jennifer's eyes and I could swear I saw an image of Sofia.

"She sees the world differently and that's what makes her even more special. It's called Asperger Syndrome and some very famous individuals are thought to have possessed the gift. Einstein, Da Vinci, Byron..."

"Lord Byron?"

"Yes, the famous poet. People on the autism spectrum have the ability to concentrate on a particular subject, such as computer programs or music, with such intensity that they become experts in a very short time. They're creative people, often inventors, and include many geniuses in the fields of technology, physics, medicine and the arts. In Sofia's case her genius is her ability to relate and make a connection with the most vulnerable in our society ... helping and healing children ... innocent victims of a horrible disease that she helps them fight and defeat."

My throat went dry, and I started playing with my hands, just like Sofia did when she became anxious.

"I ... I had no idea—" I tried to say, though in the back of my mind somewhere, I was receiving a message that this might not be true.

"It's a lot to take in," Jennifer said. "I got a book for us to look at together. It's important to understand the condition."

I nodded and stared straight ahead, unable to move.

"Remember what you told me about Sofia and your parents?" Jennifer asked, and I nodded again. "That period when she was acting angry and irrational toward her grandparents wasn't her fault. People with Asperger's can be prone to emotional outbursts when the burden of trying to act 'normal' becomes too great. They can feel everyone trying to get them to imitate the behavior and emotional responses of so called 'normal' children at school or do a better job of fitting into the family at home, and it becomes too much. They wind up having meltdowns." Jennifer's eyes glinted again as she looked at me and smiled. "Similar to the meltdown you experienced while suspecting I was having an affair with Jonathan."

"I did not have a meltdown."

"Oh really? That must have been another 'Joe' walking around the house cranky and irritable and forgetting how to be a gentleman … treating his adorable and loving wife like dirt."

"Seriously, like dirt?"

"That's the way Sofia and I saw it," she said, and laughed … that infectious and lovely laugh that put everything right.

"That's the way you and your clone saw it?" I asked.

"*My* clone? I think you mean *your* clone. A trait common in virtually all individuals with Asperger's Syndrome is a tendency to be repetitive, such as eating the same foods every day and watching the same TV shows. Besides Sofia, does that sound like anybody else you might know? A certain person, like our daughter, who eats cereal with chocolate milk for breakfast, unless I make French toast? Peanut butter and jelly sandwiches for lunch every day, and pizza or pasta for dinner every night? Is this ringing any bells at all? The man who on our first date looked at the margarita in front of him as though it contained poison and asked if he could have a beer. The man, like his daughter, who watches reruns of *The Honeymooners* and *I Love Lucy* every time either one of them turns on the TV."

"Okay, wiseass, you made your point, but you don't have to go around criticizing our wonderful taste in classic TV sitcoms. It would be like criticizing someone for looking at the *Mona Lisa* every day."

She pushed me toward the bed. "And for the record, she is very sorry about the way she acted around her grandparents."

"I know," I said. "She told me that she prays to them to forgive her and she wasn't sure if they were listening. As you know, I've told her that the proof they're listening rests with *you*. What she doesn't know is that my mother and father could never remain angry with her, especially knowing what they know now."

Jennifer leaped on me and we fell onto the bed and made love. Afterwards, Jennifer lay beside me, resting her beautiful face on my bare chest. I asked, "Do you think Sofia will ever fall in love, get married, and have a family?"

"Why would you even ask that? Sofia and I talk about guys all the time. Every straight, male doctor, intern, and nurse is in love with her. She could choose anyone she wants and have him proposing to her in minutes."

"Surely, her mother would not allow anything like that to happen? She's only eighteen years old, and how old are these doctors and interns? In their late twenties and early thirties?"

"Yes, mostly in their early thirties. At what age do you think it would be appropriate for Sofia to start dating?"

"Not for years."

"Really? And how do you plan on protecting her from all these predators?"

"Well, when she's at work I would expect you to make it clear to all those perverts that she's just a child, and that if any of them so much as try anything with her that there would be some serious consequences."

"And on the days she's not at work?"

"Don't worry about it, I'll figure something out."

"And what should I tell her in the meantime, that dating Lawrence is far more desirable than any man she might meet out there?"

"And what's wrong with Lawrence? He's a gentleman, scholarly, good looking, and he has always been there for her."

Jennifer tapped her fingers on my chest and looked at me with those big blue eyes that seemed to read my very thoughts. She started to laugh.

"What's so funny?"

"You. You're so funny. My God, you really do believe that Lawrence is the perfect match for our daughter."

"Don't be silly. But believe me I would prefer him over 99 percent of the guys out there."

"Of course you would. I bet you already have her marrying Lawrence. You've probably got it all arranged with The Little Brown Church."

"Surely would allow me to sleep better at night. The month she decided to move out was like a nightmare for me. The only comfort I had was that she had Lawrence with her."

"Wow! I brought the wrong one to see the psychiatrist."

"I'm a writer, Jennifer. My imagination is the key to my success."

"I guess so. I just never knew that Nick and you made movies in which the key demographic was children between three and ten years old."

I looked down at her and smiled, "You're such a wiseass."

"And you love me all the same."

"I do."

There were those words again, the same ones we'd said to each other at the alter not long ago. I could feel my chest expanding with love and relief. We kissed and tossed on the bed as Jennifer laughed and laughed and created a little puppet show on my chest, using her fingers to represent the hilarious wedding of Dr. Jonathan and Nurse Jennifer. I poked her arm and told her to *shaddup*.

I was beginning to see just how much of an expert my wife was at the art of diversion. She was someone who could effortlessly take a stressful situation and within minutes have everyone trading easy banter. I guess this made sense for a nurse in the field of pediatric oncology. She had me in stitches that night, and I'm pretty sure we were still laughing softly as we fell asleep in each other's arms.

I woke up late the following morning, and before I was fully conscious, I saw my wife streak past me like the Flash. I sat up and looked out the open door of the bedroom and I saw Sofia, my wife's doppelgänger, moving quickly down the hallway. A second later, my wife was kissing me and whispering into my ear, "Did I wear my baby boy out last night?"

A second later she was gone, replaced by my daughter, who hugged and kissed me and said, "Love you!"

Before she could disappear I grabbed her arm and said, "I am so proud of you." She looked at me and smiled ever so vaguely and mysteriously, like da Vinci's *Mona Lisa*.

A moment later I heard the front door close, and my wife and daughter left to spend the next fifteen hours tending to children and families who were engaged in the battle of their lives.

I laid my head back down on the pillow and fell back to sleep. Suddenly, I was back on the basketball court I had grown up on. I was alone, practicing, pretending to be Walt Frazier and Willis Reed. In the distance, walking toward the court, I saw Sarah. She was all dressed up and looking especially beautiful. She was carrying a suitcase and stopped before the chain link fence. I walked toward her and asked, "Are you going somewhere?"

"Yes, Joseph, I am moving oversees to dance in l'Opéra National de Paris."

"What the hell is that?"

"The Paris Ballet Company."

"You're moving to Paris, France?"

"Yes. Paris, France."

"Why? Don't they have ballet companies right here in New York?"

She shook her head and looked at me as though I was the stupidest person on the planet. "My God, you really are dense. You know, there is more to life than playing basketball. One day, you are going to have to grow up."

"Yeah, but why do it now?"

She smiled as tears rolled down her cheeks and replied, "Because now is all I have."

She put her face up against the fence and we kissed. She said, "You will always be my first and only love." She turned and walked away into a vista of billowing white clouds.

I turned and walked toward center court. I threw the basketball with more power than I imagined I ever possessed against the backboard of the court facing me. The ball ricocheted back and hit me directly in the face. I fell backwards, in slow motion, as blood gushed from my mouth and nose. I landed directly in the painted center court circle and in the background I could hear The Who's "Baba O'Riley" blasting the repetitive chant, "It's a teenage wasteland, just a teenage wasteland, just a teenage wasteland, just … just … just." I looked up, dazed and confused, into the faces of the many friends I had played basketball with on this very court … Howie, Jerry, Charlie, Sal, Pete, John, Billy, Mike … and they were all laughing and waving their hands and saying, "Oh, he's okay. He's okay, just give him a moment."

I woke up with the taste of blood in my mouth. I had chomped on my tongue while dreaming. I got up out of bed and went into the room that Jennifer slept in before we got married. I picked up the picture of Sarah sitting in the hospital bed, bald from the cancer treatments, yet smiling, and I said, "I hope you are enjoying Paris, dancing with Astaire and Kelly, but most of all I wish I could have helped. Oh, I so wish I could have helped."

Chapter 40

Like I said earlier, my wife was a professional at diversion. She told me just enough about Asperger's Syndrome to send me to my computer the next day looking for more details while she and Sofia were at work. I knew a little bit about Asperger's simply because the film industry had become so reliant on technological innovations and computer simulations that the studios were now packed with computer experts, including quite a few people who were on the spectrum. It was often hinted that without Asperger's, the industry might be forced to shut down. Special effects had become such a large part of the business that the effects were literally replacing the story and characters as the most important selling points. Film purist and historians would argue differently, but the box office told the only story that movie executives were interested in: Movies with superb special effects delivered big bucks, worldwide.

I had never thought of Sofia working with special effects. Yes, she knew a lot about computers. Anytime I had a problem with a computer program, I went to her for help and she figured it all out in a matter of minutes, making her technologically inept father feel like an idiot. But like her father when it came to looking at movies and TV shows she was a purist. She liked shows that presented the viewer with a good story and great characters, such as *The Honeymooners* and *I Love Lucy*.

As I clicked around on my own computer, ignoring the latest round of revisions from Nick, I learned a lot about the condition that Jennifer and now Dr. Moore were sure Sofia had. I read that Asperger's Syndrome is a mild form of autism, and that people with Asperger's are considered to be very high-functioning. Children and adults with Asperger's have difficulty in social settings. They are slow to detect social cues, such as a friend giving you a sign to lower your voice or to stop talking so much, and they have a hard time reading irony and good-natured teasing. Children with Asperger's also tend to be physically clumsy, and are more likely to be bullied at school and on the playground. On the flip side, they regularly perform much better in school than their classmates — often to the point of being labeled young geniuses.

How had I not known more about this, or noticed any of these tendencies in Sofia? And how had it never been flagged by any of her teachers? I was sitting there getting madder and madder about this when I read a passage about the way kids learn to compensate for their condition. The site I was reading pointed out that the syndrome often goes undiagnosed, especially in children who are very good at imitating the behavior of their peers. Their gallant attempts to conform to what they see as socially normal puts them under so much pressure that they often have meltdowns, like the ones Sofia had with her grandparents.

"What's wrong, Sofia?" my mother would ask as she gingerly tried to console her by softly rubbing her neck as my father looked on.

"Nothing! Nothing!" Sofia would scream at her as she shoved my mother's hand aside, closed her eyes and covered her ears with her hands, rocking back and forth. "You don't understand. You're both so stupid. I hate the both of you!"

She would then leap up from the couch and continue, "I wish the two of you would stop visiting. Don't you understand? I hate you! I hate you! Just stop bothering me and leave us alone."

She would then run off and slam the door to her room shut and wouldn't come out for hours.

I can't think of two people who deserved this type of treatment and abuse less than my mom and dad.

And the pressure leaks out into other parts of their lives. They start to miss school and are late with homework assignments. At times, it was nearly impossible to get Sofia out of bed in the morning and get her ready for school. When she told me that she did not intend to go to college I was relieved, and when she told me she was moving out, I nearly had a heart attack. Independence often becomes a major objective for teenagers and young adults with Asperger's; in this way, they are no different than most older teenagers and young adults in society as a whole.

Sofia had become so detached and oblivious to everyone who had been a part of her life that I could not even imagine her ever getting a job or joining an acting company. But she insisted on moving out anyway, and eventually I said okay and promised her a monthly allowance that was more than most hardworking men and women make in a month. The day she left with Lawrence was like a kick in the groin. I felt like a total failure as a parent.

I was blinded by Sofia's beauty and blamed her growing detachment on what I was sure was a case of raging narcissism. Yes, I had tried to get her to see a psychiatrist, psychologist, or counselor. I had even made appointments for her, only to have her refuse to go at the last minute. Every time I tried to get help for her, she brushed aside the attempt, saying, "You just don't understand."

For someone like me, who came from a blue-collar family where both parents worked, it was very frustrating to watch my little princess descend into what looked like the worst kind of self-indulgence and outright laziness. She never had to worry about money, and I gave her everything she ever asked for, spoiling her royally, "like a good Italian father should." That phrase had rolled off my tongue so many times that I was beginning to wonder if I was a big part of Sofia's problem. At times, I felt guilty that she didn't have a mother like other children did, but I was always there for her, and sacrificed everything for her. I knew that my love for Sofia had always been unconditional. And yet, it took Jennifer to figure out what was wrong and to 'correct' my misperception of my daughter.

I could see now how Jennifer's unexpected arrival in my life would have set Sofia off. She must have felt that the one person who she could count on as truly her own, who would always have her back and always love her, might be stolen from her by this lovely blond lady. The only relationship she felt comfortable with, and over which she had any real control, was in danger of being blown to pieces by Jennifer.

Thankfully, the only victim in this unlikely scenario was a shelf in my bookcase, and out of this rubble a new family was born.

The phone rang at one o'clock and it was Jennifer. It was unusual for her to call from work, but today it did not surprise me. Her intuition was uncanny. In many ways she reminded me of my grandma, whose instincts and perceptions were developed to the point of seeming mystical to the rest of us. Without any forewarning, my grandmother was able to sense that one of her children or grandchildren was in trouble or not feeling well, and she was right almost all of the time.

Jennifer pretended that she was calling because she had some free time and just wanted to hear a loving voice and remind herself that she had someone really special waiting for her at home.

"But Sofia is there at the hospital with you," I teased.

She laughed and replied, "And now who's being a wiseass?"

"Okay, I admit it."

"That's awful big of you."

"Thank you, my beautiful and loving wife. I try to please. I'm well aware that I'm the luckiest guy in the world."

"Really? Why is that?"

"You want me to say it, don't you?"

"Yup."

"Because I'm married to you."

"Bingo! You keep this up and we might have a repeat of last night."

"I don't know about that. After all, it's Sofia's night with you."

"Just another reason why our beautiful daughter might need an added distraction in her life ... such as a boyfriend."

"Now who's being the wiseass? Remember you promised to protect our lovely daughter against all predators."

"You know, I was going out on dates when I was sixteen."

"But at sixteen, you were probably already thinking like a thirty year old."

She laughed and laughed. "No, I was thinking exactly like a sixteen year old."

"But you were probably carrying a gun in your purse."

"Yeah, but then in Kentucky it's legal and I had a permit. It's a state with an open firearm law. The NRA simply loves Kentuckians. I can take Sofia down to a shooting range and teach her how to shoot and when she's ready we can buy her a nice small handgun that will fit perfectly in her purse. That way, if anybody tries to get nasty with our little girl, she can simply shoot them."

"You are joking, right?" I asked and she laughed.

"Or we can double date. You and me and Sofia and her date."

"You know, that's a really good idea. If Sofia's date is a real gentleman without any dirty intentions, he shouldn't mind one bit. We're cool, or at least you're cool."

"Did you take your parents along on your dates?" she asked with a touch of sarcasm.

"I never went on any dates, but I doubt I would have cared if they came along. They were very cool."

"Are you telling me you never had a girlfriend?"

"No, I never had a girlfriend." And then suddenly I remembered Sarah and I felt guilty. She had become so real that I started to think of her as my teenage girlfriend. I shook my head and started to think that maybe I was the one who needed to go see a psychiatrist.

"Wait. You're serious? You never had a girlfriend?"

"You're the first. Sofia's biological mother may have lived with me in this house while she was pregnant, but it would be a real stretch to call her a girlfriend. She was more like a roommate."

"Who came yielding gifts," Jennifer remarked with a laugh.

"Yeah," I replied pensively. "The greatest gift of all, Sofia."

"I'll give you that," Jennifer said. "She's a gift to us all."

"Undeniably so," I said. "I love that child more than my own life, and if she sees the world a little differently than most, all the better. Maybe we would all benefit from seeing the world a little differently."

Chapter 41

I took a cab to the hospital and arrived early. Jennifer and Sofia had discovered a new Italian restaurant next to the hospital that was getting rave reviews from their co-workers. Sofia did not shy away from Italian restaurants as much as other places. After all, they served pizza and always had a wide variety of pastas to choose from, even if she only had her pasta with butter.

I took the elevator up to the pediatric oncology unit of the hospital and as I stepped into the hallway I was at first struck by the theme park décor. Every square foot of wall space was painted with superheroes and cartoon characters, from Captain Marvel to Bugs Bunny and at least a dozen other well-known and lesser-known figures. One long wall was taken up with a giant image of Catbus from the Japanese anime *My Neighbor Totoro*, which had been one of the only newer shows that Sofia would watch in her younger years. Apparently, studios obsessed with protecting the rights of their products were sensitive enough to the struggles of sick children to give permission to reproduce their work. And the murals were only the beginning. The whole unit felt like a kid's birthday party, with helium-filled balloons floating freely along the corridors and nurses and doctors walking around wearing silly hats, while mounted televisions in a few of the corners played children's programs.

I looked into a room and suddenly the theme park décor dissipated as I found myself facing a little girl of about four or five (it was truly hard to tell). Bald and emaciated, she stared back at me from her bed with sunken eyes. From the door to the room, where I found myself frozen, I could see that a bag of clear fluid was dripping nutrients or medication into the child's body through a catheter implanted just below her neck. Three adults and two older children huddled around her, their laughter lacking mirth and their smiles etched with anxiety. It is said that a family is never the same once a child is diagnosed with cancer, and I could feel that burden weighing on every person in the room. One of the adults, who could have been the girl's grandmother, caught my eye, and seemed to look through me. I nodded to her and kept moving down the hall.

Nurses and orderlies were moving quickly in and out of rooms, pushing carts fitted with computer screens and stocked with bandages, needles, disinfectants and other supplies. I stopped at the main desk and was met by the head nurse, who asked if she could help.

"No, thank you ... Maureen," I said, glancing at her tag. "I'm just here to see Jennifer, but I'm in no rush."

"Oh, so you're the lucky guy married to that southern belle?"

"Yes, I am undeniably the luckiest guy in the world. That is the one thing I am sure of."

Maureen pointed her head toward a room, and when I looked over, I saw Jennifer, dressed in her nurse's uniform, pulling a pair of latex gloves off her hands. She looked haggard and unsettled but at the same time more beautiful than ever. I walked up to her and said, "You take all the time you need. I'll go visit with our daughter, and we'll both see you in a bit."

I walked through a pair of swinging doors and into a different part of the pediatric oncology unit. The theme park décor continued, but this part of the unit had actual playrooms where children could gather and play with toys and games and ride motorized cars and horses. The rooms were well-used, and the children in these areas did not look nearly as sick as the girl I had seen when I first got off the elevator. I wondered if this meant that they hadn't started treatment yet, or that they were close to being released and doing well.

I stopped before a well-lit room and looked in at a girl who was sitting up in bed, laughing and giggling like any normal child. Sofia was sitting in a chair next to the girl and was teaching her how to play a video game. Sofia was also laughing and giggling, her hair pulled back in a simple ponytail.

Yes, she was my child and I was biased, but at that moment I could swear there was a halo around her head, adding to the natural glow of her olive complexion. As if to drive the point home, two ladies, each with a coffee cup from the hospital's cafeteria, stopped outside the room and looked in. The first one said, "She's like an angel. My little boy cannot stop talking about her."

Then the second lady said, "My little girl is the same. It's Sofia this and Sofia that, all day, every day! Wouldn't the world be a nicer place if there were more young people like Sofia."

I turned and walked into the nearest bathroom, opened the door to a stall, and closed the door behind me. I wept as a flood of tears rolled down my face and all I could see was an image of my Sofia, my Sofia, my beautiful, my beautiful Sofia.

Chapter 42

The girls got out so late that we decided to skip the restaurant, go home, and order pizza from our usual place like we did every night that the girls worked. Sofia had her usual two slices and talked incessantly about her day. I listened to every word as though the hidden meaning of life and our purpose for being here could be deciphered from her joyous ramblings.

She got up and went to take a shower and clean up. I stopped Jennifer, as she was just about to get up and go off to do the same. I poured her another glass of wine, leaned over her shoulder, and gently kissed her on her neck. "When was the last time I told you how very proud I am of you?"

"You tell me all the time, unless of course you think I'm having a steamy affair behind your back with my gay friend." She smiled as she took a sip of her wine and I sat down beside her and took her hand.

"I watched Sofia interacting with the children today, and you were right. She is a natural. I could not be prouder of our daughter, and I have you to thank for that." I hesitated for a moment as I looked down into Jennifer's glass of wine and said, "It didn't take you long to figure it all out, did it?"

She laughed and replied, "I'm a professional. It's my job to detect the smallest peculiarities in someone's behavior."

"Okay, Sherlock ... stop being a wiseass."

She smiled and said, "That hurts."

"What, being called Sherlock or a wiseass?"

"Being called Sherlock, of course. I see myself as more of an Inspector Clouseau or a Charlie Chan."

"Have you ever been spanked?"

"Not that I can recall. Why would you even ask such a thing? I never would have thought that *you* were into kinky behavior."

"I'm not, but at times I think it might do you a world of good."

"Like you would ever hit a girl."

I looked into her bright blue eyes, reached over and kissed her. "You can be quite infuriating at times."

"Yeah, but you love me all the same. 'Undeniably so' is what Maureen told me."

I laughed, "You girls really do talk."

"Just like you guys, and just as dirty, by the way." She laughed and then added, "You're the exception of course. I can't imagine you talking dirty. After all, how long did it take you to get up the courage to kiss me?"

"I like to think that's because I was raised to respect women."

"That's not what you originally told me. You told me it was because you were so out of practice."

"Well, that too."

"And for the record, you are progressing wonderfully."

"Thank you. And now back to the original question. How were you able to figure it all out so quickly?"

"I had an idea the very first night I met her. She felt threatened by my presence in your life and yet at times she seemed distracted and unattached from the very surroundings she was so familiar with … the very home she was raised in. She did not behave like a girl who was "in love with herself," as you had said. Believe me, I have known girls who are in love with themselves and she didn't fall into that category. When Sofia looked at her reflection in shiny objects and mirrors, it wasn't to admire herself but to reassure herself that she existed. Sofia is so unusually beautiful that it is easy to misjudge her behavior … easy to simply categorize her with the same old stereotype associated with such lovely girls."

"I imagine that's a stereotype you have had to deal with your whole life."

She looked at me as a sardonic smile curled around her lips and replied, "If you say so."

"Oh, don't give me that. Doc Hollywood wouldn't have hired you if you didn't fit the qualifications, or the costume. It's not every girl who could jump into that nurse's uniform and fill it out so perfectly."

"I kind of enjoyed playing that part, and it did have its perks. After all, I got myself a rich husband out of the deal, and now I'm driving an eighty-thousand-dollar SUV and my student loans have all been paid off."

"And don't forget your car loan."

"Oh, I haven't forgot that. And best of all, I got myself the perfect daughter and her not-so-perfect daddy who, thank goodness, is trying really hard to live up to the two perfect women in his life."

"It's not easy trying to live up to such perfection."

"No, but at least you're working at it, and I give you a solid B minus for your effort."

"Wow! How generous of you … a B minus. Sheesh."

"Well, if you keep acting like a jackass you could easily work your way down to the Cs. And whatever you do, don't get too comfortable, because behind the smiles and our charming personalities, Sofia and I are both strict disciplinarians, especially when it comes to keeping the one guy in our life on the straight and narrow." She laughed and playfully pinched my cheek. "And no amount of cute or money will get you out of the dog house."

"And just when I thought the Just Like A Man movement was dead, it seems to be making a comeback."

"I don't know where you ever got the idea that it was dead. We were just giving you a little break to adapt to the new reality, which is that you are now in the minority."

"Actually, I think I have always been in a minority. Since the day Sofia was born, it has always been either her way or the highway."

Jennifer took another sip of her wine, tapped her finger on the table and said, "Of course I wasn't positive until we went to see Jonathan and he made the diagnosis."

"And how did Sofia take the news?"

"She was relieved. It's important that children or adults suspected of having Asperger's get diagnosed. It gives them a much-needed answer, an explanation for why they feel different from others."

I sat quietly for a few moments and listened to Jennifer tapping the table. Finally, I asked, "What song are you thinking of … or is it a Jennifer original?"

"How do you know I'm thinking of a song?"

"Because of the rhythmical way you're tapping your fingers."

"The Cystals' rendition of 'Then He Kissed Me.' Maybe we should make that our song?"

"I thought it already was," she replied as she leaned over and whispered in my ear, "I love you so much" and then she kissed me.

She sat back and continued, "I really wish I would have had the opportunity to meet your parents."

"They would have loved you. That I'm sure of."

"Even though I'm a legendary wiseass?"

"In spite of it." I opened the refrigerator and took out a beer and poured the wiseass some more wine.

"Thank you, sir. I just love the way you spoil me."

I sat back down, opened my beer, took a sip and said, "Sofia's grandparents did not leave her out of their will. I was just so angry with her that I told her they did. They left her the same amount as their other grandchildren: eighty thousand dollars, on the condition that she not receive any of it until I was satisfied that her behavior had changed and that she was acting like a responsible young person. I think that day has arrived."

Jennifer took a sip of her wine and smiled. "Yes, that day has arrived…"

"But…"

"There are no buts. I think your parents would be so proud of her and it would certainly relieve Sofia of the guilt she feels about the way she treated them."

"And you have no problem with me giving her all that money?"

"I have come to terms with the way money is handled in this household. After all, didn't I let you pay off my loans?"

"Yes, I was very proud of you for letting me do that."

"Of course you were," she replied with a laugh and a shake of the head. "But that doesn't mean I won't offer our daughter wise counsel in matters concerning her finances."

"I have total faith in you, my beautiful, bargain-seeking, happy hour-loving little wise—"

"Keep it up, and you will be the one getting your butt spanked."

Sofia walked into the kitchen, dressed in her pajamas and her wet hair combed back away from her face. Jennifer remarked, "Wow! Someone smells really nice and clean."

Sofia sat down and smiled at Jennifer and replied, "I started using the shampoo and conditioner you bought for me. I love the way it smells."

"I thought you might like them," Jennifer said. She finished off her glass of wine, stood up, and kissed Sofia. "And now it's time for me to clean up. You stay here and talk with your daddy."

Jennifer left as I reached over and gently took my daughter's hand. "Jennifer tells me that all the male doctors are in love with you."

"They like talking to me and I am very nice to them."

"Have any of them asked you to go out on a date?"

"Yes," she replied as she lowered her eyes and then after a long pause she continued, "I would never go out with any of them because none of them are like you, Daddy. I would never go out with a man unless he was just like you."

I was ready to give her some wise, fatherly advice and then I simply decided to let the compliment sink in and cherish the fact that my daughter thought so highly of her father. I simply replied, "That is very sweet of you to say, Sofia. Thank you."

"You're welcome. Jennifer tells them that I am way too young to be dating anyone."

"And I'm sure they listen to Jennifer."

"Yes, Daddy."

"I watched you today, working with the children."

"I love the children."

"I could tell, and it was easy to see that they love you back. Your grandma and grandpa are very proud of you."

Her eyes grew wide and I reached over and lifted her chin up. "I had a dream about your grandparents and they told me how proud they are of you and how much they love you. Remember when I told you that they left you nothing in their will?"

"Yes."

"I sort of told you a lie. They left you eighty thousand dollars but on the condition that I not give it to you until they gave me a sign that they thought you deserved the money. Well, in the dream they said it was time to give you the money."

It was like a burden was lifted off her shoulders … an affliction not of her making, not of her fault. At any moment I expected her to spread her wings, the wings not of a bird but of an angel, and fly away. I quickly placed my hands over hers and held her down because it was I who needed her, my lovely guardian angel, more than ever … forever in my life.

Later that night I sat on the couch in the living room, eating popcorn, drinking an ice-cold beer, and looking at *The Honeymooners*. Sofia sat down beside me and handed me a computer printout of the New York Knicks schedule for the upcoming year, which was going to start very shortly.

"Have you changed your mind about the Knicks?"

"Yes, Daddy, I have. I will be rooting for the Knicks like I do every year. Jennifer explained to me that the Kentucky Wildcats were a college team, and so my rooting for them would not interfere with my rooting for the Knicks, who are a professional team. She also said that she was quite certain that the brilliant Wildcats would have little problem beating the hapless Knicks."

"Did she really say that?"

"Yes, exactly that. And she told me not to forget to tell you."

I swear I could hear my wife laughing from Sofia's room, but I knew better than to get into an argument with the Bluegrass beauty. Besides, she might be right. Sofia picked at my popcorn.

"So we will be watching the games together like we do every year?"

"Yes, like every year, while eating popcorn."

"I have a strong feeling that the Knicks are going to be really good this year," I ventured.

"That's what you say every year."

"But this year, I really believe they are going to turn it around."

"Yes, Daddy, that's what you say every year and they keep on losing and you keep on yelling at the TV."

"It's not like they lose *every* game."

"No team loses every game."

"Well, I refuse to give up hope before the season even begins."

"Yes, Daddy," she said as she placed her head on my shoulder, picked at the popcorn, and watched *The Honeymooners*. After a few minutes, she was asleep, and her soft, clear breathing was like a soothing musical composition and at that moment I could not imagine life ever being any better.

Chapter 43

I leaned back in my chair as a shaft of sunlight passed through the blinds over the window in my study. I could feel a pleasurable nap coming on as I closed my eyes, and as I lingered between that empty space just before falling asleep my phone rang. I was tempted not to answer the phone and just listen to the message when I woke up but my hand reached out and I picked it up.

I didn't recognize the voice on the phone. The person was whispering, and at first I thought I might still be asleep and dreaming.

"Joe, It's me, Joshua."

"I'm sorry," I said. "Who is this?"

"It's Dr. Souter. Joshua Souter."

No, I wasn't dreaming, but this had all the makings of a nightmare.

"Doc … um, how are you? Are you out on bail?"

"No, I was denied bail but it's all worked out for the better. I'm going to be a father. Remember that night I told you about … the night I had sex with my wife and her girlfriend."

I felt like saying, "Yeah, the night you drugged your wife and her girlfriend and then raped them." But I couldn't say that. It just wasn't my style. So I said, "Congratulations!" and then immediately felt a little sick.

"Thanks! The girlfriend is the one having the baby. I thought for sure she was going to have an abortion, but she's one of those gentiles like you and actually believes it's a sin to kill a fetus."

"Wow! That's really … amazing. Do you know the sex of the baby, yet?"

"I don't know, but am fairly certain she knows. She came to visit me at the jail to tell me the happy news and then she went on a rant, swearing that it would be a cold day in hell before I ever got to see the child … that I was the devil incarnate and that once the child was born she would have a priest perform an exorcism, even before having it baptized."

Yes, this was a nightmare in real time, and it only had the potential to get worse.

"It's better this way. It's not like I would be able to spend any quality time with the child anyway. Once I was denied bail, I made it easy and simply pleaded guilty and was given twenty years. No trial, none of that headache to deal with, and just the thought of not having to see that treacherous infidel of a wife during the trial was worth the extra five years the judge added to my sentence. Believe me, Joe, it's not bad in here at all. Actually, I love it. For the first time in my life I feel loved. I feel like the stud I always imagined myself to be. I've had all the hair removed from my body and my skin is as soft and silky as one of those sweet young babes you see in commercials. I'm glamorous!"

"Glamorous!" I repeated and then for good measure I repeated it again. "Glamorous! That's really wonderful."

"I never realized the amount of time and effort that goes into being glamorous, the one that everyone desires."

The last I remember of him, that frightful day in his office before he was arrested, was that he was a short, overweight, balding man in his mid-fifties whose wife refused to have sex with him and had left him for another woman. Now, in addition to being a convicted two-time rapist whose second victim was going to give birth to his child, he was suddenly glamorous — an irresistible stud in a sea of sex-starved inmates. I guess it really is true what they say about prison, that "it changes a man."

"I have a favor to ask of you, buddy," he said, to my dismay. After all, why else would he be calling me from prison where he couldn't possibly use the Academy Award tickets I had given him every year for the last fifteen years?

"And what might that be?" I asked.

"It's just a small favor. Do you think you can pick me up three pieces of lingerie … one in red, pink, and white … and a couple of different shades of lipstick and maybe a little mascara?"

"Lingerie?" I repeated, hoping my tone of voice would convey how unlikely I was to visit a women's boutique and ask for lingerie … but apparently he didn't pick up on my nuance.

"Yes, Joe, lingerie. Surely, you know what lingerie is … a big showbiz guy like you?"

"Yes, I know what lingerie is, it's just that I have never had another guy ask me to pick it up for him."

"Circumstances change. There's a lovely boutique right there in Studio City where you live, next to the bookstore. I would like one in red, pink, and white, and please none of that cheap shit. You have a lot of money. Splurge a little for your old buddy."

The nerve of this guy, using a phrase I only associated with my lovely daughter. Just the thought of him being within a thousand yards of my daughter was enough to make me want to strangle the pervert, but since I was only on the phone with him, I simply took down his measurements.

"And how am I supposed to get all this stuff to you?"

"Just leave it at the front desk of the prison, in care of Big Bubba Jones. He's my main squeeze, if you know what I mean."

I mean, what was I supposed to do? What choice did I have? I was just happy that there wasn't going to be a trial and I wasn't going to be called in as a character witness. In a strange sense, I was happy for him; he had discovered love … sure it was in prison, but then where does it say that all love affairs have to start an hour before closing, sitting on two bar stools, in an upscale, overpriced bar in Beverly Hills? Besides, it was Big Bubba's birthday.

I typed out the list of everything the pervert wanted, got into Sofia's car, and drove to the boutique. I entered the store and was immediately approached by a well-dressed, smiling, Michelle Pfeiffer lookalike, whose first name just happened to be Michelle. I handed Michelle the list, along with my American Express Centurion Card and fifty dollars, and asked her if she could pick out all the stuff on the list and pack it in a shipping box and that I would be back in like a half hour to pick it up. I made it perfectly clear to her to pick out medium-price attire and cosmetics, nothing super expensive like that jackass wanted me to buy. The audacity of that man, saying, "You have a lot of money. Splurge a bit for your old buddy."

Michelle walked behind the counter as she looked down at the list, and just as I was about to walk out of the store, she called me back. "Just a few quick questions," she said as I turned back and looked at her and the other ten or so women in the store.

"Would you like stockings to go with the lingerie?"

"Sure, if that's what usually goes with lingerie," I replied as I suddenly got the feeling that I was being watched by every single woman in the store.

"And do you have a preference on the different shades of the red, pink, and white lingerie?"

"Whatever shade of those colors you like would be absolutely great," I replied, as I once again headed toward the door.

"Just one more question," lovely Michelle said as she pointed the pencil she was holding in my direction.

"Yes, and what might that be?" I asked.

"Can you just tell me the skin color of the lady that you are buying this attire for … fair, golden, dark? It makes it easier when it comes to picking out the correct makeup."

"The skin color…" I repeated in a much louder voice. "Why don't I just give you a description of the person? The last time I saw him, he was an ugly, middle-aged, overweight, short man with a very pasty complexion. Does that answer your question?"

"Yes," she replied as she looked down and pretended to write.

"Anything else, Michelle?"

She shook her head, gathered herself, looked up, smiled, and replied, "No, I'll have it all ready for you in half an hour."

"Thank you," I said, as I looked across at all the women in the store who immediately dropped their eyes and pretended to be shopping. I stepped out of the store and walked to the corner and entered a sporting goods store that carried the jerseys of all the professional teams (and yes, that did include the New York Knicks), as well as caps and sweatshirts. I bought four new Knicks caps in the hope that this might bring them some much needed luck. One was for my lovely daughter, one was for the wiseass, one was for me, and one was for Lawrence, who always watched the games with us. I then went one step further and bought three Knicks sweatshirts. They didn't have one in Lawrence's size.

I walked back to the boutique and Michelle had the entire package ready for me. I tipped her an additional fifty dollars because I felt lousy for getting testy with her before. I signed the credit receipt and addressed the package to Big Bubba Jones, prisoner 3458.

Michelle escorted me to the front door, all smiles, and wished me a wonderful day. Money can quickly heal hurt feelings, especially in a town like this one, where emotions are about as real as costume jewelry. The whole package cost me four hundred and fifty dollars. It wasn't bad enough that for over twenty years he was overcharging my insurance and leaving me to pay higher deductibles, but now from behind bars he was costing me even more. I dropped the package off at the jail and drove straight home, stopping at our mailbox for a moment to pick up the mail and then parking Sofia's car in the same spot it had been in since Jennifer moved in.

Jennifer had received a small package. The words "handle with care" appeared in big block letters on the front and sides. I placed the package on the kitchen table so I wouldn't forget to give it to her. I then made myself two peanut butter and jelly sandwiches and washed them down with a few ice-cold beers. The whole time reminding myself: "Never, but never, answer the phone without first looking at the display and seeing who is calling. Never!"

The girls arrived home from work at about seven o'clock, which was early for them. I had the pizza placed in the middle of the table with three plates around it and a glass of ginger ale for Sofia and a glass of white wine for the wife.

Jennifer asked, "So how was your day, dear?"

"The usual, sweetheart."

"So … a few hours of writing? Maybe a conversation with Lawrence? And drinking a few beers while watching your favorite TV shows?"

"Yeah, sort of like that. No one ever said a writer's life was easy."

She laughed and asked, "So are you and Nick finished with the revisions?"

"Yes and no. For the moment we are finished with the revisions, but for the first time in years I will be on the set for most of the shoot, and after that I'll also be in the editing room with Nick and our chief editor. The dialogue on this film is quite tricky, so I'm expecting revisions to the script throughout the entire process."

"Maybe Sofia and I can come down one day to visit you on the set and see how the magic is made?"

"That would be great. When Sofia was just a child, she used to visit the sets on some of our earlier movies. Remember that, sweetheart?"

"Yes," Sofia replied, between bites of pizza.

"Sofia is the only other person besides Nick to have ever sat in his director's chair."

"Wow!" Jennifer exclaimed. "That's some honor."

"Yes, Nick is very nice and he's always loved me. Right, Daddy?"

"Yes, angel," I replied as I looked across at Jennifer who was smiling at Sofia.

Jennifer reached over and picked up the package she'd received in the mail. She opened it and pulled out a letter, and as she read it, her face suddenly began to turn pale and ashen, and her breathing became labored. She stuffed the letter back in the package and pulled out a small stack of photos. After glancing at them for a second, she suddenly sat up and ran toward the kitchen sink. As I stood up to see if I could help, she slipped and fell to the floor, where she started to vomit violently, the retching of a poison buried deep inside and always present.

Sofia moved toward her but I stopped her. I looked quickly down at the dropped photos and saw that they were all of Sarah getting ready to go to the prom. I stepped toward Jennifer as she spewed up the last of the vomit. She placed her head down on the floor and started to cry uncontrollably like a sick kitten. The floor was covered in vomit, as was Jennifer.

I kneeled next to her and put my hand on her shoulder, but she pushed me away and said "I'll be okay." She looked across at the floor, smiled at Sofia, and said, "My God, I have made such a mess." She tried to stand up, wobbled, and before she fell back down I managed to catch her.

This seemed to almost annoy her, and she tried to push me away again, saying, "I'm fine. I'm okay."

"I think you'll have to agree that there is some evidence to the contrary here," I said, trying to keep my tone light.

She barely laughed, and dropped her head down as she rested her hands on her knees and looked up at me. "It's not just your job to be the one always helping and lending support. It's all our jobs. We're a family."

I moved toward her, put my arms around her, and felt her body relax. I picked her up, carried her into our bathroom, and gently lowered her onto the toilet seat. Then I helped remove her soiled clothes, and placed them into a laundry bag. "I'm going to throw these out and we can go shopping tomorrow."

She snapped at me and said, "Don't you dare. All they need is to be washed." I smiled, knowing with that remark that she was at least feeling a little better. I left her alone to clean up and walked back out toward the kitchen where I nearly fainted at the sight of Sofia cleaning up the vomit and spraying the area with a pine-scented cleaner like a real professional. Then it struck me like a thunderbolt. This had become a normal chore for my daughter, especially after a child had chemo.

She took the plastic bag full of dirty rags out to the trash, then came back in and washed her hands and said, "I'm going to check on Jennifer."

She started to walk toward the bedroom and I said, "Thank you, sweetheart."

She turned, smiled, and said, "You're welcome, Daddy."

You often hear people say that there isn't much difference between make-believe and real life, but as someone who has made a fortune writing make-believe, I can honestly tell you that there is a major difference. In all my life as a writer I have never cared for really sick children or been in a position to help them feel better. I've certainly never held the hands of a sick child just before they died. Jennifer, and now Sofia, occupied a world apart from mine, and I would just have to do my best to keep up.

Chapter 44

And just like that, another basketball season was upon us. My New York Knicks were off to a fabulous start, winning their first game. It was a hotly contested game, especially after my Knicks blew a twenty-point lead, but like true champs they held on and pulled it out. My two girls sat on either side of me throughout the game, wearing matching Knicks attire, while Lawrence sat next to Sofia, sporting his Knicks cap and looking handsome as usual, if a little less scholarly. I pretended not to notice as Jennifer wiggled uncomfortably in the expensive Knicks sweatshirt I bought for her.

After the final buzzer sounded and the win was safely in the books, I turned to my daughter and kissed her on her cheek and said, "You see, I told you this year was going to be different."

"Yes, Daddy, that's what you said last year after they won their first game, right before they went on to lose seven in a row."

My daughter had this amazing memory when it came to certain things, such as statistics, win/loss percentages, shooting percentages and the odds of a certain team making the playoffs. She would have made a wonderful bookie. For once, however, I wished she had kept her mathematical expertise and superb memory out of the conversation and just enjoyed this joyous moment. It was like she was deliberately placing a jinx on our team.

One month later and eleven games into the season, my Knicks still had not won their second game. The wife conveniently lost her Knicks sweatshirt and gave up her place on the couch, and after every loss, she was quick to remind us that the college basketball season was just around the corner. Lawrence went back to wearing his fedora. At least my daughter remained loyal, picking at the bowl of popcorn, and suffering through one loss after another with her daddy.

My grief over the dismal Knicks start was alleviated by the joy and happiness of the holiday season. This was a year when I had a lot to be thankful for … with Jennifer in my life and with Sofia back at home and thriving like never before, I was often reminded of the phrase, *my cup runneth over.* We decided to celebrate Thanksgiving the Wednesday before the holiday because the girls were working on Thanksgiving day. Jennifer cooked a traditional Thanksgiving dinner: turkey, stuffing, macaroni and cheese, and her mother's special, oyster casserole. Naturally, we also ordered a pizza to go with this feast. Unbeknownst to me, Sofia invited Nick and he accepted. I never would have thought of inviting my partner, simply because he was Australian and he found this particular American holiday nauseating. But since his godchild invited him, he just didn't have it in him to say no to her, whereas an invitation from me would have had him laughing hysterically before saying no.

When I asked Jennifer if she knew about Nick she replied, "Of course." And when I asked her why she didn't tell me, she said, "Oh, I forgot. Just like you forgot to tell your closest friend in the world that you got married, even though you have talked to him every day for the last three months. What, are you ashamed of me?" She laughed as she slapped the kitchen towel across my butt and said, "And now let me go change into my hillbilly overalls." I followed the wiseass into the bedroom.

Sofia was so popular at the hospital, not only with the children and their parents but also with every male employee, married and unmarried, that the administrator offered her a job. They were afraid to lose her. When she went to the administrator's office to talk about the offer, she politely told the gentleman that they didn't need to pay her because her daddy had a lot of money. Five minutes later, Jennifer took our lovely daughter by the hand and marched her right back into the administrator's office and explained the apparent misunderstanding. "Yes, she was thrilled to have the job, and naturally, she would be happy to receive a regular salary."

The administrator agreed, and arranged for her to start at eighteen dollars an hour with full benefits. Jennifer explained to our daughter that neither the children nor their parents would look upon her differently if she got paid, and that while it was wonderful that she volunteered, she deserved to be paid like everyone else, especially since she had proved herself so valuable an employee. She had also started taking counseling classes, with Jennifer, which the hospital offered.

Jennifer, dirty from cooking all morning, started taking off her clothes. I asked, "What's going on at the hospital with all these guys hitting on our daughter?"

"Seriously, Joe, are you that removed from the real world? Our daughter is gorgeous. I would be more shocked if they weren't trying to hit on her. But she has handled the situation wonderfully, without hurting anyone's feelings, and making it perfectly clear that she is not ready to date anyone."

"I just worry about her. I don't want her to get overwhelmed."

"She's much more mature than you give her credit for, and she is in a really good place right now."

"Thanks to you," I said, as Jennifer turned the water on in the shower.

"Your encouragement and support make such a difference, and I wouldn't worry about any guys taking advantage of her. She's told me she is interested in only one type of guy, a guy just like her daddy, and I can attest to the fact that guys like her daddy are one in a million." She winked at me as she stepped into the shower and behind the curtain.

I pulled the curtain slightly back and looked at my dripping wet wife and said, "And I can attest to the fact that her mommy is one in a billion." She laughed and laughed.

Chapter 45

I watched as Nick got out the back seat of his limousine and breathed a sigh of relief when no one else emerged from the back seat. The only girls Nick dated when he was in the process of making a film were five-thousand-dollar-a-night call girls. The girls were usually way prettier than any actresses you saw on screen and undeniably more intelligent than many of them, but it would have seemed a little odd to bring a call girl as a date to Thanksgiving dinner. Besides, it was Sofia who had invited him, and when it came to his godchild he was always on his best behavior.

Nick could be quite charming, and at six feet four inches, he was an imposing figure. He was ruggedly good looking, solidly built, and with shoulder-length wavy blond hair, he could easily pass for a Viking. His laugh was infectious and as long as the conversation didn't turn to movies and the world of entertainment, he was delightful. At least I did not have to worry about that problem when it came to my wife, who I was quite certain had never seen *Gone with the Wind*.

He bought a beautiful boutique of flowers for Jennifer and a box of Godiva chocolates for Sofia, with an envelope attached to the box, and one could only imagine how much money was inside the envelope. I'm sure Jennifer caught sight of the envelope, even as she was thanking Nick profusely for the lovely flowers. The eighty thousand dollars Sofia received from her grandparents was put into a long-term CD at the bank. Mommy convinced her daughter that her grandparents, who were so proud of her, would be over-the-top proud if she used the money wisely, and that for the moment, putting it into a long-term CD would be a very wise thing to do. Sofia was more than happy to follow Jennifer's guidance, and made sure to tell

Grandma and Grandpa about it in her next round of prayers. Jennifer also had Sofia's paychecks deposited automatically into her savings account, which is where I am quite sure the money in the envelope Nick gave her would also be going.

I handed Nick a large glass of white wine, and then Sofia sat right next to him on the living room couch. She told him everything she was doing at the hospital, about the children, and about how the parents loved her, and how the administrator of the hospital gave her a paying job. She apologized if she repeated herself and Nick assured her that she could repeat herself to the end of time and he would never get tired of listening to her. The entire time Sofia was talking to him, Nick's focus never shifted, and his eyes stayed glued on his lovely godchild. I could see Jennifer watching the two of them from the kitchen with a smile on her face a mile wide. It was easy to see that in the short time Nick had been there, any doubts or concerns about the big Aussie had dissipated and he had won even her over.

Days before Thanksgiving, Jennifer had made it clear that we would eat our meal in the dining room. I had to be reminded that we even had a dining room; Sofia and I had probably eaten in there three times during the past eighteen years. I tried to tell Jennifer that it didn't matter where we ate, but she was adamant that we needed to set a proper table. Apparently in the south you could be dirt poor, but when it came to entertaining friends and relatives, every family had a formal dining set to show off to their guests. Since I had no quality silverware, fancy napkins, or place settings, and since the few tablecloths we had were either mottled or too informal for the occasion, that gave Jennifer and Sofia an excuse to go out shopping for a respectable dining set for the few times when we might have guests.

The girls had gone shopping a few days before our planned meal, to make sure they had everything in hand. They left at nine in the morning and returned nine hours later. Who would have thought that buying a formal dining set, napkins, and a tablecloth could take up so much time? They'd returned home with shopping bags stuffed full of utensils, glasses for water and glasses for wine, cloth and paper napkins, two tablecloths, one white linen and the other an elaborate paisley design, and a woven gold runner with tassles at either end. Jennifer asked me how much I thought it all cost, and off the top of my head, looking at the sheer volume of what they purchased, I guessed that they'd spent about twenty-five hundred dollars. She laughed and rolled her eyes at Sofia and said, "Just like a man. Clueless. Happy to eat with plastic knives, forks, and paper napkins for the rest of their lives."

"Yes, just like a man," my lovely daughter repeated, as if she knew anything about formal dining before going shopping with Jennifer that day. The final cost for all of this wonderful dining ware was $187.30, according to Sofia's calculations. Also, according to her calculations, they saved $3,345. They visited ten thrift stores, but the savings was worth it, and now they were exhausted and it was left to me to polish all the silverware and clean all the glasses and plates.

Now that the day of our celebration had arrived and the table was decked out with dinner and salad plates, chargers, shining silverware and beautiful crystal glasses, all on top of the white tablecloth with the gold runner, I had to admit that they had done an amazing job.

Sofia went into the kitchen to help Jennifer, while Nick and I stayed behind on the couch with a bottle of wine before him and a beer in my hand.

"I was surprised to hear that you were coming to Thanksgiving dinner, and then I realized that if it was me who invited you, and not Sofia, you would have laughed and said no thanks."

"That's exactly right. What can I say? Sofia is the only girl that I have allowed to twirl me around her little pinky and mold me like a piece of putty. I cannot even begin to tell you how proud I am of her."

"Sofia sees the world differently."

"Of course she sees the world differently; otherwise, with a face like hers she would have already been on the cover of every teen magazine."

"I like to think I had a little to do with that."

"You had everything to do with that. Sure, Sofia sees the world differently, but without your love and support, things could have turned out drastically different." Nick picked up the bottle and refilled his glass.

"Jennifer has been a godsend."

"Apparently so. The way Sofia talked about her I was expecting Florence Nightingale…"

"With or without the southern accent?"

"Without, and definitely nowhere near as beautiful. Maybe I should choose a girl from down south to be my next wife. Does Jennifer have a sister?"

"No, she's an only child, but she does have some beautiful female friends she worked with back in Kentucky."

"Nurses, like her?"

"All nurses, working in the pediatric oncology department that Jennifer worked in."

"Is that so. Wow! What a difference it would be to be married to a woman whose job it was to save lives. To be married to a lady whose top priority in life is not her face, or her weight, or the color of her hair, but the happiness and wellbeing of little children who are facing the toughest challenges that anyone can face. A professional whose job each day was to give new life and meaning and hope … a future … not only to the child but to the child's whole family." Nick lowered his head and looked sadly into his glass of wine.

"It takes a certain type of person," I said somewhat feebly, unsure where this conversation was heading.

"It takes a really strong person, someone who sees the world and their place in it differently, like Sofia and your wife." He took a large gulp of wine and laughed, "Wow! You are really screwed, Joe. You already had one strong, independent young woman in your life, and now you have two! You're not going to have anyone to listen to your silly complaints, let alone show you any sympathy, especially after what those two courageous women see and have to deal with every day. It's a good thing you are going to be spending a lot more time on the set of this movie. At least on the set, you will have a whole crew to bitch and sympathize with."

And on that note, the two strong and independent women summoned Nick and me to the dining room. The table looked marvelous, fit for a queen and her entourage. Truly amazing, what a money-conscious wife and daughter can buy for $187.30. My mother would be so proud. The turkey was all carved and the side dishes were arranged around the bird. Even the pizza, which was delivered in a box, was set on a silver platter and the box tossed in the garbage. Jennifer asked, "Would anyone like to say a few words of thanksgiving?"

There was a long, awkward silence and then to everyone's surprise, it was Sofia who spoke up.

"Yes, I would." She made the sign of the cross and continued. "I want to thank God for bringing Jennifer into our lives and for giving me a mommy." I looked at Jennifer who was trying desperately not to cry. Whereas she might be strong, she was putty in her daughter's hand, and it didn't take long for the tears to start rolling down her face. Sofia looked at her and smiled before continuing. "I want to thank God for giving me the very best daddy in the world, and the very best godfather. And I want to thank God for giving me a chance to help sick children, because it hurts to see children suffering and it makes me happy to know I am helping to make them feel better. And I hope my grandma and grandpa are having a very happy Thanksgiving in Heaven. That's all."

Nick broke the silence by reaching over and kissing Sofia on the forehead and saying, "That was lovely, sweetheart."

"Thank you," Sofia replied. Jennifer excused herself and told us not to wait because she would be a few minutes, so we didn't. Sofia grabbed a slice of pizza, Nick chose a turkey leg, dressing, and some of the side dishes, and I filled my plate with white meat, dressing, and a slice of pizza. Like my daughter, I couldn't resist Italian food, even on this most American of Holidays.

Jennifer returned, looking refreshed and as beautiful as ever, and sat back down. I poured her a glass of white wine as she served herself a little of everything, including a slice of pizza.

Nick turned to Jennifer and said, "I just recently finished reading Siddhartha Mukherjee's *The Emperor of all Maladies: A Biography of Cancer*. Have you had a chance to read it?"

"Yes, it's a wonderful book," Jennifer replied as she took a sip of wine.

"Yes, I thought it was especially enlightening and I was very impressed with his ability to keep it simple. It's not like you had to be in the medical profession to understand the terminology or the concepts."

"I think that is the real beauty of the book and why it has enjoyed such widespread appeal. These days you would be hard pressed to find a person who has not had a family member or friend affected by the disease."

Nick and Jennifer carried on this conversation throughout most of the dinner and Sofia listened with rapt attention while I listened with disbelief. Like most great directors, Nick is exceptionally intelligent and well-read, but his knowledge of all the different types of cancer, the treatments available, the drug trials, and the misinformation put out there by tobacco companies and manufactures was astonishing. He went toe-to-toe with my wife on a number of topics, including differences of opinion within the oncology community about research and treatment options, and I could sense that Jennifer was impressed.

It wasn't until dessert was served that the topic changed from cancer to Jennifer's beautiful girlfriends back in Kentucky. Jennifer promised that once the movie we were working on was finished, she would invite a number of her friends up from Kentucky and they would all go out. She just worried that he wouldn't find them very interesting. They really didn't know much about the entertainment business and their jobs were all-consuming. Nick said that was exactly the type of woman he would be most interested in meeting, and that he could only hope they spoke with the same southern accent she spoke with.

"Oh, he didn't have to worry about that. They made her sound like she was from New York City."

Nick left shortly after dessert but not without first speaking alone, by the pool, with his favorite girl of all, Sofia.

Later in the evening as I watched my wife go through her regular ritual of cleaning her teeth, she mused about our first dinner with Nick. "I was quite impressed with him. I was expecting a much different person. Has he ever talked to you about cancer?"

"If he has, he certainly didn't go into the same depth he did with you. I remember he used to joke with Sofia about making her the next Sophia Loren, but in private he was appalled by the prospect that she would ever go into show business. He only said those things because he thought she wanted to become an actress. He is so proud and happy that she has chosen the path she has."

"Usually someone who knows that much about cancer has either suffered from the disease himself, or has had a close family member affected by the disease."

"He's never mentioned anything like that to me, and since he has never had any children of his own, I don't know of any contact, if any, that he has had with children who have had cancer."

Jennifer rinsed her mouth and smiled. "I surely hope you are learning something by watching me every night cleaning my teeth."

"Yeah, I've learned that you are an obsessive-compulsive when it comes to your teeth or for that matter anything you love and care for deeply."

She threw her arms around me and remarked, "Kiss me, and honestly tell me if you have ever kissed a girl with cleaner breath or nicer teeth?"

"Well, in all fairness, you are the only girl I have kissed in eighteen years, but I can't imagine a mouth tasting any better than yours. In fact, I still can't believe I am married to such a wonderful, beautiful, and minty-fresh creature."

"Okay, enough with the sweet talk, even if you are funny. I cried my eyes out after the beautiful words our daughter said about me at dinner. Please, no more crying for me tonight."

"You did manage to get hold of that envelope Nick gave Sofia with the chocolates?"

"You bet your life I did. Into the savings account it will go. Not only is she the most beautiful and loving creature out there, but also I intend on making her the most responsible young lady possible."

"A carbon copy of yourself?"

"And is there anything wrong with that?" she asked as she laughed.

"Not a thing," I replied as I kissed the girl with the cleanest mouth in town.

Chapter 46

The hospital had its annual Christmas Party for the children, their parents, and the staff early in December. Santa Claus flew in for the occasion and handed out gifts to all the inpatient and outpatient children. For the children who could not get out of bed, or had chemo or radiation that day, Santa made a special trip to their rooms. And for the children whose immune systems were severely compromised because of intensive chemo treatment, Santa had to don a gown and mask to protect them from infection. The staff and parents all had to do the same. A mother could not so much as hug or kiss their child during this period.

Jennifer and Sofia came home early on the day of the party. The party was in the early afternoon, and since the girls were off that day, they were home by mid-afternoon. Sofia came into my study and pulled up a chair beside me. I asked her if she had a good time and she replied, "I had a wonderful time and the children were all very happy."

"And did Santa give you a gift?"

"No, Daddy, the gifts were all for the children."

"Not even a bag of popcorn?"

"We have all the popcorn we need right here at home. I don't need any gifts. I only wish the party was closer to Christmas, not three weeks away."

She lowered her eyes and bowed her head and I reached under her chin and lifted her head. As I looked into those big brown eyes, I immediately knew it was going to cost me money. Amazingly, I even guessed what it was about. Anticipating the question, I suggested that she could have a Christmas Party at the house and invite whomever she wanted. She kissed me on the cheek and ran off. A few moments later, my wife appeared with a big grin on her face and said, "Heard we're having a party. How exciting! Eggnog and rum, mistletoes and kissing."

"I figured we could use the money that Nick gave Sofia for Thanksgiving to pay for the party."

She walked over to me and sat down on the chair just vacated by our daughter and said, "That is such a bad idea."

"Is that so," I said, as she laid her head across my lap and looked up at me with her big blue eyes and a hurt expression.

"Are you actually trying to sabotage my efforts to train our daughter to be a responsible young adult?"

"No, I'm trying to teach our daughter responsibility. She wants to have the party and she has quite a stash in the bank and the responsible thing for her to do is pay for the party she so desperately wants."

"No! No! No!" she replied and with a wave of the hand dismissed my stupid idea. "The responsible thing to do is for her daddy to pay for the party and show her how much he appreciates all the hard and unselfish work she has put in to help ailing little children. That's what a responsible, rich parent would do."

"And how about the responsible, rich mommy?"

"You don't see me making claims to any of your fortune. In fact, I would say that I have increased that fortune by spending money wisely, not with the blatant disregard to which you are accustomed."

"You have all the answers, don't you?"

"I like to think so," she replied.

Chapter 47

My lovely daughter spent the better part of two days on her computer, researching ways to transform the house into a Christmas wonderland. The pool was drained of water and in its place stood a twenty-foot Christmas tree. I must admit the smell of fresh pine is invigorating. Fake snow was spread across the entire bottom of the pool. Santa's house, aka the pool, was bigger than my first apartment after moving to Los Angeles, and it was filled with so many gifts for the children that they might still be opening them until next Christmas … or not. A reliable Santa Claus was hired — the same one who visited the children at the hospital — and my daughter told Mr. Claus that if she smelled so much as a tinge of alcohol on his breath she would kick him back to the North Pole.

The Christmas tree was decorated with more lights and ornaments than any tree I have seen besides the one at Rockefeller Center. Sofia had individual, custom-made ornaments for each child, each one laser-printed with a picture of the child sitting on the lap of a miniature Santa Claus.

The inside of the house was decorated with four six-foot Christmas trees, and Jennifer saw to it that a mistletoe hung from the top of every door frame. Even the bathrooms were decorated with elves and garland and miniature Christmas trees.

The outside of the house was so lit up that you would have sworn that it was a movie set. There was no need to give the guests the address of the house; guests were given the street name and told to look for the house with a million lights, and if they still couldn't find it, to look up in the sky and the blinking star of Bethlehem, above the house, would lead them right to our door.

The one contribution I made to this wonderful wonderland that my daughter designed was setting up a fully stocked bar, with plenty of Jennifer's apparently world-famous eggnog and rum (since this was our first Christmas together, I had to get up to speed on her fame in this area). I hired my old friend Fernando from the Smoke House Restaurant to tend bar. I'd known him for twenty years, ever since Nick and I would go after work to the restaurant–for drinks and dinner. I knew I could trust him to keep the parents of the children happy, but not too happy.

Before any guests arrived, I took my beautiful wife on a tour of every doorway in house that a mistletoe hung from, and I had the pleasure of kissing the most perfect wife in the world a grand total of eight times. Then I realized that we had enough time for a second go around, and I got eight more. One needs to take advantage of such opportunities.

Sofia stood by the front door ready to greet the guests as they arrived. When I noticed that she was nervously clenching her hands, I took her aside and told her that I thought it would be better if Jennifer greeted the guests. I reasoned that if the little children saw her as soon as they got to the house, they would want to stay with her, and they wouldn't get to enjoy all the festivities and games she had set up for them. Jennifer readily agreed to take over, and just like that, Sofia relaxed. I then took her on the same tour as Jennifer and got eight kisses on the cheek from my very special and beautiful daughter.

The guests started arriving and from the way Jennifer was greeting everyone I could not help but feel that my wife had dipped her glass into the eggnog a few times already. She was naturally warm and charming, but there was an extra degree of perkiness in her greetings that made me slightly suspicious and a bit jealous.

The children, at least a dozen in total, slid away from their parents at the first opportunity, and when I looked outside I saw a gang of bald-headed children, with smiles a mile wide, following my daughter, dancing and singing ... and never in my life did I hear a group of children sing so poorly, so out of tune, and yet sound so heavenly.

I sat at the bar after most of the guests had arrived and talked to Fernando about basketball. He was an LA Lakers fan, and like my New York Knicks, they weren't faring so well this year. But I was quick to remind him that my team had not won a championship in nearly forty-five years, whereas his team had won about a dozen championships ... so I had very little sympathy for his team's less-than-stellar year. I was a 'long suffering fan,' whereas he was suffering through one bad year.

I observed the guests, many of whom I had previously met while visiting the hospital. Strange, how different individuals look when you see them dressed in regular clothes and not in the uniforms you are used to seeing them wear at work. Many of the nurses and orderlies I had met on a number of occasions I had trouble remembering, but thankfully my wife was quick to toss me helpful hints.

Jennifer introduced me to her friend and psychiatrist, Dr. Jonathan, who was there with his husband, Bruce. Jennifer was right: I had nothing to worry about. They were both very nice and Jonathan was quick to tell me that my daughter was not only special, but also quite likely the most gorgeous young lady he had ever seen. I felt like asking him if there was any chance that he got her diagnosis wrong. The way I understood it, people with Asperger's Syndrome were socially awkward, but my daughter didn't seem to have the least bit of trouble attracting male suitors from all over the hospital, and I don't care how beautiful someone is — that type of following usually only occurs when the girl in question is also an expert in the art of flirting. I had learned that from over twenty years in the entertainment business. But I played it safe and kept my mouth shut even as I looked out at the pool area and saw Sofia talking quite affably to two very handsome gentlemen while a dozen children were pulling at her each and every way.

Jennifer, Jonathan, and his husband went off to mingle with the other guests and as I turned to Fernando to order another beer, Nick sneaked up behind me and asked Fernando for a Macallan 12 neat.

"My God, twice in my house in less than a month. Is that a first? My little Sofia really does have you wrapped around her little finger."

"I admit it, I'm powerless when it comes to my godchild." He looked around the room and outside at the pool area and continued, "You really went all out with this party."

"Not me, Sofia. She drew up the blueprints, right down to the decorations on the trees, and the workers simply followed her instructions."

"So not only is she Florence Nightingale but she's also another Dante Ferretti," Nick remarked as he took his drink from Fernando and said, "Thank you, Fernando."

"Very nice to see you, Mr. Jones."

They shook hands and Nick said, "How many times must I tell you not to call me Mr. Jones. I don't want anyone to get the wrong idea and actually mistake me for a gentleman. Nick, simply Nick."

"Yes, Mr. Jones." Nick shook his head as Sofia came rushing up to him, followed by the twelve elves. She hugged and kissed him and then she went on to introduce him to each child. Nick, at first, seemed slightly taken aback and then he went on to shake each child's hand, making little jokes here and there, and acting like a clown like he used to do with Sofia when she was their age. Nick had one of the firmest handshakes of any person I knew, but when it came to shaking each child's hand he was as gentle as I have ever seen him … as if in the frail hand of each child was a precious gem … the gem we refer to as 'life.'

Nick and I followed Sofia and the children outside. It was time to meet Mr. Claus and I don't know who was more excited, Sofia or the children. Nick and I sat at a table on the other side of the pool, away from the house, but with a clear view of Santa, Sofia, and the children.

The guests all gathered around the pool, many of them holding cameras. Nat King Cole's version of "A Winter Wonderland" played in the background as Sofia directed the action below, placing the children in a line. One by one they went to sit on Santa's lap and they all received too many gifts for any one of them to carry, but they tried their hardest, and with a little help from their parents and other guests they succeeded in carrying away all their loot. Sofia, holding her camera, clicked away like a professional photographer, and with the other guests also clicking away it was as though the children were walking down the red carpet at a movie premiere. The only difference being that the children were real-life heroes.

After a few hours, most of the guests and the children had left, and Nick and I were still sitting at the same table. Fernando walked over to us carrying a bucket of beer and a bottle of Macallan 12. I handed him an envelope with a thousand dollars inside and Nick reached into his pocket and pulled out two hundred-dollar bills and reached out to hand it to him and then pulled back and said, "What's my name?"

Fernando laughed and replied, "Nick, Nick."

Nick handed him the money and Fernando naturally said, "Thank you, Mr. Jones," and quickly put the money in his pocket and said goodnight.

"Remind me to stiff him the next time." Nick remarked.

"Really, like you would ever stiff anyone."

"There's always a first time. Look, I've visited your home twice in a month and you never thought that would happen."

Nick poured more Macallan 12 into his glass and I opened an ice-cold beer.

"My wife was highly impressed with your vast knowledge of cancer treatments and research."

"Is that so," Nick remarked as he took a sip of his whisky.

"She also said she had never known anyone with that type of knowledge who had not had a personal, intimate experience with the disease."

"Your wife is not only beautiful but quite wise and perceptive."

"Meaning…?"

"Meaning that she is right. Back in Australia, when I was first starting out, I had a child with my first wife … a little girl named Nicole. She was a precocious, beautiful little creature. She wanted to wrestle crocodiles when she got older. I spent more time with that child than I have probably spent with any other person in my life, including my mother." Nick took another sip of his whisky and looked out into space, back to a time that would always be with him.

"Occasionally, I had to go away for a week or so to shoot some stupid-ass commercial in the interior, and back then you couldn't get any type of cell service out there, so I had no contact with the family. When I finally got back home, my wife but not my daughter greeted me at the front door, which was highly unusual. I asked her where Nicole was and she said, 'Oh, she hasn't been feeling well and is upstairs in her bed.' She then went on to tell me that she had been running a slight fever and vomiting on and off and complaining of headaches, but that the doctor said there was nothing to worry about … it was just a case of the flu. When I went up to see her, I nearly had a heart attack. The child was semi-conscious, sweating profusely, and had vomited on herself. I looked at that stupid bitch of a wife and yelled, 'Nothing to worry about. Will you look at her…?'

"She was going, 'But the doctor said…' and I just said, 'Fuck the doctor and fuck you.' I wrapped the child in clean blankets, got into my truck and drove to the nearest hospital and straight into the emergency room. After numerous tests showing nothing seriously abnormal, I took my shivering child and drove like a manic to another hospital where they finally diagnosed her with leukemia. Once they were able to stabilize her, I had her airlifted to a specialized cancer hospital in Sydney where I would spend the next four weeks by her side. The doctors had told me that her form of childhood leukemia was the most common and that the cure rate was very high. After just a few days of chemo and radiation, she was already starting to look better and talking about the crocodiles she was going to wrestle when she was a little older.

"The doctors had warned me that before she really got better it was going to get worse, a lot worse, and at one point she would be put into isolation because for a short time she would have no immune system due to the chemo, but that after that things would start to improve.

"And just like the doctors said, it did get worse. She lost her hair, and at times was vomiting all the time, and I doubt if she weighed twenty pounds. But she was a fighter; after all she still had crocodiles to wrestle and nothing as stupid as cancer was going to stop her. My wife flew down a couple of days at a time and for the sake of the child we pretended everything was great between us, whereas when I was alone with her, I was tempted to strangle that useless piece of shit to death. The only thing that woman ever loved was her refection … a wannabe, dumbass actress.

"After my daughter's immune system hit rock bottom, she was removed to an isolation ward, and in another day she was to get a transfusion of stem cells and slowly her immune system would recover. The cancer was gone. The doctors allowed my wife and me to see her, dressed in protective gowns, face masks, and protective foot wear. At no time were we to take off our masks, but my wife, pretending that she loved the child, took off her mask and rushed toward the bed wanting to hug and kiss her baby girl. I grabbed her before she got to the child and flipped the stupid bitch out of the room. That night my beautiful little daughter caught a cold, a common cold, which she couldn't fight off because she had no immune system. That night my wife also came down with a cold but before I could get my hands on her she skipped town.

"My sweet, darling little girl died from a cold which, if she'd been healthy, wouldn't have slowed her down for a moment."

Nick shot down the last remaining whisky in his glass, and quickly refilled the glass. I'd been listening closely all this time, and sat there in silence until Nick continued his story.

"You never get over losing a child, Joe. Never. All the money and fame in the world can never take away the pain. As the saying goes, 'We are put on this earth to bury our parents, not our children.' Shortly afterwards, I had a vasectomy. I could never get past the idea that my child was a victim of a flawed hereditary trait in my DNA and the idea of having another child of mine go through the same suffering as Nicole did was something I just couldn't handle."

Nick shot down the whisky in his glass and poured himself another. It was a lovely night and the stars were out in full force. The Christmas tree swayed gently and Santa's house was still lit but no one was inside. The sound of a bouncing basketball got our attention and as we looked over at the basketball net I had put up we saw a little, bald headed child trying to shoot, but he could barely get the ball half way up and into the goal. We walked over to him and I asked him if his parents had left him behind. He said no, he was sleeping over in Sofia's room and his parents were going to pick him up in the morning. His name was Stephen, the same name as my father and I guess he was around nine or ten. It was hard to tell.

He continued to try to throw the ball up toward the net but he was just too weak and it continued to fall way short. I asked him where they had his catheter and he pointed to his upper chest. I told him I had an idea as I bent down and gently picked him up and placed him on my shoulder. He was skin and bones and I doubt he weighted 60 pounds. Nick handed him the ball and he threw it up and through the goal.

He told us that he used to be able to shoot the ball through the hoop from down on the ground, but then he got the cancer and he became too weak. But he said the doctors said once he was all cured he would be better and stronger than ever. Nick continued to feed him the ball and he continued to throw it up and through the net like a true champion.

Sofia came up beside us and said to Stephen in a gentle and soothing voice, "Young man, I been looking for you for half an hour. I promised your parents you would be in bed by ten o'clock and it's almost eleven."

He smiled at her and whispered into my ear, "I want to marry Sofia. Do you think she will wait until I'm older?"

I replied, "She would have to be a fool not to wait."

Sofia took him by the hand and they walked toward the house. He turned, waved and smiled, and yelled out, "Thank you."

I walked Nick to his limousine and watched him drive off. Shortly after that, I saw off the ambulance and its crew, which the hospital supplied just in case they were needed. I turned and looked at the lit-up house and the blinking star of Bethlehem and said a little prayer.

Chapter 48

A little less than a week before Christmas, we flew to New York for a couple of days. It was what Sofia wanted for Christmas. I rented a car at the airport and drove to the Bronx and through the gates of Saint Raymond's Cemetery. I parked across from where my parents were buried and Sofia, holding a Christmas wreath, got out of the car. She told us she wanted to be alone for a little while with her grandma and grandpa. Beside their grave, she made the sign of the cross, bent her head, and prayed. She then tied the wreath around the tombstone, kissed the engraved faces of Saint Joseph and baby Jesus, and walked back to the car.

That night the three of us went to Rockefeller Center to look at the great Christmas tree. We drank hot chocolates and gave our varying opinions on just how much bigger the tree at the Center was than the tree in our pool. We all agreed that our tree definitely had more lights and a lot more ornaments.

Chapter 49

Finally, after months of hearing my wife bragging about her Kentucky Wildcats and how she could beat me in a one-on-one basketball game, it was time, once and for all, to bring this Bluegrass beauty back to reality. We had tried to have this match two other times, but it was as if the universe didn't want it to happen until we'd been married a little longer. The first time we were supposed to play, Jennifer was called in to work a shift for another nurse who'd fallen ill. The second time, Nick called me onto the set to deal with some last-minute scene changes. Now that we finally had a day to ourselves and no work obligations, it was time to get this challenge underway. I was not going to show her any mercy and no amount of flirting would distract me from my mission to literally wipe the basketball court with her pretty behind.

We got up early and walked to the park, which was only a few blocks away and had four regulation basketball hoops. My wife was dressed just as I suspected she might be. She had on short short gym shorts, like the ballplayers used to wear when I was growing up, and a cut-off Kentucky basketball jersey. She looked hot, as always, but this morning she made sure she looked super hot, no doubt in an attempt to throw me off my game.

And then there was my daughter, wearing short shorts like mommy and a baggy Kentucky basketball sweatshirt. I looked at her and said, "I don't believe you. At the very least, you could have worn a neutral sweatshirt." My God, I loved my daughter more than life itself, but women simply stayed together and there was no denying it, and with Lawrence always siding with his girlfriend they had a veto-proof majority.

Sofia lifted her baggy sweatshirt to reveal a New York Knicks jersey underneath. "It was just easier to fit the Kentucky sweatshirt over the much smaller Knicks jersey. When you score, I am going to pull up the sweatshirt and yell out Knicks, and when mommy scores I am going to point to the sweatshirt and yell out Wildcats."

"Well, I can guarantee you that you will not be calling out Wildcats very often."

We arrived at the park and shot around for a little while. I have to admit my wife had a lovely shooting style and she didn't miss; whereas I was a little rusty after not playing for years except in my dreams with Sarah. I had little doubt that it would all come back once we started playing, and once I put a hand in my wife's face, she wouldn't be hitting her shots so effortlessly.

The game was to sixteen by ones. The first to reach sixteen won, and after hitting a shot, you kept the ball. In short, I could literally hit sixteen shots in a row and the game would be over, but I didn't see that happening, especially since I still hadn't hit a shot during practice.

Jennifer got the ball first after hitting a do-or-die shot from the top of the key. If she'd missed, I would have had the ball first. She smiled as I crouched down to guard her. She dribbled right, put the ball between her legs, pivoted left and easily put in a left-handed layup. Sofia yelled out, "Wildcat!"

She took the ball out again at the top of the key, faked right, stepped back and hit a jump shot from twenty-five feet out, nothing but net. "Wildcat!"

Once again, she took the ball out and without even faking, hit another jump shot. Swish. "Wildcat!" "Wildcat!" "Wildcat!"

Before I knew it, I was down by eight baskets and I had not even taken a shot.

Once again, she took the ball out at the top of the key and asked, "Are you sure you've played this game before?" Now she was talking trash and even worse she was backing it up as she drilled another one from twenty-five feet out. "Sweet. I just love the sound of the ball swishing right through the net. Music to one's ears."

She took the ball out again, but just as she was about to open her big mouth, I stole the ball from her and hit a layup. "Knicks," my daughter finally yelled out as she lifted her sweatshirt to show her Knicks jersey.

Finally, I had a chance to take the ball out. I faked left, went right, lost the ball and watched as my wife easily laid the ball in. "Wildcats!"

It was at this point that I seriously considered faking a sprained ankle, but then it occurred to me that my opponent was a nurse and that would really make me look bad.

She won sixteen to three and went around the court hooting and hollering and celebrating. I said, "It's not nice to brag."

And she replied, "Who said so?"

And then she threw her arms around my neck and kissed me passionately and said, "I love you so much, so much."

A moment later, my daughter placed her head on my shoulder and said, "And I love you so much." And never did such a trashing on a basketball court feel like the biggest victory of my life.

Chapter 50

As in every other household where the females outnumber the males, I was no longer the king of the castle but instead subservient to two independent, intelligent, loving and caring women. At least they didn't take away all my privileges; I was still allowed my Budweiser beers as long as I continued to run every morning, and I was allowed to watch my classic TV shows anytime I desired, and the study was my man cave, off limits to all, as long as I was working.

The wife and daughter went to an animal shelter to rescue a stray kitten they saw on the Internet and instead brought home a litter of kittens, five in total, and they were named Bogie, Bettie, Carney, Jake and Dixie. Jennifer and Sofia promised me that they would find new homes for at least three of them, but by the time they found a co-worker at the hospital who wanted to take two, I had fallen in love with all five. I was not the type to separate a family, so we kept them all, and it became my job to clean the five different litter boxes scattered about the house.

And at any time during the day or night, there might be gang of bald children running around the house and they were as adorable and beautiful as any children I have ever seen.

Resources

The following books were extremely helpful in giving me a more complete understanding of pediatric cancer, Asperger's syndrome, nursing, and cancer research in general:

22 Things a Woman with Asperger's Syndrome Wants Her Partner to Know by Rudy Simone

Asperger's and Adulthood: A Guide to Working, Loving, and Living With Asperger's Syndrome by Blythe Grossberg, PsyD

The Complete Guide to Asperger's Syndrome by Tony Attwood

Critical Care: A New Nurse Faces Death, Life, and Everything in Between by Theresa Brown

The Emperor of All Maladies: A Biography of Cancer by Siddhartha Mukherjee

First Survivor: The Impossible Childhood Cancer Breakthrough by Mark Unger

The Gene: An Intimate History by Siddhartha Mukherjee

The Laws of Medicine: Field Notes from an Uncertain Science (TED Books) by Siddhartha Mukherjee

My Child Has Cancer: A Parent's Guide to Diagnosis, Treatment, and Survival by Della L. Howell, MD

The Shift: One Nurse, Twelve Hours, Four Patients' Lives by Theresa Brown

This Narrow Space: A Pediatric Oncologist, His Jewish, Muslim, and Christian Patients, and a Hospital in Jerusalem by Elisha Waldman

Acknowledgements

A special thank you to all my friends I grew up with in Parkchester, especially Howie, Eric, Jerry, Charlie, Pete, John, Billy, Frank, Mary Ann, Brian, Opie, Lenny, Kevin, Howie Weiss, Carl, and Mike. The many hours we spent together on the basketball courts, and in the hallways in Parkchester, were among the happiest years of my life.

Once again, a special thank you to little Ava…. Courage comes in all shapes and sizes.

To Dixie, Jake, and Malé…. Cancer does not discriminate.

A big thank you to the staff at Iguana Books, especially to my editor, Lee Parpart, who made this book a lot better than I could ever have imagined. To Heather Bury, whose help toward the end of the process was greatly appreciated, and to Meghan Behse, who makes everything possible and is a real gem.

Finally, to my lovely wife, Melissa, whose caring, love, and compassion are just a few of her wonderful qualities.

www.ingramcontent.com/pod-product-compliance
Lightning Source LLC
Chambersburg PA
CBHW020401210626
46816CB00006BB/2075